House
of
Shadows

Walter Spence

Published by Full Moon Publications

PRINT VERSION

Cover Photo: © Zinaida / shutterstock.com

Walter's Photo: © Deborah M. Spence

Copyright © 2012 by Walter Spence

ISBN: 0985483709

ISBN 13: 9780985483708

This book is dedicated to the memory of my father,
George Lee Spence

I lay in darkness on cold dank stone and remembered the day I died.

Prior to death I did not appreciate true darkness, the total absence of light. It is like drowning in a limitless ocean of black ink. And with the absence of light came the absence of sound. No noise, not even the ringing of the ears for company, as though my head had been stuffed with clay. In my mouth my tongue lay desiccate, like a worm pulled from the earth and left on a hot sidewalk to broil. No scent either, not even the odor of my own flesh as I waited for the process of corruption to begin.

But then came sensation.

It began as a sense of pressure against my back, stronger even than the winepress of the dark. From there it spread to the backs of my thighs and buttocks, my arms and palms, the prickling of grit against bare skin.

Following this came sound, the soft whispering of many-legged insects growing steadily louder as they approached my body, locked in rigor mortis. Soon they would crawl over my hair, my face, my eyes.

I lay there and remembered, it had been my choice to die. . . .

*   *   *

I first met Penelope Ember on a hot overcast day in July of 1975.

I was standing knee-deep in the garbage dumpster of the Sneadsville Fruit and Produce Company while sifting through trash in search of gold,

1

cardboard boxes containing cans and jars of food (many broken but some still whole), pickled eggs mostly that day. A wholesale distributor to convenience stores, the occasional damaged box had no retail value and so it was almost always thrown away. The rumor was that Marvin Snead (the owner) would not allow his employees to keep any unbroken items remaining from a dropped box on the theory that doing so might encourage vandalism for scavenging purposes. So the oxen were muzzled and everything was discarded.

It was a Sunday afternoon, so the warehouse was closed, but my sister stood watch just in case. At eleven she was two years my junior and too short to clamber into the bin, so that job fell to me. Our mother had left that morning for the beaches of Kitty Hawk with a 'friend', and there was little in the house to eat except for a loaf of bread and a jar of salad dressing. In a better neighborhood the sight of two unsupervised children rummaging in a dumpster might have prompted intervention from someone, the police or maybe Social Services. But this was East End, a thatch of decaying rental houses dotted by the occasional homeowner. You could identify them easily enough, their yards were more frequently mown and their front porches decorated with large orange and black plastic signs that read 'No Trespassing', mostly elderly couples who minded their own business with missionary fervor.

But not always. Which was why, when I heard the voice, I clambered out of the trash bin in a hurry.

"Hey, little girl!"

Before she could even think about moving I got between Barb and the speaker. He was of medium height and broad, with thick fingers and a barrel chest, his brown hair cut so close to the scalp you could see the white skin underneath. He stood beside the driver's door of a long silver car with smoke-tinted windows. I had never seen a Mercedes, but I recognized the emblem.

"Get in the house, Barb," I told her through clenched teeth.

She looked at me, then back at the stranger. "But—"

"NOW!"

She turned and fled. Since we lived next door to the warehouse, it did not take long for her to reach safety. She looked over her shoulder, one small act of rebellious defiance, before disappearing inside.

The man watched her vanish, then turned back to me with his head lowered, bull-like, as though about to charge.

"I don't know what she was doing here, I told her to go home. She didn't do anything," I said as convincingly as I could.

"Charles?"

The lilting feminine voice confused me. I refocused on the car, still keeping the Sherman tank of a man in the corner of my peripheral vision. The rear window on the driver's side, too dark to see through, had slid down about halfway.

The man turned. "Yes ma'am?" he said deferentially.

"Charles, you are scaring the poor boy half to death and that will not do. Just step back now. You!"

My shoulder muscles tensed and I ducked my head, ready to run. "Yes ma'am?" I said, mimicking the almost reverential tones of 'Charles' in the hope that a soft answer would turneth away wrath, though the voice did not sound angry. If anything, it sounded amused.

"Please come over here, young sir. Now don't dawdle, I'm not going to bite. Though I have been known to take a little nip now and then." She chuckled at her joke. "There now, that's better."

I peered into the car, still keeping half an eye on Charles. In the rear seat a young woman sat, watching me. She wore a cream-colored summer dress decorated with small pink flowers. A short veil hung from the brim of her white straw hat, though it did little to obscure the cotton candy pink of her cheeks and her cherry red lips. A pair of Wayfarers hid her eyes. Over her freckle-dotted shoulders flowed hair the color of a sunset, a dark red mane as full of waves as the incoming tide. She looked like a catalogue model, as fresh as an April morning.

"Please pardon my driver, he was hired for his predilection for paranoia," she said. Her accent was as southern as my own, but it danced with her vowels as lightly as a sunbeam, nothing like the molasses thick drawl of most of the people in this part of North Carolina.

"It's okay," I said with a nervous shrug.

She tilted her chin in the direction of my house. "Your sister?"

I tensed again, but kept my voice friendly. "Yes ma'am."

She lifted her veil and removed her sunglasses, then turned the full weight of her gaze on me. Her eyes reminded me of a late evening sky full of stars. "You love her very much, don't you?"

"I suppose so," I replied, wondering what answer she might most want to hear, what I could say that would keep those violet eyes fixed on me forever.

She nodded, then fumbled with her purse. My heart sank as her attention focused on something other than myself. "My driver and I are new to this area and he is still learning his way around." She pulled a piece of paper from her purse and checked it. "Do you know where 362 Berry Street is?"

Take me with you and I will guide you right to the front door, I wanted to say. Instead I told her, "Just keep straight until you come to a T-intersection, then make a left, then take the next right. That's Berry Street."

She smiled, and the darkness of the car's interior shredded like cigarette smoke in the wind. "Well, you are just a lifesaver, aren't you?" she gushed. "And though it's small reward, please accept this token of my gratitude."

Before I could move, her fingers caught my hand and pressed something into the palm. She wore white gloves of elbow length, silk or maybe satin. Her fingers gripped mine with such strength that I experienced a moment of terror (hope?) that she would not let me go.

Then she returned her hands to her lap. "Charles?" she said. "Back in the car now, there's the boy."

The man took his place at the steering wheel with no wasted motion as the lady smiled at me once again. "Please pardon me for my lack of good manners, but we have yet to be properly introduced," she said. "And by what name are you known, my young white knight?"

It took several attempts to clear my throat. "My name's Eugene," I told her, choking on every syllable.

Her bright laugh sent a raw red flush from my collar to my ears. "My, my, your mother must harbor a sincere grudge against you. Or your father."

"I wouldn't know. We've never met him," I said after lowering my gaze, wanting nothing more at that moment than for a hole to open beneath my feet into which I could disappear forever.

She smiled once again, a curling of the lips that reached all the way to her eyes. "Well, we are—none of us—responsible for the sins of our parents. Never forget that! And to prove this is so, I hereby rename you Ace! That sit well with you? Ace?" The smile again.

I shrugged, unable to hide a grin as it fought its way out. "Sure."

She nodded, apparently satisfied, then looked past me again. "You do love your sister, don't you?" she repeated.

I nodded. "Yes."

"And family is everything, isn't it Ace?"

I nodded again, fiercely this time. "It ought to be."

And though the wattage was lower, the smile she gave me then seemed to run deeper, down to the bone. "My name is Penelope Ember, Ace, and I have a feeling we will be seeing more of one another, you and I." And with that she leaned back as her window closed, separating us. I stood by our narrow one-lane street and watched as that silver dream of a car disappeared into the distance.

Only then did I look at the crumpled green wad in my hand and unfold a one hundred dollar bill.

That was our first meeting. Our second came a little more than a year later.

*   *   *

I was walking down a deserted highway on a blazing hot Friday in early September. The hundred dollar bill I had been given the previous summer was long gone, but some leftover change still jingled in my pocket. From that I had found a dime to 'loan' Jimmy Saunders while we stood in the schoolyard waiting on the bus drivers.

Once the dime had changed hands and Jimmy (along with his shadow, Richard Satterwhite) had walked across the street to grab a candy bar, a hand had fallen on my right shoulder. "Come with me."

It was the vice principal, who firmly escorted me to his office where he accused me of 'matching dimes' (i.e., gambling). I told him that I had simply given Jimmy the coin (no pretense about loaning), and after continued protestations on my part he finally released me. I ran back to the parking lot and discovered that my school bus had already left.

When I returned to the vice principal to inform him of this, he asked for my address, consulted his schedule, then told me that Bus 32 would be returning shortly and that Cedar Street (where I lived) was on its second route, so I needed to take it.

There were few students on Bus 32, the pleasant circumstance of which allowed me a seat alone for a change. I watched while the other students got off at their respective stops, ultimately leaving me as the last passenger.

A few minutes later, as we drove down a country highway I did not recognize, the driver slowed to a stop at a crossroads. Back then students did most of the bus driving, and this one — Calvin Jason Hobbs — played offensive tackle for the Sneadsville High Vikings. "Here you go."

I looked around. "Huh?"

"I said we're here, genius, Cedar Lane."

I shook my head. "I live on Cedar Street. I've never heard of Cedar Lane."

"Well, Cedar Street's not part of my route and you're the last one on this bus. I've got a football game tonight and you're damned sure not going home with me, so hop off."

He did not look happy, so I exited the bus and watched it disappear down the road. Since I had no idea where I was, I started walking in the same direction for lack of a better one.

There was little room on the narrow shoulder, just a few feet between the shimmering asphalt and a deep ditch thick with weeds, broken beer bottles and other assorted trash. My choices were limited to the risk of being sideswiped by a car due to walking too close to the highway or getting tetanus from a rusty beer can if I stumbled into the ditch, so I paced the middle ground as best I could.

A strong wind ruffled my sweat-soaked shirt, and I looked over my shoulder. A dark thunderhead had raced up behind me and now filled the sky. Lightning flashed deep within its interior, and a curtain of rain hung from its leading edge. I faced front again, picking up my pace.

It had just occurred to me that it might be safer to cross the road and face oncoming traffic when the ridiculously loud blare of a horn behind me caused me to spin, fists clenched defensively as I fought to avoid a spill into the aforementioned ditch. Heart thumping a mile a minute, I faced a familiar mirror-bright Mercedes sliding to a halt next to me. The passenger window, still sunglasses dark, lowered.

"Well well now, if it isn't my young white knight!" said Penelope Ember from the far side as she gave me the up and down. "Though not so young anymore. My word, you look as though you've grown a foot! And what, pray tell, are you doing walking down this god-forsaken country highway begging to become yet another depressing traffic statistic?"

My breath caught in my throat and it took a moment for my lungs to relax sufficiently to allow speech. I had forgotten how intoxicating that melodic voice had been. "Wrong bus," I choked out, feeling like an idiot for my situation as well as the fumbling coarseness of my tongue in comparison to that lilting soprano.

She frowned, a pretty little moue with a hint of a pout that made my heart flip flop. She wore a lemon yellow sundress with matching sandals baring her slim white feet. A straw hat with lime-green ribbons sat perched atop the auburn cloud of her hair. "My dear sir, do you even know where you are?"

I shrugged. Since I already looked the fool, I could hardly do myself greater harm in those luminous eyes. "I figured I would keep walking till I found a store where they might let me call home."

Penelope tsked. "Ace, the closest Quick Mart is another four miles. How you managed to end up abandoned on this wayward lane is a tale to be told over the ice cold Coke Charles will fetch you once we arrive there. Now hie thee into my chariot, young sir, and mind you open the door only so far as is absolutely necessary for egress. My eyes are very sensitive and cannot handle too much light. In fact, bide a moment while I put these on," she said as she removed a pair of sunglasses from her purse.

I waited until she motioned impatiently for me to get in. Cracking the door just enough to slip inside, I huddled against it while Penelope looked on, obviously amused, as the window shut once more.

The interior was dark and blessedly cool. The car accelerated so quietly it took me a moment to realize we were in motion at all.

"Yes, Ace, you certainly have grown," she said with a nod as she looked me over again. "How old are you now?"

I swallowed. "I turned fifteen a week ago. My mother told me I was born on Labor Day."

Penelope laughed, almost a bark. It was the only less than perfect thing about her, though I was more than willing to overlook it. I had read once that Persian rug makers always included a flaw in their work, since perfection belonged to God alone. While not a true bray, it did make her a bit more human and thus almost approachable.

"Oh my dear Lord," she said once she had regained her breath. "And how many days did it take for you to grace our presence?"

I grinned with her. "Three. Practically four she says when she's piss—uh, ticked off with me."

She shook her head. "Don't believe a word of it. We women are deceitful and manipulative creatures with husbands and children, though few of us have yet to master that trick where lovers are concerned."

I was quite thankful for the shadow-drenched space as it hid the flames of my burning cheeks at her use of the word 'lovers'. "Um, where have you been keeping yourself, Ms. Ember? I haven't seen you since last summer."

"Miss, if you please. I despise the modern convention of obscuring a lady's marital status. I wish there to be no doubt as to my availability where romance is concerned. And to answer your question, I have been spending considerable time abroad, mostly in Europe where much of my family yet resides."

"Europe?" I could feel my brain shifting gears. "But I thought you lived . . . I mean, that you were from—"

"Oh, I have lived in the South for sufficient years to acquire a touch of its accent in my speech, which has given my Ma—my mother no end of amusement. That white haired lady can sit like a stone listening to me jabber for any length of time. And speaking of time, we have arrived at our destination. Charles, fill the tank, then get my young man here a Coke and something sweet. Fruit pie?"

I did not care for fruit pies, but did not want to appear ungracious. "That'll be fine."

"Fibber. Make it a Twinkie. God forbid I serve you anything with even the remotest hint of nutritional value. No, nothing for me, I shall break my fast later."

"So," Penelope continued, "How is your sister? Barb, I seem to recall you having said. Is that short for Barbara?"

"Um, no ma'am. Don't tell her I said so, but it's actually short for Barbie."

This time Penelope laughed until her eyes streamed. "My, my," she finally managed. "I suppose 'Eugene' is not quite so bad then, is it? Sounds to me you narrowly missed becoming a 'Ken'!"

I could not help but laugh with her. "Yes ma'am."

"Oh please, let us lose the 'ma'am'. I already feel old, let us not go from ancient to antique."

"You're not old," I said in a rush without pause. "You're beautiful." And as soon as the words left my lips I almost choked beneath a wave of self loathing. Who was I to tell this literal goddess she was beautiful?

But before I could sputter out an apology for my effrontery, she gave me a smile so coy and unpretentious that my throat clamped shut. "Really, Ace? You think I'm beautiful?"

I have had considerable time to ponder the events of my life of late, and I have often reflected on those snowy woods moments where two paths diverge, this being one of them. Had I given a different response, how might that have changed the future course of events? Where would that less-travelled road have taken me?

But no, I took the easier path, and here I now lie.

"You are the kind of woman men die for," I said, giving my hormone-soaked brain free access to my mouth. And though every ounce of common sense told me I was seven kinds of a fool for admitting it, I could not regret saying so. Even now, as I listen to the rustle of some multi-limbed creature in my scalp, part of me still believes those words.

I am the proof of it, after all.

She stared into my eyes. "Strong words, Ace," she said finally, a shadow of her smile returning. "But let's not talk about death today and return to my question, which you still have yet to answer."

A fog had claimed my brain and I could not think clearly. "What question was that, ma'am?"

She sighed in mock exasperation (at least, I hoped it was mock). "Again with the ma'am! From now on Ace, you will refer to me by my God-given name, Penelope."

I could not suppress a smile. "God-given?"

"You have no idea. Now, once again, how is your sister?"

"She's fine. Growing past her years, our mother says."

"Is she now?" The driver's door opened and Charles slid wordlessly inside, then handed Penelope a brown paper bag, its bottom dark from the moisture of the sweating bottle it contained. "Here's your soda, thank you Charles," she said.

"Thank you," I repeated to her driver, who gave no indication by look or sound that he acknowledged my presence, much less my gratitude.

9

"Girls mature faster than boys—I should know—so I can understand your mother's concern," Penelope continued. "What about you, Ace?" She gave me an appraising look. "Do you have any concerns?"

My sister was already quite pretty, attracting attention not only from boys her own age but even the odd glance or comment from my mother's 'friends'. Usually the remarks embarrassed her and she would flee to her room and hide for the remainder of the evening, which disturbed our mother not at all. But there were times when my sister would blush in a way that bothered me, as though she found the attention not completely disgusting, which angered and confused me.

I came out of my reverie to Penelope's slow nodding. "Girls need male approval at that age, not to mention guidance, and if I remember correctly you said your father was *in absentia*?"

I nodded. "We've asked, but mom won't talk about him. She just says that he doesn't care about any of us or he would be helping out."

"Well, there are always two sides to every story and oftentimes more than that," Penelope said. "What about other family? Grandparents? Uncles? Third-cousins twice removed?"

I smiled despite the depressing topic. It felt good to talk with someone who seemed to care, though I knew the answers Penelope sought could only lower me in her eyes. Still, she listened without appearing judgmental and even conveyed the impression she gave a damn. "No relatives I know of. We have an aunt somewhere but the way mom talks, they don't like each other."

"That's too bad, Ace. Family should be the center of a person's life, those whom one can count on when the world itself is against you, people whom one is connected to by bonds which death itself cannot break. Do you not agree?"

I do not know where they came from, and later I would recall their sudden appearance with a sense of shame and self-recrimination, but tears started flowing down my cheeks. I refused to openly sob, so instead I sat there and wept in rigid silence.

"Oh, Ace," I heard Penelope say. She placed one slim arm over my bony shoulders, and that almost made me lose control right there. But I had had considerable practice in my life containing misery, learning how to cry on the inside in the presence of others, which had served me well in life.

As it does now in death.

My tears burned runnels into my skin and more than anything I wished for a moment of privacy so I could dash them away. Instead Penelope held me even closer, the fingers of one slim hand stroking hair I knew to be in desperate need of a trim.

"Ace, my heart goes out to you, and to your sister as well. We live in a very unfair world, you and I. There are wonderful parents out there, men and women of means and status who are saddled with the most ungrateful and selfish brats for offspring, while deserving young men like yourself—well, it's a shame. No, not a shame. It's a crime."

Part of me wanted to speak up, to defend my mother against the unspoken allegations that hung in the air between us. But memories of being left alone for days at a time while our mother kept company with her 'friends' rose in my throat like bile, and I remained silent.

"A crime, truly," Penelope continued. "Someone should do something about it. And you know what? Someone damned well is!"

"Excuse me?" I said.

"Yes indeed." She removed her sunglasses, then looked down into my eyes. The smile she gave me then would have chased away any night's worth of darkness. "You and your sister have now become my personal pet projects. I will see to it that the doors of opportunity are thrown open for you both. I will not carry you, mind, I expect you to walk through them under your own power. And if at any moment I sense you attempting to take advantage of my generosity, then away I'll fly and that will be the end. Do we understand one another?"

The seriousness of her tone and her mien cowed me, and I nodded without speaking.

"Very good. Oh, one other thing, you must keep this a secret between the three of us."

"Why?" I asked, despite the thrill of terror running through me that my question might cause her to retract her offer as quickly as it had been made.

"Well Ace, I could repeat the biblical admonition about giving in private rather than in public, and there would certainly be truth in that. However, I must confess that self interest plays no small part here as well."

"Huh?"

Penelope clucked her tongue. "My dear sir, how to explain to one of your tender years? Blunt is best. You see, I am a lady of no small social standing in the world, and were it a matter of public discourse that I was playing benefactress to a very handsome and very *underaged* young gentleman, the consequent wagging of tongues would stir a breeze from here to the borders. Have I made my concerns plain? Or must I be even less decorous?"

"No, no ma'am!" The sliver of disappointment that shot through me at the line she had drawn between us was ameliorated in large part by her emphasis of the word 'handsome'.

"Very well. Now, let's get you home. Keep an eye on the mail for anything with the return address 'Light's Hope'. It's a charity of the Ember family, but sounds enough like a religious organization that it should not arouse too many suspicions. When we arrive, have your sister step outside. I'm a good judge of sizes and I think we can do the two of you better than these Salvation Army hand-me-downs."

I did as she asked. When we got to my house I ran inside and searched for Barb. I found her at the kitchen table with a package of Saltine crackers and a jar of peanut butter. Just the sight made my mouth dry out. I motioned for her to follow me, then sauntered outside with her in my wake to the open car window. "Barb, this is Penelope Ember. She wanted to meet you."

"Indeed I did," Penelope replied as she lowered her sunglasses. "Bend forward dear; let me get a good look at you."

My sister blushed, but did as she was told. "What a little beauty!" Penelope exclaimed. "I see your family's good looks were not completely exhausted on your brother. Why, you look delicious enough to eat with a spoon! And so petite! I'm guessing, what, a size zero? If that?"

Barb shrugged and looked over at me, her gaze puzzled and a bit panicky. "Sounds about right," I said, even though I had no idea what a size zero was.

"Well, I do enjoy a challenge," Penelope said. "And as Charles here can attest, shopping for me is more than a hobby, it is a vocation. Take that little cupcake back inside Ace, before the sun fries that milk white skin to a crisp, and I shall be in touch with both of you very soon now." And with those words her window closed, separating us.

I stood in my front yard for quite some time after she left, staring into the distance in which she had disappeared, my heart floating in my chest. I knew, in the way only the faithful do, that an angel had come into my life and changed it forever.

Three years passed before I saw Penelope Ember again.

*   *   *

Of course I had no way of knowing this ahead of time. June came each year warm with promise, followed all too soon by the cool disappointment of autumn and still no Penelope.

How did I know she would come only with the summer's heat? I cannot say. I simply *knew*.

The first packages came three weeks after that last visit, one for Barb and one for me, both full of clothes for the coming winter. And brand new, not used with stains that refused to come out or zippers that frequently stuck halfway up, when they worked at all. Shirts, sweaters, jeans, socks, shoes, all packed between crinkly sheets of tissue paper into two enormous leather and brass footlockers sturdy enough to stand on, with locks that were not merely decorative but actually functional.

Two more packages arrived four weeks later and each subsequent month afterwards, over time establishing a pattern. Every three months we received packages with new clothes for the upcoming season, the sizes always right. Other months the boxes were smaller ones which might hold any number of surprises (as well as money, always discretely hidden). Once Barb's included a small bottle of perfume, and as soon as she opened it I recognized the scent. The container was crystal, as elegant as an orchid, the label a mystery in French. Barb was tightfisted with it, but would sometimes relent (though never when our mother was home) and dab a bit behind her ears before sitting next to me on the sofa to watch television. I would close my eyes and imagine Penelope sitting between us dressed in silk, her slim legs clad in shimmering hose, one knee resting against my own, that familiar knowing smile on her face.

The sender was always listed as 'Light's Hope', as she had said it would be. Nothing else, not even a return address. The packages were postmarked, however, and displayed a wide variety of cities: San Francisco, New York,

Las Vegas, Chicago, Boston. Los Angeles appeared multiple times. And cities outside of the US as well: Milan, Venice, Cork, Athens, and one place called Livoire se Andolé.

Our mother's brow furrowed when the first packages came, though she accepted my story readily enough about a charity list I had signed Barb and I up for at school. We could see the reduced strain Penelope's generosity had placed on Mom's pocketbook when we were no longer being sent into the Quick Mart with one dollar food stamps and instructions that each of us purchase a nickel piece of candy so she could buy a pack of cigarettes with the remaining change.

But no matter what other wonders we might find in our monthly packages, books were always included. Leather bound editions gilded with gold, volumes upon volumes by such authors as Arthur Conan Doyle, Jules Verne, Alexandre Dumas, Rudyard Kipling, Charles Dickens, and many, many more.

I devoured them, then turned to my sister's stacks: The Brontë sisters, Jane Austen, and others whose names I cannot recall.

But I will never forget that first book, primarily because the main character was also named Eugene. It was Thomas Wolfe's *Look Homeward, Angel*. And though no note had been included, I was convinced that Penelope was sending me a message with its inclusion, that I need not be ashamed of my name, a name that (at least in my case) had led to more than one schoolyard brawl.

Prior to that first parcel from Light's Hope I had slunk into my classes, avoiding the eyes of my instructors and barely acknowledging my classmates who were almost all strangers to me (Sneadsville was our seventh move over the past ten years). This too had become part of a pattern. New kids are typically bullied when coming to a new school, but I was no one's victim and had avoided that fate by savagely attacking anyone brave enough (or stupid enough) to test me. I did learn early not to wait till after school for a fight when the buddies of my fourth-grade classmate and would-be tormentor Eddie Pritchett decided to join in after his victory appeared questionable, bloodying my nose and face as well as knocking out a tooth (thankfully not an obvious one).

So the next year, after one more move to yet another school, when the kid behind me started thumping the back of my head, I simply leaped out of my seat and bore him to the ground, my remaining teeth in his ear. The presence of the teacher (who dragged me off to the principal's office) saved me from a possible group beating, and I suffered the week long suspension with relief. Eventually, at each subsequent new school, I would be left alone as too much trouble to bully, instead being simply ostracized.

But when I got on the bus that following Friday morning after receiving my new wardrobe, I noticed a difference in the looks I got as I made my way down the aisle. The glances continued all the way to my first class. The teacher, Mrs. Brannigan, looked up from her desk and actually smiled. "My, don't you look nice today!" she said.

My cheeks flared at the unexpected compliment, and I mumbled a reply before slinking to my seat. Someone tittered and I slouched as low as I could without hitting the floor.

As soon as I got home I dug into the non-fiction selection of Penelope's books, which I had so far only glanced at before setting to one side. I found the one I was searching for and sprawled on my bed with its squeaking springs to stare at the huge volume's cover: *A Gentleman's Guide to Dress & Deportment*.

I spent a good part of the weekend reading it. Much of it was a blur, since I could only absorb so much, so I took to skipping back and forth, focusing on whatever caught my attention. At one point I put the book to one side and stepped into the bathroom where I examined my nails and thatch of hair, both ragged and unkempt. How was it I had never seen myself before? And if I saw this, then what the hell had Penelope Ember seen to make her take an interest in me?

She saw something no one else ever has, a voice in my head replied. *She saw potential. And we are not going to disappoint her, are we?*

I shook my head and tightened my jaw. "No, we are not." I swore that when Penelope did finally return, she would find a gentleman waiting for her, not some poor white trash lacking the self respect to take decent care of himself. For all she had done, and for all she continued to do, I would demonstrate with word and deed that her efforts were neither disrespected nor unappreciated. I would prove beyond the shadow of any possible doubt that the seeds of her generosity had been scattered on fertile ground.

So I scrubbed myself well, trimmed my nails, then took some of the money she had sent and walked with Barb to the closest hair salon I could find. The two women made much of my curls, but went into ecstasy over my sister's long blonde tresses, pulling out one fashion magazine after another while debating how best to do them justice. By the time they were done (and with our new clothes) I almost did not recognize either of us, the transformation was that dramatic.

When I returned to school the following Monday I attracted stares once again, but not like the previous week. Those had been tinged with amusement, as if a chimpanzee had suddenly shown up at school dressed in a tuxedo. Not this time. These were accompanied by a series of open-mouthed gapes that, over the day, evolved into hostile glares from other males and amazed (and sometimes coy) glances from the girls. I pretended not to notice any of it while secretly exulting.

I allowed myself a week to revel before getting back to work in order to match the inner man with the outer. I threw myself into my schoolwork as never before, my hunger surprising even myself and dumbfounding my teachers, who stared at me as if I was some curious new life form. I saw myself as a lump of clay being molded into a sculpture worthy of Penelope's interest and attention.

Suddenly the world expanded into a much larger place, filled with both mystery and promise. I opened my textbooks with new eyes and saw things I had never seen before. Math became a puzzle to be solved, History a novel in its own right, and English Literature a drug with infinitely addictive properties.

When I returned as a junior, the difference from the previous year was noticeable. People who had looked through me before now spoke to me in the hallways, asking me to sit with them during lunch and on the bus. And the gazes of the girls (which had once slid over me without pause) now occasionally lingered as they spoke to one another in hushed whispers accompanied by shared giggles and smiles completely unlike the ones I had grown accustomed to. A few even flirted openly, which confused me. How to respond? What would Penelope's reaction to my having a girlfriend be?

That I saw this as something to be concerned about says something about my level of naiveté. Deep in my heart I knew that Penelope's interest in me went no further than her show of compassion (though 'pity' might have been more descriptive.) I also knew that the idea she might harbor feelings for me as a man (other than amusement at the notion) was ridiculous. But despite this I could not rid myself of the impossibly slim hope that one day maybe, just maybe. . . .

So whenever girls flirted with me I casually flirted back but never took things any further. A few of them appeared to consider this a challenge and grew quite bold. It got harder and harder to keep saying no (and a friend warned me that at this rate people were going to start talking), so after a while I came up with a story about a summer love I was saving myself for (a tale with more truth in it than fiction.) And while this tale did not completely discourage those (mostly) unwelcome attentions, it did have the benefit of not alienating the majority of the girls, who over time grew to admire my steadfast loyalty to my 'true love'. Which did not prevent some of them from testing it, though.

As time went on, I spun many a tale to explain Penelope's continuing absence, each more fantastic than the last. I daydreamed about running away to search for her after finding a clue that she might be in trouble, then rescuing her from any number of perils, each more outrageous than the last, ultimately basking in the fullness of a gratitude that (as time went on) required me to lock my bedroom door for privacy's sake.

Senior year came, then high school graduation, but still no Penelope. That was the worst, and for the first time I grew angry at her. While many of my classmates had taken off for a weekend celebration at Myrtle Beach, I spent that time at home, my temper flaring. Barb, who knew my moods better than anyone, kept her distance while I brooded. Here I was, hanging on the hook of a dream after three years for someone who did not care enough to show up for what was (at least, up until then) the most important day of my life?

So I kept to my room and fumed. What now? While my friends (well, classmates) had been busy making post-graduation plans, I had done nothing but watch the horizon for the ghost of a silver sedan.

Then, when the next package arrived, it included something none of the others had, a note. Granted it was not much of a letter, just one single word.

Soon.

And with each following monthly delivery came other messages of similar brevity:

Patience.

Trust.

The one which broke me came with the cooling days of fall, and when I read it I wept.

Delayed.

For months my life had been on hold. I had believed, had been *convinced*, that my relationship with Penelope meant something wonderful was about to happen now that I was a man, something incredible. I had believed this as people of faith believe in God.

And now? I wallowed in the mud of my own self pity, flagellating myself.

Moron! Imbecile! Idiot! You really think she ever shared any of your feelings for her? You deserve to be abandoned. Oh, no doubt she intends to come back one day, but something will come up like this past time, and then something else, on and on, and as the years go by she will just forget about us, not even remembering to tell whoever is sending those packages not to bother anymore.

I got drunk that night (in those days the legal age limit was eighteen). I sat on the steps of my front porch next to a growing pile of empty beer cans and stared out into a darkness as empty as my future prospects, wondering what I was going to do now.

Then the screen door banged open and my sister stuck her head out. "Telephone."

The weight on my chest vanished and I leaped to my feet. It had to be Her, if for no other reason than no one else ever called for me.

I raced to the phone, then paused to catch my breath, unwilling to sound as anxious as I felt. "Hello?"

"Eugene Evans?"

The voice was male. "Yes," I replied, heart sinking to the floor beneath my feet. "Who is this?"

"This is Mr. Price."

Then I recognized the voice, with its nasal cadences and theatrical flair. Mr. Price taught English, Speech and Drama at the high school, and I had taken several of his classes. His amazement at my grasp of the works of William Shakespeare (stemming almost entirely from repeated readings of the annotated edition of his collected works Penelope had sent) had both pleased and embarrassed me. There were rumors he had once performed on Broadway, which I questioned. Why in the name of God would anyone leave New York City to teach English Lit in Sneadsville? "Yes, Mr. Price?"

"Interested in taking a trip to New York?"

Though still heavy, my heart rose to belly button level.

Every year Mr. Price organized a trip to New York City during the fall. Those trips had become the stuff of legend in our small town. "One of our group had to drop out suddenly, and I remembered you saying in class how much you wanted to see New York," he said. "The bus ticket and hotel room are already paid for and non-refundable, though you'd have to pay for your own meals and personal expenses. What do you say?"

For a moment I stood, phone in hand, jaw frozen.

What are you waiting for? He's offering you a free trip to New York! Stick a crowbar in your mouth and say yes!

But what about Penelope? What if she shows up while I'm gone?

Good! You've spent the entire summer and half of fall waiting for her to grace us with her presence. Let her wait on us for a change. Then maybe she'll show some respect and not keep taking us for granted!

An angry rush of heat sent a flush from my neck to my cheeks. "When?"

"The bus leaves from the school parking lot at eight am this coming Wednesday. We're staying at a hotel in Manhattan, near Times Square, and will head back Sunday after breakfast."

I took a deep breath to silence the niggling doubts bubbling below the surface of my so-called brain. "I'll be there."

*   *   *

I rested my forehead against the glass of the tour bus window while recalling my departure; Barb's nervous questions ("You're coming back, aren't you?"), my mother's angry demands ("When you bring your sorry ass home, you'd better march it right back out that door and start looking for a job so you can help out around here!"), and Penelope's continuing absence.

She's going to come while I'm gone, I repeated to that inner voice which had now gone silent. She's going to come back and I won't be here. Then she'll meet someone else, somebody better, smarter, more deserving of her time.

Maybe she already has, the voice whispered back.

The thought made my throat close up, and I spent the rest of the trip imagining one such scenario after another.

Then skyscrapers peeked over the horizon and I lost myself in the wonder of New York.

When we arrived at the hotel, I marveled over the cavernous lobby. And when I reached my room, I marveled again at how small it was. There was a lesson there, I knew, but I would think about it later.

We ate at a local restaurant, then gathered back at the hotel for the first of our events, a showing in Greenwich Village of New York's oldest running musical, The Fantasticks. Mr. Price told us the production had been active for so long that the actor who played the son had returned decades later to play the role of the father. The smallish theater surprised me, and I wondered how they could sell sufficient tickets to pay the performers enough to live on.

When the show was over we were told to meet the following evening in the lobby of our hotel after dinner, and from there we would walk to Broadway's Circle in the Square Theater. Till then we were left to our own devices, and I spent that next day exploring the city and staring in amazement. Everywhere I turned someone was selling sex in one form or another. Adult bookstores, topless bars, live sex shows, posters for a play called *Oh! Calcutta!* I gawked at it all.

We met at the hotel as a group, then wagon-trained to the theater to watch the play. After all I had seen that day I half-expected the actors to shrug out of their clothes by intermission, but the closest thing to nudity I saw occurred when the ingénue, a beauty by the name of Roxanne Hart, stripped down to her underwear.

Once the show ended and the audience left, the actors kindly showed up for a brief question and answer session with our group. After that we went to a local restaurant. It was very crowded and noisy, full of people talking and laughing. I had never seen anything quite like it. The prices were high, though, requiring me to be careful with my dwindling cash.

I ate while alternating between listening to the talk at our table and people watching. I saw the redheaded actress who, two hours before, had been traipsing about the stage in her bra and panties. She waved at some people she obviously knew and made her way to their table. I followed her with my eyes, trying to be inconspicuous, and wondered how one might survive long enough to live in this fascinating and exciting city.

Then I saw Her.

I cannot say how I could possibly have missed her until then. She made her way from the bar, a small clique in her wake, and headed for the exit. I watched as one of her retinue, an elegant man in his twenties, opened the door while smiling at her in a smitten way I was very familiar with. Penelope smiled in return and stepped out, leading by the hand a young woman who was as beautiful as the man was handsome.

I was out of my seat and through the door in a moment, looking around frantically, no idea what I would say even if I did catch up to her.

There! At the corner, next to the open door of a taxicab, the young man and woman both chattering away with her as they slid inside.

"Penelope!" I cried.

I saw her head tilt, like a bird's, as her eyes turned in my direction.

And stared straight through me, as though I was a windowpane.

Then she was gone.

*　　*　　*

I do not remember much about the trip home. I could think of nothing but the beautiful couple, so elegantly dressed and so very far above my station. I remembered how they had hung on Penelope's every word, their faces glowing with the joy of simply being in her presence.

At some point we arrived back in Sneadsville. I retrieved my suitcase and walked home, then closed my bedroom door and sank into a black depression. My mother grew so worried that she almost stopped yelling at me.

I do not remember how long this went on, the blending of day into night into day again, until one evening my sister grew brave enough to stick her head (just barely) into my room.

"Someone's at the door," she said before vanishing again.

I dragged myself out of bed and walked through the shadow-strewn hallway without raising my head. And when I did, there She was.

I blinked to clear my vision. Still there.

She nodded at me. "Hello, Ace. Let's take a stroll, you and I. We need to talk."

Without waiting for a reply she turned and strode away. The night was chilly, and all I had on was a t-shirt and an old pair of Levi's. Barefooted, I followed her into the night.

We walked to the edge of the street, where Penelope turned to face me. She was dressed in black evening wear, a choker of pearls circling her throat, a small black purse clutched in her hands, her hair piled high like an auburn thunderhead.

"I thought we had a deal, Ace."

Her voice was cold, almost devoid of emotion. And I knew I should be quailing in the face of her obvious anger, but I wasn't. I was angry myself.

"Well?" she said, her jaw tight, her eyes as black as her dress.

"Well what?" I replied, not intending to sound as ill-tempered as I felt, but failing.

"The deal was that you would not make public any connection between us. I had already told you I was coming, eventually, but no, you somehow managed to chase me down to New York where you started yelling my name across Times Square. You have no idea how fast I had to talk to convince my companions that they were mistaken, that no, I had no idea who that was yelling after us, and that no, the so-called gentleman in question had not been crying out 'Penelope', for if he had and if it had been anyone I knew, I would certainly have had the good manners to acknowledge him. I despise lying in others, and even more from myself and those who force me into such. And while I believe myself fortunate enough to have convinced them of their mistake, I cannot say the same for any other large ears which might have overheard you braying 'Penelope!' all across downtown. So tell me," she said, folding her arms, her voice even colder, "How long have you been stalking me?"

"Huh?" I replied, now genuinely confused. "Stalking?"

"Don't lie to me, Ace."

"I'm not lying!" I said. "How could I stalk you? I don't even know where you live!"

"Really? So you just got hungry and decided to drive to New York for dinner? Ace, do you take me for a complete fool?"

"I was with Mr. Price's group! They go to New York every year! Somebody canceled and he asked me if I wanted to go! I didn't even know you were there! I've been sitting around here waiting for months, for years, for you to come back, and I . . . ."

At this point I lost my grip on all of my accumulated anger. A sob choked its way out of my chest, and I hated myself for it, but could not hold it in. "I didn't even want to go, in case you came back while I was gone. But it's been so long, and you didn't even show up for my graduation, and I was so mad at you. So I went, and then I saw you with those other people, and I couldn't help it, I . . ." And at this point my throat swelled shut and I stood there, silent and miserable.

She stared at me. "Do you mean to tell me that your sudden appearance right under my nose was nothing more than a coincidence?" She shook her head. "I don't believe it."

"It's true!" I all but yelled. "You can ask Mr. Price. He called me!"

And then Penelope's face broke and she laughed. "Oh Ace, I didn't mean—that is—oh this is just too much." She laughed, a merry peal that went on for so long I could feel a smile forcing its way to my own lips. "That is a tale of such outrageous proportions I am inclined to believe it must be true."

"It is!" I insisted, my own anger having melted away in the relief that she appeared to accept I was telling the truth.

"Oh, of that I am quite convinced, Ace. No one could make up such a preposterous lie and expect to be believed." She wiped her streaming eyes. "But that does not excuse you for violating the trust I placed in you," she said, her voice serious once again.

"I'm sorry," I told her. "I really am. I've just missed you so much, and you kept promising to come back, and you didn't, and when you sent that note 'Delayed' . . ." I trailed off, the misery returning.

"That could not be helped." She turned her back on me. I forced my mouth shut and waited.

Then she turned to face me once more, a broad smile on her face. "It would seem I have underestimated the power of my charms," she said as she stepped towards me, her long lashes shadowing her eyes. "And for goodness sakes, when did you grow so tall?"

I swallowed the lump in my throat. "It's been three years."

"So long? My, the days have just flown by, haven't they?" She halted a breath's distance away, standing well under my chin as she looked up at me. "And you have grown into quite the young man, haven't you?"

"I've worked hard," I said. "I wanted to make you proud of me, to show you that you haven't been wasting your money. . . ."

"Oh pshaw, what is money?" Penelope said with a wave of her hand. "One day you will see its minor role in the grand scheme of things. Now, what I see is a young man who feels he has been wronged . . ."

"No! I mean—"

She waved her hand to cut me off. "No, no, I have treated you quite shabbily, and mean to make amends. Tell me, might there be an opening in your social calendar into which you could squeeze me? Say, tomorrow night?"

"Tomorrow? I, ah, I think I could manage that," I said, trying to match her humor.

"Splendid! I will send Charles for you at, shall we say seven pm? And your sister as well."

"My sister?" I said, my voice sounding thick and stupid even in my own ears.

"Yes. We are going to have a little dinner party, so dress accordingly. You see—" and here Penelope lowered her voice to a soft whisper. "There is something you and I must discuss, as one adult to another." She rested her right hand over my heart. "Please assure me that this time I may have full confidence in your complete discretion?"

I nodded fiercely. "You can count on me."

"We shall see." She turned and walked back to her Mercedes, idling quietly as it waited for her. "Until tomorrow."

*   *   *

The next day I got up early to fix breakfast for Barb and me before dragging her downtown to Alice's Beauty Den. She kept asking what the occasion was, but I had pledged silence to Penelope and had no intentions of breaking my word. So I told Barb to trust me ("It's a surprise!"), and so she did.

Fortunately this was the weekend, which meant that our mother had made plans that did not include either of us, which in turn meant no bothersome questions about where were we going and when would we return.

The hours crawled by, but pass they did, and finally I heard a knock on our door. It was Charles.

"Ready?" he asked.

I nodded, then went to find my sister, whom I found sprawled on her bed writing yet one more letter to some boy she had met at school. I rolled my eyes and told her the guy was an asshole and she could do better. She snorted before muttering "Takes one to know one," as she walked past me. I made to pinch her on the butt and she squealed "Leave me alone!" while flying out the front door past Charles, who simply stepped to one side and waited while I followed her out. He then opened the rear car door as I stood by and let my sister slide in before joining her.

She turned to me. "We're going to visit Miss Ember?" I did not reply, still holding to the letter of my promise, instead simply shrugging.

"How long will it take to get there?" Barbie asked our driver, since I refused to say anything.

"An hour or so, give or take," Charles answered as he slid behind the wheel, then waited while tapping the steering wheel with the massive and ornate golden signet on his right ring finger. "Seat belts?"

Barb frowned (she did not want to wrinkle her dress, the nicest she had yet received from Penelope), but she obeyed, as did I.

It was already dark, and the air cold. We huddled in our coats until the heat finally kicked in. Charles took us out of town and onto a two-lane country highway I was unfamiliar with.

After an hour of various turns and forks Barb nudged me and mouthed, "Where are we?" Since I had no idea, I shrugged again. Our mother rarely took us anywhere if she could help it, so our circle of familiarity pretty much ended at the city limits.

Perhaps sensing our growing boredom, Charles reached over and switched on the radio. The music was unfamiliar, but soothing, some type of classical orchestra music.

We knew we must be close when Charles turned off onto a gravel road. Trees bordered the narrow lane, huddling so close I wondered what would happen if we were to meet a second vehicle coming from the opposite direction. Barb looked out into the thick copse, the darkness at odds with the glare of our headlights, and visibly shuddered.

After several minutes the trees pulled back and we spotted the outline of an enormous mansion, its lower windows filled with a golden light. I spotted a small structure on one end that looked for all the world like a tower. It was the biggest house I had ever seen.

The circular drive led to a large set of double doors. Charles slowed to a halt, then got out and opened the rear door for us. I got out first, then reached down to help my sister, who was wearing high heels for the first time outside of our own home and therefore still a bit unbalanced.

"Follow me," Charles said before heading for the entrance. The steps were composed of large stone blocks, and worn smooth. I held Barb's hand to steady her. We crossed the threshold and paused, looking up.

The high ceiling left us both gawking. Huge timbers crisscrossed, real beams, not wooden planks nailed together to simulate such. A crystal chandelier hung glittering like frozen candle fire over the foyer. Multiple oil paintings hung on the walls in huge wooden frames, some of the portraits quite old. One in particular caught my eye, a young woman not much older than myself, with white blonde hair and eyes as blue as a winter morning. Her stare appeared to be focused on a spot over my head, and I resisted the urge to turn and look behind me.

"Well, here you are!"

I did turn then. Penelope, dressed in green satin, a necklace of red gems (Garnets? Rubies?) circling her white throat, approached us with open arms.

"Barbie, my dear, how perfectly lovely to see you again." She embraced my sister, kissing her warmly on each cheek. "Such an angel!"

Every human being I have ever known has drawn nothing but a look of scorn from my sister after hearing her given name fall from their lips. Everyone, that is, but our hostess. "Hello, Miss Ember," she said demurely, while I looked on in frank amazement at her uncustomary good manners.

"You do take after your brother, don't you? Penelope, please dear. And speaking of the young man, well, my my. You do clean up nicely, don't you?"

My cheeks flamed as though they were on fire. "You flatter me," I said in my best courtly manner, bowing slightly.

Penelope looked at me as though seeing me for the first time. "Oh, you will do just fine, just fine," she murmured. "Come; let us retire to my sitting room. And please pardon the furniture. I myself am a strong believer in the admonition that form should follow function, which one would never guess after an unsuccessful attempt to sit comfortably on one of these grand monstrosities. Yet I am an Ember, which means I am a slave to tradition, and these chairs have been in my family for more years than I care to count. There's a dear, take your seat in that one, it's by far the least uncomfortable of the ménage. No, Ace, you come sit by me."

I sat next to Penelope, across from Barb. "Miss—Penelope, you have the most beautiful home I have ever seen!" my sister said. "It's like something out of a movie!"

"Why thank you, my dear—Charles, please prepare our guests some refreshments—we stole the designer from Charles Biltmore. Or so I've been told, that is. After assisting in the construction of that lovely chateau in Asheville, many of those craftsmen settled there to live. If you ever visit the town, you will see their influence all over. My family persuaded one of his budding young architects to come here and practice his magic. True, it's a bit solitary — we own all the land between the lake and the river — but the Ember family has always preferred a quiet existence as far outside of the mainstream as possible. Thank you, Charles, please make preparations for dinner."

"How many rooms?" my sister asked, her head swiveling non-stop.

"You seek to make a liar out of me, don't you? I truly cannot recall for certain, but if you would like to try counting for yourself, please feel free to do so. You see," and here she patted my knee, sending an electric shock through me, "I have some matters to discuss with your brother, quite dull but necessary, and while it goes against my sense of etiquette to leave a guest to her own devices, I do promise to take as little of his time as possible. With your permission?"

"Huh? Oh sure," Barb said. "You say I can look around?"

"Pry at will, my dear. All of the family skeletons are securely locked away, so do not fret," Penelope said as she stood. I immediately got up as well. "I recommend you make the library your first stop. The upstairs is far less interesting, but consider any unlocked room fair game while I steal your sibling away for a short time. Ace?" Penelope extended her arm, which I took. She looked up at me, her eyes sparkling, as she led me away.

We turned down one hallway, then another, before pausing at a heavy wooden door. "We will not be disturbed here," she said and stepped inside.

The walls were wine red, the furniture dark wood and more modern than the gilded antiques filling what I had seen of the house so far. A cream-colored love seat rested beneath a huge window with dark green curtains. Penelope reclined into it and patted the cushion beside her. "Sit down, Ace. We have important matters to discuss, you and I."

I sat next to her, all nervous energy. "Okay," I said and waited for her to speak.

She leaned on her elbow against the back of the settee. Lamps with shades made from stained glass cast a soft glow over the room and her features. "You know, Ace, I have practiced this conversation, and how to begin it, multiple times over the years, and I must confess I am still at a loss how to begin. So I hope you will forgive me if I express myself less than elegantly."

I nodded. "It's okay. What did you want to ask—uh, I mean, what did you want to say?"

She sighed. "Well, quickly said is quickly done, and I know you are dancing on pins and needles, so no more procrastinating." She placed a slim hand on my thigh and held my eyes with her gaze. "Ace, one of you, either you or your sister, is going to die tonight."

As I stared into Penelope's unsmiling eyes, a familiar sensation stole over me, one that I remembered from a dream in which the world got smaller and smaller like a rapidly shrinking hallway, until I could not move. Animals during the Ice Age must have felt the same way after wading into a mirror bright pool of water to slake their thirst, only to sink into the morass of a tar pit, while a saber tooth tiger crouched at the water's edge, its yellow eyes gleaming.

"What?" I whispered after finding my voice. Wait, what was wrong with me? She was kidding of course. This was just her strange idea of a joke.

"I know this is going to sound odd," she said, "But as I have said before, I have issues with modern social conventions. You being the eldest, I see it as your place to decide which of you it is going to be."

I stared into her eyes, searching for something, anything, any reason for this sudden burst of madness. And found nothing.

"Are you crazy?" I choked out.

"No, Ace. Please believe me when I tell you that I am perfectly sane. Now granted, were I sitting where you are, I would ask the same question. In fact, you could say that—in a way—I once was in your position, though the circumstances were quite different."

I wanted to slide away from her, but I could not move. "I told you I was not stalking you," I said with as much calm in my voice as I could manage, which was very little. "Ask Mr. Price. I swear! . . ."

She laughed. "Ace, you think this is about New York? No, my dear, if it makes you feel any better, tonight has nothing to do with that. I have been planning the itinerary of this evening for the past three years. Well, maybe four. Now granted, your sudden appearance in the hubbub of Times Square has forced me to modify my schedule somewhat, but the end result has never been in doubt."

At this point my paralysis broke and I stood, backpedaling away from Penelope as fast as I could. "No!" I said.

She shook her head. "Yes, Ace. Now, let me tell you how this is going to go. You have two options. You can pick whichever one of you is to die. The other will live, and I will see to it that the one who survives enjoys a life of such luxury that he or she could only dream of. The second and only other option is for both of you to die. Those are your choices. Now, I know that this comes as quite a shock, so I do understand that you are going to need some time in order to collect your thoughts."

I had stood next to this woman only minutes earlier. She was almost a foot shorter than me and I had to outweigh her by at least seventy pounds. She had no gun, not one that I could see, and no place in that outfit to conceal one, so how did she plan to kill either me or my sister? I could knock her out or something . . .

She shook her head and chuckled. "Ace, you are as transparent as air, and I must warn you before you attempt something stupid. While I can assure you that the notion you might somehow overpower this fragile female sitting before you and attempt an escape is a foolish one, for a moment let's assume you could, just for the sake of argument. You cannot seriously think you could overcome Charles? The man could snap you in half like a twig and we both know that. But before he did, I guarantee you he would take your sister's life in a messy and highly unpleasant fashion while you watched helplessly, knowing you were next. Really, Ace, this is not rocket science. One or both? There is only one sensible option. Now, I have heard that there are multiple stages of grief when faced with death, and had we a week or so to work through them I would be willing to grant you those days. But time is of the essence, and I require an answer now. Who lives, and who dies?"

*   *   *

We walked back into the sitting room, Penelope's arm on my own as she chattered about things I had no concept of, the use of color to create desired moods as she pointed at the walls. Barb sat on a delicate sofa in front of a coffee table of black ebony, her eyes shining. Charles stood just behind her, his large square hands resting lightly on the back of the couch, his fingers silently drumming. A silver tea service took up the small table. It looked very old.

There has to be a way out of this, my inner voice kept repeating over and over. There has to be . . .

"You just sit right here next to me, Ace, there's the fellow. Now, while the Japanese have raised the serving of tea to an art form which must be seen to be believed, we do have certain customs in this house to which we hold. Now, here are the two I mentioned. This is Formosan Oolong (Oolong being Chinese for 'Black Dragon') and this one is English Breakfast. Twinings, of course. You pick one, and we shall serve Barbie the other, so that the two of you share completely differing experiences. So tell me, which shall it be?"

There has to be a way, there has to be a way . . .

Penelope stared at me, her chin resting in the V of her slender fingers. "Ace?"

No way. Oh my God, this is really happening! No way . . .

I looked at my sister, then turned away. "I'll have the English Breakfast."

"Really? Well then, I suppose that leaves the dragon for Barbie. Milk and sugar with that, dear? Oolong has a bit of a bite, it's a tad on the bitter side, but with a sweet aftertaste."

"You said it's black dragon?" Barb said cheerfully. "Well then, I will take it black!" She laughed.

"A lady after my own heart! Here Ace, milk and sugar for you, I know it is a bitter brew. Drink up, my dears!"

I swallowed my tea, my eyes fixed on Barb as she studiously tried to mimic Penelope's dainty manner. I watched as my sister listened to Penelope's endless stream of talk, her eyelids drooping as her head nodded. Eventually, with a soft sigh, she reclined on the sofa and did not move.

Penelope watched her for a moment. "Charles?"

My fingernails bit into my palms as the man gently shook Barb's shoulder. No response.

"Very good. Gather her up, and see to it the young lady gets safely home. She should sleep straight through till morning, but one never knows how a given individual will react to certain soporifics. Call me after you get there, I have another matter for you to attend to."

More than anything, I wanted to rip my sister out of that monster's arms, but to do so would condemn us both. So I watched him leave with her, knowing that I would not see her finish growing up, that I would not stand with her one day at the altar to give her away to whatever man might be fortunate enough to win her heart, and that I would never see the children she always spoke of having with such passion. ("They will have much better lives than we've had, I can promise you that!")

I listened as the front door closed with a heavy thud. "How long?"

"Hmm?" Penelope turned back to me. "How long what, Ace?"

I gritted my teeth and wondered what it would feel like to wrap my fingers around her throat. "How long before the poison takes effect?"

"What?" She shook her head. "Ace, I did not put poison in your tea."

Now I was confused. "But you said you put . . ."

"I put something in your tea, yes. But I never said it was poison."

My head spun. "I don't understand—"

"I know, dear."

"You said it was going to hurt—"

"Of course it will. Dying usually hurts. Unless it happens so quickly one does not even have time to realize it. That will not be the case here, I am afraid."

"Then what?—"

"As far as you are concerned, it does not matter. Trust me in this."

"Oh, why wouldn't I trust you?" I said bitterly. "You've been so honest and truthful up to now."

"My, what a mordant streak you have developed. And that was a completely unfair remark, to say nothing of being untruthful. I have never lied to you, Ace. I have a very strong sense of ethics regarding honesty."

"You said you're going to kill me!"

"And when did I ever say I would do no such thing?"

I realized I was arguing with the insane, so I stopped trying to make sense of her, or of my situation. "So if you didn't poison me," I choked out, my gaze once more taking in the difference in our sizes and her lack of any sort of weapon. "Then how?—"

"You will see. I do have one favor to ask, however." She bent forward, sliding her high-heeled shoes from her pale feet. "I so rarely have the opportunity for an indulgence such as this that I would like to experience it as fully and completely as possible."

I cannot explain why, but a sudden unreasoning terror gripped me, despite the ridiculousness of the situation. Most of what was left of my sanity wanted to spit in her face, but deep within one flickering part still — crazily, perversely — wanted to please her. "What?"

Penelope leaned towards me. I watched as her pupils swallowed first her irises, then the whites of her eyes, now dark as coal. She smiled and her teeth . . . oh God, her teeth . . .

"Would you run?" she whispered.

I did as she asked. I could not have done otherwise. Her laughter chased me down the hallway. Then a mocking silence, followed by the padding of her bare feet as she pursued me. And when she caught me, her body hit me from behind with the force of a truck. A small table rushed up to greet me, and I heard a sickening *crunch* as my head slammed into the marble top. She pinned my arms to the floor like a bug in a science project, and I heard my own screams. Her teeth ripped open my throat, and I watched the spray of my own blood spatter against the wall.

"Thank you," she murmured. "That was—exquisite."

Penelope had not lied. Dying did hurt. It hurt a lot.

And it took a very long time. . . .

*　　*　　*

I listened to the diminishing echoes of the voices in my head. The faces, so clear only a moment before, had vanished in a blur of silvery light. They had told me something, something important that I had to remember, something I must not forget.

But I did forget.

And then they were gone, and all that was left was darkness.

I lay still, unable to move. My heart had stopped beating, my lungs had ceased to swell and contract. Time stretched ahead of me like a desert highway long deserted, its narrowing length vanishing into the distance as I counted each and every step, with no destination in sight. Lying there felt like being buried alive, but lacking the cold comfort of knowing that death must come eventually, bringing relief or — if not relief — at least release.

I wondered, as I listened to the minute scratching of small creatures crawling over me, is this Hell? And if it is, how long before what's left of my mind crumbles like a rotten tooth, leaving . . . what?

But then came sensation.

It began as the faint movement of air against the hair of my arms and my legs. Then — an eternity later — I felt against my back the cold, gritty texture of the stone on which I lay, unable to move.

First sound, then touch. So what comes next?

Light.

It began as a blurring of the darkness, an encroaching gray at the edge of my vision, growing steadily brighter.

And then a voice.

"Yer happy, skipper, sure that they don't spare you the time of day. But I hear them. I hear them pissing in the woods, farting into the wind. And the only answer is to burn them pure. Hey, what the fuck is this?"

A moment of silence, followed by a second voice. "Don't touch that!"

I should know that voice, I thought. But I did not.

"Weeping and wailing, you're all the same. And I'm telling you that none of it matters, you hear me?"

There followed the meaty sound of something heavy slapping against flesh. "None of it matters!" the first voice screamed. "Now, I have to speak pure or else the wiggins there'll be to pay! There a key?"

Another moment of silence. Finally, "There is no key."

"There's always a key!" the voice cried. "Seekers of knowledge do not bloody their knuckles on the door!"

More blows. A low moaning when they stopped.

"I'll prove it to you," the first voice said. Now a rattling, followed by the squeal of hinges. "Aha! You will regret your obstruction, toll taker!"

A spitting, the clearing of a clogged throat. "No, I won't," the second voice said. "Would that you could say the same."

I heard the hollow sound of feet on wooden stairs. "We shall continue our conversation of before, and you will give forth light in the burning! I—"

Then there was a darkening of the gray, and shadows swirled into the outline of a gaunt face edged by a scraggly beard. "What the fuck?—"

A wave of sensations crashed over me, submerging me like a house-high ocean wave, drowning me. I watched in dim horror as the emaciated limbs of a naked man wrapped themselves around the stunned tramp above me, bearing him down to the floor. I listened to the hobo's screams as teeth ripped open flesh and raw red meat gushed forth a fountain of blood. I watched the torrent slow to a stream with wet, sucking sounds, a bright red tongue licking desperately to catch every possible drop, and the sickening realization that, sweet Jesus Christ, that monster, it's—

It's me.

*   *   *

Sanity returned only by inches. When it did, and I realized what I had done, the knowledge struck me like a blow to the face. Trapped between horror and need, I forced myself away. The man lay sprawled, eyes wide with terror, his scraggly hair and beard soaked with blood. His blood. I watched as a dribble of it pulsed from what remained of his throat.

Conflicting desires warred inside me. One, to vomit out the blood I had consumed, stomach heaving until I choked on my own bile. The other? To return to the cooling corpse so I could lick the wounds clean.

Corpse! Good God, I had just killed a man, murdered him in cold . . . well, certainly in blood. What there was left of it.

"Hello?"

The second voice. Elderly. Terrified.

"I heard screams! What's going on?"

He was going to call the police. Or the sheriff's office. Christ, what was I going to do?

"Can you help me?" the quavering voice said. "The bastard tied me to a chair and I can't get loose!"

Bound. Frightened.

Helpless. . . .

I shook my head. Goddammit, had there not been enough insanity for one day?

You can't let him go. He'll be grateful for being freed, but once he sees the dead body in his basement, you know what he's going to do.

Basement. I looked around. Stone floors. Brick walls. Wine racks filled with hundreds of bottles, thick with dust. On the left a stairway, leading up to a sliver of light. And in the center of the room a massive stone table, the outline of a man's shape clearly visible on its surface. My shape.

Where was I?

"Please help me!" the voice cried out.

Maybe he was hurt. Maybe he was dying.

Maybe he was bleeding. . . .

I shook my head again. What if the old man was injured? Could I trust myself to help him? What if—whatever it was that had just come over me did so again, only this time leaving me a bit more sane, more aware of what I was doing all the while?

Penelope Ember, what have you done to me?

Until that moment I had not thought about my one-time benefactress. The sudden awareness that she might be upstairs turned my muscles into water. I remembered my death, how she had killed me, the joy she had taken in my murder, and my helplessness in preventing it.

But you're alive!

No. I remembered dying, the agony of her teeth in my flesh, and the sounds they made scraping against the bones in my neck. The slowing beat of my heart, and the moment that beating ceased. I remembered when the pain stopped, when everything stopped, as a growing darkness sucked me down into . . .

What?

I sat for a long time on the floor, my face in my palms. Eventually the voice started up again.

"Please! Is anyone there?"

Now was the time for calm rational thinking, something I felt incapable of. I wanted to pick a direction, any direction, and run until I could not run anymore. But there were no windows, no other doors. The only way out led up those stairs.

I began searching. I needed something to defend myself with in case Penelope was somewhere up there, hidden. Waiting.

There, next to the stairway, a broom. Not much, but better than nothing. I snapped the handle over my knee, the wood splintered to a jagged point. Now I had a weapon, and a good idea how best to use it.

I moved to the base of the stairway and looked up, poised to run if necessary. (Though where would I run to?) The door above stood ajar maybe an inch, enough to allow for one thin wedge of light. My eyes had adjusted well though, I had no trouble seeing.

I rested my weight on the first step, my feet far to the side to minimize creaking. Slowly, with my left hand on the rail and the broomstick handle in my right (point forward), I made my way up.

I paused at the top and peered through the opening. The room I saw was almost the size of my house. In the center rested a granite island large enough to seat a family of twelve. Enormous cabinets of dark wood covered the walls. On the far side I saw a farmhouse sink big enough to bath a six year old in. Dual ovens perched near an eight burner gas range. And nearby stood a refrigerator easily twice as wide of any normal icebox. The kitchen.

I stayed where I was, my gaze sliding over the stainless steel appliances, using them as improvised mirrors. No one there.

Will she cast a reflection?

My brain backpedaled fast from the implications of that thought. I shuddered, then stepped through the doorway while spinning to face the other direction, my teeth bared in a defiant and terrified snarl.

Nothing. More cabinets. Packages of frozen food melting on the stone countertops. And nearby, a complicated and expensive-looking device with what had to be the smallest coffee pot I had ever seen.

I stepped around the kitchen island. Several knives lay there. I put down my makeshift spear and picked up the largest. Then I looked around. Double doors, no knobs. And on the other side, breathing, with a bit of a rattle in the throat. I hefted the knife and pushed open one of the doors just far enough to glimpse through.

A massive dining room table filled the available space. It could have seated twenty people, with room for more at the ends. Enormous oil paintings covered wainscoted walls. Below the portraits rested several large china cabinets, one devoted entirely to crystal. At the far end a window stretched from floor to ceiling, shrouded by heavy drapes the color of dark wine. Below the window, a chair. In the chair a man, wrinkled and gray, his arms and legs tightly bound, his face bruised. Blood flecked a day old beard.

Blood. . . .

I stuck my left index finger into my mouth, biting down hard, and did not let go until tears started to flow. I had killed once. I was not going to do it again.

The head lifted. "Someone there?"

I stepped through the door, the knife in my hand. Even I did not know my intentions. The man gasped as he saw me.

"You! I—I—Please don't hurt me!"

I looked down at myself. Naked, blood streaking my chest (and likely my face as well), a large knife in my hand. Christ, it was a wonder I had not killed him just with the sight of me.

I shook my head. "He's dead," I said, indicating the way I had come with a jerk of my head before tilting my chin in the old man's direction. "Did he? . . ."

He swallowed, nodded. "He was going to set fire to the house, burn it down. He made no sense, jabbering like a crazy man."

"I couldn't help it," I said, waving the knife for emphasis before I realized how I must have looked. I lowered it, but did not put it down. "Where is she?" I whispered.

"Huh?" The old man looked confused. "Where is who?"

"The woman who lives here. The owner. She—last night—I . . ."

The man shook his head. "No one here but me," he said. "And I've lived here alone for over a year now, since the missus . . ." He choked up and fell quiet.

Of course. Her house, eh? A lie. Pardon me, another lie, just one more to crown Penelope's stack of them. And a man sent to destroy the scene of the crime, and any evidence of what she had done along with this old fellow, whose voice still sounded maddeningly familiar.

"Self defense, that's what it sounds like to me," the man said. "I see you overcame him. Hope he didn't hurt you."

Hurt me? He did struggle, I recalled, the way a small child might struggle when it does not wish to be held. And near the end a relaxing, as though he knew death was inevitable and simply surrendered.

"Now sir," the man said, "If you would untie me, we can see about making things right. I thought I heard voices outside not long ago, perhaps our would-be arsonist has friends."

I nodded, that made sense. "I'm sorry," I said, gesturing at myself before making my way to the chair. "I've been attacked twice now."

The man nodded, his eyes locked on my right hand. Ah, the knife. I put it down on the table, reluctant to give it up but unwilling to terrify the old geezer any more than he already had been. "I'll just undo the knots," I said as I bent over him.

I started with his ankles, bound to the legs of the chair so tightly that the skin below the ropes had turned blue. I heard him gasp in pain as I turned my attention to his wrists. He shook so hard the ring on his right hand rattled against the arm of the chair as I loosened the last of the ropes.

The ring . . .

I bent forward after freeing him, my eyes fixed on the multi-colored stone in its golden setting, and I remembered where I had seen it before, tapping against the steering wheel of a silver Mercedes. And as I recognized the ring, I recognized the voice as well.

I looked up into a pair of rheumy eyes, now wide with terror. But how had he grown so old?

I did not know. And I did not care.

"*Charrleess,*" I whispered.

He tried to bolt. I grabbed him by the front of his shirt, lifted him out of his chair, and smashed him into the wall beside the window.

"Goddamn you, you son of a bitch!" I cried as I pushed my face into his, my need to rip open his throat warring with my need for information. I compromised, slamming his head backwards as I emphasized each word. "Where—is—my—SISTER!"

His hands flew above his head, as though surrendering. Then his arms jerked down.

And I screamed.

I had felt pain before. When Penelope tore open my throat, only to rip away at the flesh beneath, I thought I had never felt such pain in my life.

This was worse. My eyes exploded as though a foot long needle had been jammed into each one. I howled as I fell to the floor, my fists jammed into my sockets. The pain dimmed, but just barely.

"Hurts like hell, doesn't it?" The clucking of a tongue. "They told me it feels like having your eyes put out with hot irons. No damage though, or so they claimed, at least not initially. Prolonged exposure, now, that's another matter."

I heard diminishing footsteps, followed by the creaking of someone taking a seat on the other side of that bright, fiery wedge of agony. Or so what was left of my senses told me.

"Now the Lady, *she* could go out during the day, though never without sunglasses and a veil, so long as she stayed inside the car with them shaded windows. Trained herself for it, she did, though she could only do it for brief periods of time. The sun was a killer for her too, though not like in the movies where you burn up like a sheet of flash paper. It's a slow death, like being roasted alive. Not sure how long it takes."

I sobbed in my pain and fury, unable to move, wanting nothing more. "I'll kill you!" I howled.

A pause. "Well, that may be true," he finally said. "And it may not. But either way I have a job to do, a job I've been waiting on for a while now. So let's get that out of the way first. Then we'll see about any killing that must be done."

"And since I cannot imagine you hearing (much less understanding) much of what I say while being in that much pain," he continued, "we're going to deal with that first. I know you can't move your hands away from your eyes, so what I want you to do is use your elbows and knees and move to your left. Once you reach the wall crawl backwards until you find the corner. That'll take you out of any direct sunlight, but you should still keep your hands over your face. You're not the Lady, after all."

Despite (or, to be more truthful, because of) the pain, I did as Charles advised. I could tell when I found the shadowed corner, since the pain receded, though not completely. I huddled there, face against the floor.

"Good. Now, after we've had a chance to play catch up, I'll see about putting those drapes back. Until then they stay down, on account of the way I see it, that wall of light between us is the only guarantee I have of you staying where you are and being a good boy. We understand one another?"

I gritted my teeth. "Yes," I growled.

"You don't sound all that convincing, but I'll let that slide for the moment. Now, first things first. Your sister. . . ."

I stiffened, suppressing the overwhelming urge to leap through that burning space between us, fire be damned. "Where is she?"

"Calm down, no reason for you to get all anxious on me here. Fact is, she's fine. Better than fine. The Lady kept her word, like she always does, took good care of her. Your sister married a prince."

I could not have heard what I thought I had heard. "What?"

"Huh? Oh, sorry, I didn't mean she married a *real* prince. She married one of the Durham Princes. Nathaniel Prince. Family made their fortune in tobacco, then went into pharmaceuticals and made another one. Lady Ember saw to it that your sister got a scholarship to Duke University. Not exactly an honor student, but one heck of a cheerleader. That's where she met Nate. He played shooting guard for the Blue Devils. Third string though, he was a walk-on. Team went to the NCAA finals their senior year, as I recall."

"Married?" I tried to wrap my brain around the word.

"Yep. Two kids. I hear they're a comfort to her, what with her husband passing on and all."

Passing on? "How long?"

"I think Nate died two years ago or so. Oh, wait, maybe I misunderstood you. She got married in, what, 1988? Or was it '89?"

I dug my nails into my face to remind me what would happen if I moved my hands. I could tell by his voice he understood what I was asking, he was just toying with me. "How long?"

Charles sighed. "Now don't you go and get stupid on me here, ok? It's been about thirty years."

No.

No. . . .

"You're lying."

"Nope. It's the year of our Lord 2009. October 31st. Halloween, if you can believe it." He chuckled.

At that moment I could not have moved even if day had turned into night. "What did you do to me?" I whispered.

"What did *I* do? Boy, I haven't done anything."

"You know what I mean," I hissed.

Charles did not speak for some time. "There are a few things you need to learn," he finally said, no banter in his voice now. "First thing you need to know is this, you don't know shit, understand me? You may *think* you do, but you don't! You absolutely do not have one fucking clue. Which is why I'm here. You've got a lot to learn, and I'm your teacher. And even at that, I'm pre-school only. Then after we're done here you go straight to college, God have mercy on you. Because They won't."

The pain dimmed a bit. A cloud passing overhead, perhaps? What time of day was it, anyway? "They who?" I asked.

"Well, there's a lot of different names for them, just don't call them vampires. That's like calling a black man a nigger. They have their own name for themselves in their own language, but when speaking in English they refer to themselves as the Breed."

I felt light-headed, as though the world had been flattened and stretched thin.

"This can't be true," I whispered.

Charles went on as though I had not spoken. "I'm sure you've read some books, seen a lot of movies. Maybe you think you know what you are. I'm here to tell you that you don't."

The tramp in the basement. "You're going to tell me that vampires don't drink blood?"

I felt him flinch at my use of the 'V' word. "No, that part's true."

"So what isn't true? Am I damned? Have I lost my soul? If I die, what happens to me now? Do I go straight to Hell? I didn't choose this!"

"Well, not being a religious man, I can't answer any of those questions. Personally, I stopped believing in God a long time ago. But that's just my opinion, I could be wrong. Sorry, that show was after your time."

In all honesty, I had begun to have such doubts about the existence of God myself. But if I really was a—vampire—did that mean God did exist? And if so, did He hate me now? Could I step into a church without bursting into flames?

"I didn't choose this," I repeated.

"No you didn't," Charles said. "You were chosen."

What? "Why?"

Another long silence. "Well, that's a tale for someone else to tell, not me. And that person is Lady Ember herself."

Penelope. Oh God, and I could not even uncover my eyes long enough to see her coming. "Where is she?"

Again the pause. "I wish I knew."

Relief flooded over me. "She's not here?"

"She's not anywhere. I haven't seen or heard from her for over a year now. And if what I suspect is true, that makes you the last."

Huh? "The last what?"

Charles sighed. "Boy, unless I am mistaken (and believe me, I wish I was), you are the sole surviving member of House Ember."

*   *   *

I watched from the corner as Charles adjusted the curtains, blocking the last bit of light. I wanted to bear him down, listen to his screams as I did to him what Penelope had done to me.

Then what would be the difference between you?

That is not the same thing! He knew what she planned to do. He *helped* her! He deserves to die!

Oh, so now we decide who gets to live and who dies? And we were so concerned about the state of our soul a moment ago.

Shut up!

"What are you mumbling about, boy?"

"Nothing," I muttered.

Charles shook his head. "We need to get you cleaned up. Follow me. There's a room set aside just for you to make use of."

I followed him, wondering what kind of noises he would make while trying to breath through a set of teeth clamped onto his windpipe. "Does it include a coffin?"

"Hah! That's better. No, the Lady did not sleep in a coffin. Fact is, she never slept at all that I know of. But I didn't spend every waking moment in her presence, more's the pity."

As we walked, we passed through a now familiar section of the mansion. I saw the heavy table with its green marble top which had broken my skull. We continued on. Charles led me to a room in what must have been the opposite wing of the house. Like the mansion itself, the room was large and decorated with antiques black with age. "Here you are. Might be a few cobwebs, but I try to keep the place neat. It's a suite, bathroom is the door to the left, closet's the one to the right. You'll find clothes in there, and shoes. Socks and underwear are in the dresser.

Charles walked to a large desk next to the closet door, then opened a drawer. "How're your eyes?" he asked.

I blinked. Tears still streamed from the corners, and I had a pounding headache. But my vision had steadily cleared, once the sunlight was gone.

Charles nodded as he watched me returning his gaze. Then he placed an object on the bed. "There it is. I watched her write in that thing for almost thirty years. She said if you 'woke up', and she wasn't around, that I was to give it to you."

I sat on the bed, my legs still shaky. "A book?"

"Yep. I've got groceries in the kitchen that still need to be put away. I suggest after you wash the blood off your face you start reading that. I'll be back later." And with that, Charles left.

Blood on my face? For a moment, the idea of looking into a mirror terrified me. What would I see?

When I did look, the sight was just unsettling. Yes, I could still see my reflection, though it was cold comfort. The entirety of my face was stained dark with dried blood. My chest was awash with it. My hair stuck up in clotted spikes, and where I was not covered in blood I was layered with dust.

I shuddered, then crawled into the shower. I turned the hot setting as high as I could get it and still the water felt cold. A bottle of liquid soap rested on a ledge, I used half of it. When I could finally hear my hair squeak and my skin was no longer covered with filth, I got out and dried off. Then I stared once more into the mirror.

The image still looked like me, though older, as though I had aged years during my so-called 'sleep'. No wrinkles, but a sharpening of the features. Also thin. Very thin. And as pale as a ghost.

Next to the door hung a soft robe. I pulled it on, then padded out in bare feet to look down at Penelope's book. The covers were cloth, the spine leather. Unfamiliar symbols decorated the front, gold edged the pages. I stared at it as though it was a snake before picking it up.

I reclined on the bed and opened it. The old leather crackled and the scent of dust tickled my nose as I turned to the first page.

*   *   *

December 26, 1980

Hello, Ace.

As I sit here at my desk, pen in hand, I am picturing the circum-stances under which I will be forced to communicate with you via this journal. They are not pleasant circumstances to imagine, and if you bear me any ill will then you may take comfort in the knowledge that if you are reading this, there are two assumptions you may safely make. First and foremost (if you will forgive the priority to which I assign these matters), consider it a given that I am no more. And if recent events continue in the same fashion as they have thus far, Charles will have no clue as to my ultimate fate.

Now, while I cannot with confidence predict your current situation, I will assume that you have recently awakened and are therefore quite con-fused. It is also quite likely you are in denial, so let us deal with that first.

While we deplore the term, yes, you are now a vampire. Under more typical circumstances, adjusting to this change is a process for which con-siderable time is allotted. Unfortunately, time is a luxury you can ill afford. For you are in considerable danger, and if you are to avoid my own probable fate, you must act with great haste.

If you regard these words with suspicion, I can certainly understand why. I did murder you, after all. But it was for a good cause, and should you find your new existence so disagreeable that you choose to discontinue it, well, that is your choice (albeit not a pleasant one, which I shall elaborate upon later.)

I chose you for a reason, Ace, because I saw in you one whose innate gifts and ambitions placed him far above his fellow man; admittedly not an arduous task. And if you take this indictment of your former brethren poorly, fret not; for with the passage of time they shall give you more than ample cause to similarly regard them.

I gave you your name for a reason as well. You are my ace in the hole, my own personal insurance policy. The fact that you are reading this allows for the second assumption you may make, that you are the last surviving member of House Ember. And if you cannot discover who our enemies are, and subsequently defeat them, then the previous four hundred years will have all been for naught, and a noble family which has endured adversities beyond your comprehension shall cease to exist.

We are the Breed, Ace. We have lived in the world, yet not of it, since the dawn of civilization. And while our own history is no less flooded with drama than that of human beings, we have risen above it to establish cultures and traditions which have endured even as the empires of humanity have crumbled into dust.

Our society consists of twelve great Houses. Not all have endured since the beginning, our own House is a product of more modern times, having its roots in what is euphemistically referred to as the Age of Enlightenment. The eldest of our Houses is Winterfax, a family of such ancient lineage that no one alive (well, so to speak) was present during its founding. We, House Ember, are sept to Winterfax. I was fostered there by its Visconté, Andracéil, the White Lady, who has ruled the halls of that ancient Seat since before Christopher Columbus had yet to be weaned from his mother's teat.

And yes, I did use the word 'family'. We are a ancient people, and rarely add to our numbers. Future prospects for potential inclusion among our kind are typically evaluated among the topovar, and if through tragedy or malice we lose one of our own, another is chosen from among them to rise and take his or her seat alongside us.

Topovar is, of course, a new word to you, and requires a bit of explanation, as well as the dispelling of a few preconceptions. We of the Breed do not kill to feed. While I can already hear your protests (which I played no small part in validating), do not consider your own experience to be in any way typical. For us to blithely slay for regular sustenance would be more than foolish, it would be suicidal. While we are a formidable species, we are—by choice—few in number, and no quicker path to extinction could be found than to randomly slay humans right and left to sustain ourselves, even if there were need. And there is no need.

The topovar are the answer to our twin concerns, to feed free of the fear of discovery and to have those among us from whom the best might be selected when or if it becomes necessary to add to our numbers, fixed by ancient tradition. We walk amongst humanity, considering prospects from which to add to our flocks, and from them we feed. We do not slay them, but take only enough blood to sustain ourselves.

In exchange, we give much. You have seen for yourself how we nurture our prospects (for yes, you and your sister were being so evaluated at the time of our first meeting). And there are other benefits, not the least

of which is the possibility of being elevated to our level, though such oc-
currences are rare and even among the topovar are the stuff of legend. You
should feel privileged that you have been included among our kind. And
one day, I am confident, you will.

I can hear the mordant tones of your denial in my head as to how we
sustain ourselves. For I did slaughter you, and in a most cruel fashion. But
as with all that I do, there was a reason for it.

Now, I would be quite dishonest if I were to claim that the taking
of your life came hard. It was, I must confess, a private indulgence on
my part. For while we are more herdsmen than hunters, and have been
so for thousands of years, there still beats within us (if you will pardon
the awkward metaphor) the heart of a predator. Few are the opportunities which allow us to embrace our hidden nature to hunt, to pursue, to
feel the quiver of our prey as it surrenders its life to our needs. And since
you had to die, I allowed myself that one pretty pleasure. For after the
botched incident of New York, I was convinced we had drawn the attention of unseen others who may have suspected I had plans for you. Those
persons had to be convinced that you were nothing to me, not even a
prospective topovar, much less a candidate for elevation. You had to appear a mere dalliance, for had your true purpose been divined then your
likely death would have been of a more permanent nature, this being the
most optimistic of all the potential outcomes. I shall spare you the possible alternatives.

Despite your B movies and trashy popular novels, one does not ascend
to our ranks by dying from our feeding. No, to become one of us, one must
consume a quantity of our own blood. You will remember I told you that
your tea contained a foreign substance, and it did. When you drank it, you
drank my own blood, and thus began the process of transformation.

Once set in motion, this process can only be undone by the most
violent of circumstances involving the destruction of one's physical form.
Normally the siring of a new family member is a process requiring a month
or so to complete, as the living body alters and is transformed.

Unfortunately, while there are rumors of those among our kind who
have devoted great amounts of time and significant resources to learning
more about our nature as a species, I must confess I am not one of them.
But I do know that even among ourselves, the slaying of a human who has
tasted our blood, this followed by the subsequent rising of his or her lifeless

corpse into a new existence, is — well, the stuff of fireside tales. No one I have spoken with has ever seen it done, though all have heard the stories. So yes, this meant there was a possibility of your lifeless condition becoming a permanent one. But after New York I had no other option, and decided to make the best of a bad situation. If it worked, then House Ember might yet escape annihilation. If not, well, you would hardly know any different now, would you?

Ace, in your mind I know I have given you no reason to trust me, and every reason to hate me. I can only say that what I did, I did for my House, that it might not perish from the face of the earth. You are young still, but with time you will come to see that there is no greater tragedy than for a parent to witness the death of her children, to see one's family perish, to endure the end of a legacy and be forced to drink that cup to its bitter dregs before the coming of one's own end. For this has been my fate. Unseen and unknown enemies have, one by one, destroyed the members of the Ember family, striking from the shadows at those who have looked to me for protection, all of whom I have failed. And now my last hope lies in my basement, sleeping a sleep that has lasted far longer than our tales say it should. The sole balm to my anxiety has been that your body has not suffered corruption. Yet still you lie, cold and unmoving. What should have taken a day, according to our tales, has exceeded a full year. Earlier today I stood over you, marveling at your still unblemished perfection, searching for wounds now long closed. Yet still, you sleep.

As I stared at you, I could not ignore the niggling worry which gives me no peace. For you should not be, and yet you are. Which prompts a question, Ace.

What are you?

*   *   *

There was a knock at the door. "Yes?"

"May I come in?" Charles asked.

I entertained a wide range of possible responses, then filed the best ones away for future use. "Yes."

He entered with an empty laundry basket. "These clothes and towels have been waiting on you for quite some time. I figure they could do with a fresh wash and a bit of fabric softener. Can't do anything about the styles, but no doubt you'll be wanting a new wardrobe anyway, so we'll just make do with a pair of Levi 501's and a white button-down for now. Far as the sneakers are concerned you're lucky, Chuck Taylors are popular again. Jack Purcells too, but you'd be hard pressed to find those any larger than a thirteen, and a small thirteen at that. So with those feet I wouldn't bother."

My eyes went to the drapes on the far side of the room. Somewhere there had to be a hammer and nails. "Thirty years?"

"Um hmm," he said as he collected the wet towels from the bathroom's marble floor. "You know, in all the years I knew my Lady, never once did time touch that perfect face. Then you failed to rise after the first day. And then the days became weeks, the weeks turned into months, and the months into years. I remember her first wrinkle, a cobweb in the corner of her right eye." He sighed, a heavy wheeze that ended in a cough. "She started avoiding mirrors after that."

A multicolored mixture of emotions overflowed my chest. I clenched my hands into fists to defend against the flood. "What happened to her?"

"Well, after your 'death', she stayed here, communicating with no one except her lambs (that's what she always called us), like Arthur and Tracy Bingham in New York. The three of us were the last of her little flock here on the east coast, not counting the topovar of other family members already listed amongst the missing and presumed deceased. The Lady couldn't sustain herself with just me, and it's a long flight out to Los Angeles where Melanie and George live, so she flew to Manhattan once or twice a month. By then you had become an obsession with her, so she only left the house when she had no choice.

"Last year she took another trip up north. She was depressed, and appeared to have given up all hope of ever seeing you rise. She always contacted me after her arrivals, so when I didn't hear from her within a reasonable amount of time I called the Binghams. I remember a young woman answered the phone, their daughter. She got her mother, who told me they were in a panic, that her husband had went to the airport but our Lady never got off the plane." He sighed, a deep exhalation that left him shrunken, his shoulders bowed. "Since then we have spent a large and quite literal fortune searching for her, but we know no more now than we did back then."

I tried to make sense of what I was feeling, but could not. So I squashed my emotions down, far down, until I felt nothing. "She was the last of her—family?"

Charles pulled a handkerchief from his back pocket and coughed into it, a phlegmy racket that went on forever. "So she said, and I have no reason to doubt her. The Breed, well, they don't experience time the way we humans do. In my entire life I've only met two other Embers, Joshua and Priscilla. Those were their common names, I have no idea what their family names were."

I watched Charles as he pulled items of clothing from the chest of drawers and the closet. "What happened to them?"

"Same thing that happened to the others, they simply disappeared. Family matters are rarely discussed with topovar, and never with outsiders, but the night before the Lady left that last time she just started talking, confirming a lot of what I had picked up on over time.

"According to her, it took a while before the Embers realized anything unusual was going on. It wasn't uncommon for years to go by without hearing from a given family member. Eli was the first to go missing, but he had a reputation as a daredevil and a risk taker. His topovar had no contact information for any of the Embers, so when he failed to come home one night they didn't know what to do. They couldn't call the authorities, rule number one among the Breed is to minimize human contact. So they did some investigating of their own, but it was like Eli had dropped off the face of the earth.

"But like the rest of the Breed, the Embers are people of tradition, and one of those traditions is a family reunion every ten years. Mostly to discuss House business, but for social purposes too. There are no acceptable reasons not to be present, and even if one existed the potential absentee would be expected to contact his Visconté and beg for permission to be excused. And if permission was denied, you showed up, no matter what the circumstances might be."

I remembered that word from Penelope's journal. "Visconté?"

"The Lady's official title as House matriarch. The Visconté is responsible primarily for family matters, things like interpreting House etiquette in cases where there's a dispute about what's proper. That might not sound terribly important to you, but understand, the Breed doesn't really have what you would call 'laws'. Laws would require some sort of power structure, but the various Houses are laws unto themselves. Traditions, customs, etiquette, these are the things which define their social structure. Normally there's a Valyar as well, a House patriarch who deals with the outside world and how it affects the family. But something had happened to the last Valyar Ember. Couldn't tell you what, though, that was way before my time. Understand, the Breed does not marry. But somebody has to manage House affairs, so each has a matriarch and a patriarch. And if something happens to one, then another is chosen from the lower ranks by the remaining head of the family, though Houses have on occasion allied with other Houses by taking on a new Valyar or Visconté from another aligned House, or so the Lady told me. Very rare though, since it's considered a sign of weakness. The impression I got was that Lady Ember had been very close to the previous Valyar and was resisting pressure from the other members of the House to name a new one.

"So when invitations were sent out for the next family gathering, and Eli failed to respond to his own, the Lady hired an agency to investigate. But they came up empty, and after a while the final consensus was that Eli's disappearance was just one of those mysteries which never gets solved. The search never truly ended, but Eli had few friends in the family, some old falling out that never got fully resolved, and after a while all efforts to find out what had happened to him became token ones.

"Juliet was the next to go missing, and according to the Lady that did stir up a hornet's nest. She was the family historian, and very close to Joshua and Priscilla, who were brother and sister to one another before they were ever sired, supposedly by Juliet herself. That appeared to be more of an accident that anything else, plane she was in went down somewhere over the Arizona desert. Found the plane, never found her.

"You have to understand something. The Embers were a small family to begin with. Bringing in a new member is as serious to the Breed as electing a president is to us. More so, you could say, because a president can only hold office for eight years. The Breed do not age, so long as they have access to blood, so siring a new family member is a decision that could theoretically affect a House forever. And from what the Lady told me that night, there have been times where a House has risen or fallen based on the consequences resulting from a new addition to the family. They take these things very seriously.

"Then the mansion burned down."

I watched Charles place the now full laundry basket on a nearby dresser before he sat, obviously weary. "What mansion?" I asked.

"Family seat. Somewhere in Western Europe. Happened at another Decennial. Only Joshua, Priscilla and the Lady made it out."

"For someone family matters were not discussed with, you seem to know an awful lot," I said.

Charles grunted. "When one keeps his ears open and his mouth shut, it's amazing what one can learn. More folks should consider giving it a try."

I chose to ignore the sarcasm. "So what happened then?"

"The brother and sister stayed here for a while with the Lady, them and their own little flocks. I remember when the three of them closeted themselves in the library, and the rest of us knew what was being discussed. Someone was going to be elevated. And sure enough, someone was. Young girl, Anatolia, a favorite of Priscilla's. I gathered that there had been a regular broohaha over who the new addition would be, judging from the tension between the siblings, but of course we were never included in any of that.

"So the choice was made, and the process begun. They took a trip together, and as I understand it, something happened to Anatolia. Never found out what exactly, but the Lady came back alone, and very shook up. She stayed here for a while, like she was waiting for Joshua and Priscilla. But they never showed.

"That was when she hatched her plans for you. This was not long after we met you and your sister for the first time. After your 'death', she made plans, dealt with some lawyers, had this house and some other properties and investments put into a trust, with me in charge and you as the beneficiary. If anything ever happened to her, then I was to consider you the master of House Ember and serve you accordingly."

I stared, trying to comprehend all of this. "You're crazy," I whispered, knowing I was repeating myself from what was (for me) the night before, yet unable to do otherwise.

"No, I assure you I am quite sane." He hacked once again into his handkerchief, then picked up the laundry basket and walked out, closing the door as he left.

Okay, I thought, so now what?

Stupid question, you know what you have to do. Get away. Escape.

But the thought of facing a still risen sun froze me in place. Sympathetic tears flowed again at the memory of that searing light frying my eyes in their sockets.

No, of course there was no escape, not while it was still daylight. And as I thought about it, I realized something else, where could I go? I had no clue where I was, Barb and I had been driven here after dark, along unfamiliar highways and country roads. How far was the closest house, or store? And what would I do if I found one?

You're trapped here.

I clenched my fists, nails biting deep into my palms. No. Somehow, someway, I was getting out.

Then I had an idea.

I searched for Charles, getting lost twice. How big was this house anyway? Eventually I found him in a laundry room not far from the kitchen. "You say you work for me now?"

He squinted, then shook his head. "Understand this, boy, I do not 'work' for *you*. I *serve* House Ember."

I nodded. "And I am the last Ember, so far as you know?"

He nodded in turn, albeit far more slowly.

I took a deep breath. "Very well, here is the first thing I want. Come nightfall, you and I are taking a little trip."

He stared at me, eyes narrow with suspicion. "Where are we going?"

"We're going to pay my sister a visit."

*   *   *

But first, there was a body to dispose of.

Charles went outside ("Gonna check the storage building for a tarp.") Dying rays from the setting sun fanned over the grass like bloody razor blades. And while I could not approach the floor-to-ceiling windows of the appropriately named solarium to monitor him, if I stood back far enough I could look outside without harm. The danger appeared to lie in direct exposure.

As I watched Charles disappear into the estate's utility building, I recalled once sitting on the front porch of my old home in early July, watching the sun set. In the summer that golden orb beat down mercilessly on those weathered boards with their peeling paint, but not that day. I remembered the creaking of the porch swing, the air drunk with the scent of flowers as I gently swung back and forth, the sun's rays warming my face. A feeling I was never going to experience again.

A plan, my inner voice whispered. *You need a plan, one that doesn't include him. He cannot be trusted. You* know *that.*

I did. But what were my alternatives?

Like it or not, my mobility was now limited. I could only move about freely by night, which meant if I got away from Charles I would have to find a hiding place by dawn. And what would happen if I was discovered? (I did not allow myself to consider what would happen were there no hiding places to be found.)

"Right now our—well, *your*— enemies are sticking to the shadows," Charles had said before walking out the back door. "I say 'your' because, as far as I can tell, whoever is behind all of this appears to be leaving the top-ovar alone. Don't get me wrong, I'm not saying that we're being shown any particular mercy. Most likely we're just too insignificant to bother with, so far as they're concerned. And after thirty years, I'm hoping they're as blind to you as we are to them—at least for now—and that our downstairs guest was just a local nutcase."

"You knew him?" I had asked.

"He used to hang around the top of an exit ramp near here, carrying a cardboard sign with 'Homeless, Please Help!' on it while panhandling from drivers waiting at the stoplight. I had no idea he even knew where this place was.

"And while I'm thinking about it, something else you need to understand, particularly if you keep insisting on this little family reunion notion. If for any reason you reveal yourself as what you are, whether deliberately or by accident, then you had better find a quick way to commit suicide. Because not only will you be advertising your existence to whoever has been waging war on House Ember, you're gonna have the Breed after you too. And they'll want to make an example out of someone that careless, or that stupid. So whatever punishment they come up with, you can count on two things. One, it will involve the kind of pain that'll make the Spanish

Inquisition look like a game of Slap and Tickle, and two, they will ensure it takes a very long time for you to die. Assuming, of course, they allow you to die at all. Believe me, you have no idea how cruel they can be to someone they view as a traitor. Or a threat."

It never occurred to me that any of this might be a lie, since it made perfect sense. So whatever I did, whatever I might do, I could never reveal what I was now to anyone. Especially my sister.

All of which meant that running away was not a viable option, at least for now. And while I desperately wanted to find Barb (if for no other reason than to confirm Charles's story), meeting with her might put her in as much danger as I seemed to be in.

So what were my alternatives?

You could simply end it all. Rob that lying bitch of her hopes and dreams and end her little dynasty right here. It's not like anyone will miss you after thirty years.

Kill myself? Just give up and surrender? Allow my life, at its end (well, its second end) to mean nothing?

No, it means you do not allow the thing you have become to rule you, to define what you are. One last noble act of selflessness. Be practical. Think how many lives you might save by taking your own.

I found a chair, then pulled Penelope's journal out of my back pocket and scanned its vellum pages. She had mentioned something about this, hadn't she?

I turned to where I had left off and read, keeping half an eye out for Charles's return.

* * *

January 1, 1981

Four am. New Year's Day. Outside of my window, the revelers are long disbanded, having left a carpet of refuse in their wake. Music from the rag end of Dick Clark's New Year's Rockin' Eve still blares from the distant television, its froth a counterpoint to my memories of Guy Lombardo and his Royal Canadians playing Auld Lang Syne, of men in tuxedos and women in evening gowns dancing while wearing their silly hats in the ballroom of the Waldorf-Astoria.

I can only imagine Jester's cynical laughter at my nostalgia's expense.

Please pardon my maudlin muses as I contemplate yet another shiny new year. How many have there been, passing like eye blinks in the long stare of my life?

Yes, I am aware of the ridiculous metaphor. Work with me here, Ace, because I cannot remember the last time I pondered such notions. For many decades, the years have passed for me like a thread in an endless ball of yarn. But now I find myself noting each passing day. And why?

Because of you.

Since I am depressed, I might as well exploit this opportunity and address a depressing topic. While the thought fills me with dismay, I must acknowledge that you may be unable to cope with the realities of your new-found existence. You would certainly not be the first. And, endless movie sequels aside, our kind most certainly can be destroyed. The difficulty lies in that very word: Difficulty.

The walls of secrecy which protect our kind also serve as a barrier to human sciences. Our culture of minimal contact has impeded us from a greater understanding of our own physical nature. We are a society of Luddites, dwelling within a sphere of willful ignorance, and very suspicious of change. I am, among our kind, considered to be a maverick as regards an appreciation of such things as science and technology, but even I possess neither the education nor the aptitude to fully understand who and what we are.

But for all this, there is much we do know. Our regenerative capabilities are preternatural, which means we are very hard to kill. For this reason, the intentional termination of our own existence, while possible, is unpalatable.

You need to understand this, Ace. For a human, life is sufficiently transient that it may be ended with minimal pain. We, however, have no such option. Our bodies resist destruction to such an degree that the willful ending of our existence is not only an agonizing but also a time-consuming process. To be sure, it is not unknown among us, but the suffering required to achieve such an end is nigh unimaginable. Not to mention that our unique biochemistry renders the use of analgesics moot. Remember this, for while you will quickly heal from levels of trauma which would extinguish the life of a typical human being like a candle's flame in a storm, you will have no relief from the consequential pain.

And even though you might survive even the most well-planned and executed attempt to end your life, you may not heal well. While we can regenerate lost organs and even body parts, that does not mean we are guaranteed to spring back to the image of our former selves like a child's doll. Sufficient trauma can cripple us, rendering us invalids for decades. Or worse.

One of the more ghastly of our tales concerns a certain Margaret, who kept an appointment with the guillotine during the French Revolution. Intentionally, it is said. The constantly blinking eyes of her severed head terrified the multitudes, who stared at it in fascination for hours, or so the story goes. Someone finally tossed the offending object into a bonfire, unaware that the flesh of the Breed resists flame. Note I said 'resists', not 'defies'. I do wonder, in my darker moments, how long did it take for her brain to surrender consciousness? Such musing is almost certainly academic, though, since by that point I doubt there was enough of a mind left for it to matter.

*　　*　　*

I closed the book and pondered what I had read.

"You okay?"

I looked up. Charles stood in the open doorway, tarp in hand. In the distance, the setting sun cast a crimson stain on an overcast sky. Soon night would fall.

"Smartest thing, I figure," Charles said, "Would be the simplest. We take the body and leave it in the woods. I know a good spot, not far from the county landfill. Lot of dogs running wild out there. By the time they get done with our friend, no one's gonna have a clue how he really died."

I stared past his head into the growing darkness. "Why?"

"Well, you see, I have this aversion to the words 'life without parole. . . .'"

I waved his jest away. "No, that's not what I meant. I'm asking, why drink blood from human beings at all? What's the point? Blood transfusions

56

have been around for how long? If you and your friends are so fucking concerned about maintaining secrecy, why engage in behavior that just piles risk on top of risk?"

Charles shrugged. "You probably think I have all the answers regarding the Breed, so if I plead ignorance, then I must be lying by default. Sorry to disappoint you, but that's not the case; you're gonna be surprised by how little I know. I will say this though, there must be a reason. I guarantee, if the Lady could have kept blood on ice, just as a hedge against an emergency if for no other reason, she would have."

That made sense, though I was hesitant to admit it. Perhaps there was something essential involved in the direct consumption of blood from a living host, some unique property either lost shortly after the blood left the body or only present when consumed directly from living flesh.

Or was it simply a matter of cultural identity? A ritual now so ancient and imbedded that, as a species, they were virtually incapable of change?

While I puzzled over this, Charles pulled up a chair and sat across from me. "Now, you and I need to talk."

I felt my eyes narrow. "About what?"

"About you going to see your sister. Now, don't look at me that way, I can tell you are bound and determined to do this. But before you do something boneheaded and get one or, worse, both of us killed, I want you to sit and think for a minute.

"First off, have you thought about what you're going to tell her? She knows nothing about the Breed, or anything concerning them, and that state of ignorance is one you'd be wise to abet."

My fists knotted. "I have no intentions of telling her what that—what Penelope did to me."

Charles nodded. "Okay. Next thing, how are you going to explain your sudden appearance, and you not looking a day older than when she saw you last? Think that won't prompt a question or two?"

The truth of his words made me squirm. "I could do something. Maybe use some stage makeup. . . ."

"Watched a lot of that old TV series Mission Impossible when you were a kid, eh? Boy, take it from someone who did a lot of amateur theater when he was your age—or rather, the age you appear to be. In real life you can't realistically make yourself look thirty years older anywhere other than on a stage with controlled lighting and at least fifty feet between you and the nearest observer. Anyplace else, forget it. It'll look fake as hell."

"Not to mention the biggest danger," he continued. "You're assuming that Mr. Schizo in the cellar was a solo act. But what if he wasn't? What if somebody suspects something, maybe knows about you and your sister's connection to the Lady? Could be someone's keeping an eye on Barb right now, just waiting to see who or what might show up. Yes, it's been a long time, but like I said, the Breed don't think about time like you're used to. Assuming they're involved, which may not be the case, though I can't imagine anyone else with the resources or the knowledge to carry on a vendetta like this. Might be the only thing keeping her safe is her being used as bait. Want to put her at risk? And her kids too?"

My rising anger wrestled with the truth in his words. "You're telling me I can never see my sister again?"

"No, I ain't stupid. I know you don't believe me, you want to see with your own two eyes that she's all right. I get that. But if you wait long enough, and don't feed, then at least the age thing will take care of itself."

"How so?"

He clicked his tongue. "The Breed doesn't have eternal life. What they have is eternal youth, but only so long as they feed. After doing without for a while, you're going to start aging visibly. Won't happen all at once, you're not gonna wake up tomorrow looking like me, but after a few weeks you should prune up enough that you wouldn't look too out of place at your high school reunion. Which is this coming spring, by the way. Saw it not long ago on the Internet."

My thirtieth high school reunion. I remembered *being* in high school a few months earlier. "What's the Internet?"

He cackled. "And that's something else, a lot has changed. For one thing, we have a black president now. Truth to tell, though, I'm not too worried about your ignorance regarding things like history and science. Lots of people in this country can't tell you who won the Civil War and twenty five percent still think the sun revolves around the earth. It's pop culture that concerns me. Music, movies, television, stuff like that. Right now you are a fountain of unspoiled ignorance, which in this situation makes you a danger to everyone, your House, the Breed, but yourself most of all. Now I know you're smart, the Lady would never have picked you otherwise, but you have three decades of catching up to do. And I would recommend you come up with a story about being abroad, to make up for the inevitable holes in your 'memories'."

Then he shrugged. "But of course, it's all up to you. So tell me, what now?"

I stared at him, wondering if he could feel the hate radiating from my eyes. Making me wait to see Barb was, of course, a trap of some sort. And the worst part was that I had to step right into its jaws, knowing it was going to take my foot off. But what choice did I have?

No choice at all. Not yet. But later . . .

"Okay," I said. "We do it your way."

For now.

Charles nodded. "You don't trust me, yet you can still see the truth in what I'm saying and get past that. The Lady was right, you are smart. So here's what we are going to do. After we get done taking our friend to his final resting place, I suggest you hole up in the old study. There's a T3 line running into this house (we own the local cable company) and I just got a new computer, now that Windows 7 is out. Custom-made job. Sixty-four bit processors, two of 'em, and a set of hard drives so big you could store the Library of Congress on them, with room enough left over for a porn collection that would give Larry Flynt a permanent stiffy."

I understood not one thing he said (except for the Library of Congress reference), but nodded anyway. While I had no direct experience with a computer, I had seen them all the time on TV while watching Star Trek reruns with Barb. How hard could using one be?

*   *   *

Damned fragile devices, I grumbled silently while watching Charles assemble the second computer in as many days. Yellow and black trade paperbacks, each on a different topic (but all prominently displaying 'for Dummies' in the title) lay scattered atop the enormous mahogany desk anchoring the study.

"It's not a washing machine," Charles muttered as he pressed the glowing power button. "Kicking it when it stops working doesn't help." He harrumphed. "At least I had the brains to move everything to the cloud before turning you loose on it."

"I didn't kick it," I muttered.

"Punching it, then. And try to avoid that particular remedy in the future, at least till you have some appreciation of your own strength. Though you won't have to worry about that for long if you continue starving yourself. I know you want to fool your sister, but if you keep on like this, the hunger is going to end up controlling you, rather than the other way around."

I clenched my jaw in lieu of shattering his. "I'll manage."

"Suit yourself." He went back to plugging various cords into the back of his new beige box.

I shut my eyes. Even the talk of feeding hurt. Hunger clawed at my gut, and once more the weakness of rationalization bubbled in my brain. It would not be an assault. Charles was willing, almost pathetically so, though I had yet to understand why.

But the image, even the simple thought, of feeding on Charles sickened me. Not only that, my belly still rolled from the memory of some leftover roast beef I had consumed two nights before in a desperate attempt to calm the burning emptiness. The end result reminded me of the first time I had gotten truly drunk, the night of my high school graduation, when I had vomited until I thought I would spit out the lining of my stomach.

Except the experiment with the roast beef had been worse. Much worse.

"Here you go," Charles said as he stepped away from the monitor. "Remember, Google and Wikipedia are your friends. And for Christ's sake, don't download any files without checking with me first, or else we'll have a hard drive so infested with viruses it'll be easier to buy a new computer than to clean this one."

I rolled my chair forward as Charles left the room. The glowing screen promised to distract me from the carving knife in my abdomen, and so I gave myself over to its promise.

One of the early packages Barb and I had received from Penelope had been a brand new set of World Book encyclopedias. Frequently I would pull a random volume from the shelf I had cobbled together to hold them, then lie in bed with it resting open on my chest, as though floating in a warm pool on a summer day.

But this thing, the Internet, was like riding on the waves of the ocean. And for the next few weeks, I drowned in it.

*   *   *

The aging face stared back at me, a cobweb of lines threading their way from the corners of its eyes. I analyzed the gaunt face with its cheekbones like blades, the skin so pale it was literally white.

The hunger remained, eating away at my insides, but somehow we had come to terms with one another. I wondered what that might mean.

From behind me Charles sighed. "I know I can't talk you out of this," he said in a low voice. "But I want it understood that I think this is the mother of bad ideas."

"Noted," I said as I buttoned my shirt. My fingers trembled, making the last one difficult. I took a deep breath (even though I no longer required air, the action itself had a calming effect), then fastened it.

How to find my sister, that had been the question. Charles had to have known, but I would rather have died again than ask him, putting me even further in his debt, before exhausting all other options. After many days spent learning how to navigate the breadth and depths of the Internet, I had begun searching for specifics. And found them.

The wedding topped the search engine lists, it had apparently been an event of considerable social import. There were many pictures of Barb, including one of her standing atop a cheerleading pyramid in her college days, her arms wide, a dark blue 'D' staining one pink cheek. Her eyes shone so brightly, her enthusiasm and happiness in the moment so infectious, I could not help but smile in turn.

But the one image now burned into my brain had been taken on her wedding day. This was the first photograph where our age difference had truly struck me. No longer a girl, she posed in her bridal gown on the worn stone steps of Duke Chapel, a woman taller than her college years, more slender, and so beautiful it made my heart ache.

The question, how to communicate? I could find no contact information for her, no telephone number or street address. Aware of my knowledge handicap, but resisting anything which might put me further in his debt, I finally asked Charles for assistance. He sighed and surrendered a single word.

"Facebook."

After some minutes of explanation (and several tugs on the reins to keep to the subject at hand), I sat in front of my monitor with my own brand-new Facebook account and an empty message box staring at me as part of the initial process of becoming 'friends'. That Charles himself used an account of his own to communicate with and keep tabs on my sister should have surprised me, though it had not. In her innocence, he must have seemed one of her few remaining connections to me.

Now, what to say?

*　　*　　*

My Dearest Barb,

While I have mustered the courage to sit at this desk and compose this message, the words themselves are coming hard. How does one explain a thirty year absence in a few paragraphs?

I do not know. And trust me when I say I do not have the first idea where to begin. I will say this, despite whatever horrors you might have imagined, the truth of my disappearance is, sadly, quite banal, and so laden with self indulgence that I find myself embarrassed to repeat it.

I worry that, after an initial moment of relief, you will be angry with me, perhaps even hate me, for not having communicated with you before now. I hope you will find it in your heart to get past that anger, and take this, my outstretched hand.

I anxiously await your reply.

Your Loving Brother,
Eugene.

The reply I received, though quick to arrive, had been less than encouraging.

To Whom It May Concern,

You should be made aware that this is the fifth time I have been contacted by my long-lost 'brother', though I give you points for no tale of woe about your dire straits in Nigeria and your desperate need for money.

I must admit, however, you do sound a bit like him, as though you've spent the last hour French kissing a thesaurus. So I'll give you the same chance I gave my other four long-lost siblings.

What did I say to you the day you walked in on me getting dressed for your high school graduation?

I had a moment of genuine panic at that point, since I could not recall anything in particular that stood out about that day, though the scene itself was clear enough in my mind. My clearest memory was of her clutching the nearest article of clothing to her chest amid the screaming that followed.

Then an idea occurred to me, and I smiled as I composed my reply.

Dearest Sister,

I must confess I cannot recall one particular comment that stands out from that five minute tirade on the sacredness of privacy, respect for another's boundaries, etc. I do, however, remember my own contribution to the conversation when I asked at what age was it no longer appropriate to wear Tinkerbell underwear?

The reply which followed had been encouraging in its brevity.

What was my pet nickname for you?

That one had been easy.

Well, there were so many. Dumb Bunny (later the more abrasive 'Dumbass' after you grew your first breasts). And who could forget 'Super Pair of Underwear'? Gods knows I have tried. I attribute that one to a combination of extreme youth and an appalling taste in cartoons.

I suspect, however, that you might be referring to the time when our mother began referring to me as the Son of Satan, after which you started calling me 'Damien'.

Have I the right of it?

*   *   *

The responding email had included no other text than a date (November 30), an address (the Carolina Inn at Chapel Hill), a location (the lobby) and a time: 8pm.

Charles had shaken his head after reading the printed copy. "No way we can make this trip on the same day. Even with the tinted windows in the Land Cruiser, and the darkest pair of Ray Bans I own, it'll still be too much sunlight for you on the way up, especially considering how weak you are."

A quick remedy to that particular problem occurred to me, which I suppressed only with great difficulty. "I am going."

"Oh, I know that. All I'm saying is that to make this work means we drive up the night before. Get a room in the same hotel, to minimize possible problems. A room without windows, if they have one, blocked if they don't. You're not thinking clear; best to play this cautiously."

And what makes you think you're invited, I almost said before reconsidering. Getting away from Charles was still my top priority, but second to seeing Barb again. And if I had learned anything over the past weeks, it was my endless depths of ignorance regarding the modern world, how much I did not know. Time enough to consider other options later.

Then something occurred to me. "Charles?"

He turned on his way to the door, eyes wide at the sudden strain in my voice. "Something wrong?"

I watched my nails extend. They were sharp now, and very hard. I could imagine the wattled flesh of his throat parting with one casual swipe.

"You said the Breed feeds on the topovar." I flexed my fingers. "Barb. Did Penelope ever? . . ."

His confusion melted away, and he shook his head. "No. Were you born stupid? How could you expect your sister to buy your mysterious disappearance having nothing to do with the Lady if Barb had known about the Breed, and that Miss Ember was one of them?" He shook his head again, as if in disgust at my obvious lack of intelligence, before taking his leave.

The drive up was uneventful. I had never been inside the city limits of Chapel Hill, though I had often dreamed of attending the university Thomas Wolfe had once called home. People lined the streets, most of them students, many of them attractive young women who strolled along the sidewalks chatting and laughing with one another. The growing hunger burned like acid in my gut, and I bit my lower lip to take away its edge.

How long do you think you can go on like this, until you reach the breaking point? Only this time it won't be some homicidal arsonist bum. It might be that little brunette over there, somebody's daughter, wondering how she did on her English test the moment before she's dragged into a stairwell, her throat ripped open as she tries to scream. . . .

I bit down harder, but could not cause enough pain to rid myself of the image of that soft warm body struggling in my arms before relaxing as it surrendered its life to sustain my own.

This cannot be how my life turns out, I told myself. There has to be a solution. There *has* to!

"You all right?" Charles asked.

"Fine," I replied, my tone as rigid as my spine. There was my strength. No matter what, I refused to validate any of Charles's predictions about how great a mistake this trip was going to be. After we returned to Penelope's mansion, maybe then we could work something out. Because he was right. I could not continue like this. The hunger grew worse with every passing day. I felt it rising like floodwaters inside my brain, and no matter what I told Charles, I knew at some point I was going to give in. And if someone had to suffer because of my weakness, I knew who I wanted it to be.

"Here we are," he said as we pulled into the parking lot. "Now, just as a precaution, I recommend I be the one to check in. It's been a while since I last visited with your sister, but it's not unusual for me to do so either. I'll scope things out, then come back for you when I'm satisfied everything is safe, or as safe as this harebrained scheme can possibly be." He looked over the back of the seat at me. "I can trust your self control enough to leave you out here alone, now, can't I?"

Oh, so clever. I knew he was manipulating me. What truly angered me was that despite this knowledge, the tactic was still effective. "I'm nothing like the rest of Penelope's kind," I said in as frigid a tone as I could manage. "I won't be murdering anyone in cold blood for my own amusement. Take as long as you like. Have some coffee. Make them brew a fresh pot."

Charles grunted as he slid out of the vehicle, and I watched him cross the parking lot. Streetlights and shadows pressed against one another, light and darkness, each clearly defined.

In the distance a couple strode along the sidewalk, hand in hand. Neither spoke as they walked into the bright circle of an overhead streetlight. As they stepped past its warm glow she moved closer to him, her shoulder brushing against his.

He would not protect you. Perhaps I would kill him first, just to watch the terror in your eyes fade into hopelessness, the dim recognition that in a moment's time, you would soon share more than a handclasp.

I looked away, then forced my eyes shut. This was not me. I grew up reveling in the tales of heroes, however flawed. In my daydreams, I was always the white hatter, the rescuer of innocents. Not the monster.

Maybe death *is* the answer, I thought. Maybe that is what a real hero would do. If you know you cannot resist the evil grinding away at you, simply find the courage to accept your weakness and do the honorable thing.

It would be nice to strike a final blow, though. Leave behind some written record of these—things. Reveal their existence to the world.

Yes. And while you're floating in the afterlife on your cloud of noble self sacrifice, think about what you're going to tell Barb when she joins you. Shouldn't take long. . . .

Fuck.

No, I could not risk it. No matter what fantasies of revenge I might indulge in privately, I could see that her life and well being were always going to be the control keeping me passive, silent, and cooperative, for as long as she lived.

I kept my eyes closed when I heard approaching footsteps.

Maybe it's not him. Maybe it's a carjacker, or a thief, someone who has hurt numerous people, someone who deserves to die. . . .

"Taking a nap?" Charles said.

I grimaced. He knew perfectly well that I never slept, not any more. Discounting my thirty year impersonation of Sleeping Beauty. "Anyone in the lobby?"

"Not a living soul. Oh, sorry. No, no one except the desk clerk. That's why I planned for us to arrive late; the fewer people who see you, the better. Room's already taken care of, here's your keycard."

I got out, pulling the hood of my sweatshirt over my face to hide my features. Part of me still did not believe a word Charles had said regarding House Ember's mysterious 'enemies', but until I knew otherwise for certain, better to be cautious.

The interior's bright light stung my eyes, making me glad for the 'hoodie' I wore, which blocked the worst of it. We slipped by the attendant, who gave us no notice as we made our way to our room.

Nothing left to do now but wait.

*   *   *

I stood before the mirror as I adjusted the band of my Timex Mercury. Barb had given it to me as a graduation present, and I had been wearing it the night I died. Charles had returned it to me before we left Penelope's mansion, along with several other personal items he had put away for safe keeping. The watch hung low on my thin wrist. Thankfully, the twisting intensity of the hunger had subsided under the weight of my agitation. What was I going to say to my sister? What convincing lie could I tell her about my whereabouts for the past thirty years? Why had I not communicated with her? Did she hate me now? How could I keep her safe?

"You going?" Charles asked.

"Of course I'm going!" I snapped in reply.

"Don't bite my head off, I was just asking, seeing how it's ten after eight."

I checked my watch. He was right. Where had the time gone?

"I'll be back," I said as I headed for the door.

"You and the Terminator, eh?"

Over the past month, Charles had developed the habit of baiting me with pop culture references. I assumed this was yet one more I was ignorant of, so I treated it as I had the others and ignored it.

I headed down the hallway towards the lobby, my stomach in knots, and my brain as well. I still had no idea what I was going to say. I focused instead on the scenic wallpaper, the crystal chandeliers that looked at least a hundred years old, the pale green rugs depicting grasshoppers and moths clambering over twisted vines.

Then as I turned the corner, I paused, stunned. There she stood.

I first noticed the lines in her face, obscured by her makeup. Her honey-blonde hair hung in a pony tail down the center of her back, pausing at her waist. She was a study in contrasts, her jeans faded and worn, her blouse black silk and expensive looking. She balanced on high heels with the poise of a ballerina, reminding me of the first time I had seen her wearing such shoes. She had just turned seven, and had raided our mothers closet. The dress had hung to her ankles, and the bright red stilettos had swallowed her feet. These were sandals, black like her top. She stood at the entrance to the lobby, her lower lip caught in her teeth.

"Barb?" I breathed.

She spun in place. "Damien?"

She did not move. I could not. The six feet between us yawned like a canyon.

"You look—wonderful," I stammered.

"Why, thank you," she replied with a shaky laugh. "You, on the other hand, look like shit."

Both of us kept our distance. We had never been given much to open displays of affection, and thirty years had not changed that. I shuffled my feet. She studied the wallpaper.

"Well, we can't stand here in the hallway all night," she finally said, breaking the long, uncomfortable silence. "You have a room?"

"Yes. That is—" I hesitated. "Do you?"

She nodded. "I stay here sometimes when I'm in town to see Penny."

I froze. "Who?"

"My daughter? Short for Penelope."

I swallowed the acid in my throat. "I thought her name was Althea," I said, recalling the birth announcement I had uncovered during my Internet search.

"That's her first name. My husband insisted, to honor his grandmother. No one who knows her calls her that, though. Penelope's her middle name. Penny's a bit of a joke, like Damien. The girl has very expensive tastes, which makes it even more of a puzzle why she wanted to come to school here, instead of Duke. Kids." She shrugged.

"What about your son?" I asked.

"Richard? Who knows. I only hear from him when he needs money." She crossed her arms. "Listen, we could stand out here all night playing catch up, but it's been a long day and my feet are killing me. Now that I can see you're you, how about we go up to my room?"

I nodded. "Lead the way."

As I followed her, I could not help but notice the casual elegance of her stride, as opposed to the stumbling child playing dress up. How much of her life I had missed!

"You thirsty?" she asked while pausing in the open door. "Nothing in here but a coffee maker, and I remember you couldn't stand the stuff."

My whole body clenched in response to her question. "I'm fine," I replied with a calm I hoped sounded sincere.

"Wise choice. I'm still the only woman I know who can ruin boiled water. I've already eaten, by the way, but if you're hungry, we could go grab a bite."

The relief I had felt on seeing her was fast ebbing away at the innocence of her nails-on-chalkboard questions. "Can we please talk about something else?" I asked.

Her eyes narrowed. "O-kay. Change of subject, then." She sat in a nearby armchair, crossing her arms and legs. "Suits me. Let's start with 'Where the hell have you been for the past thirty years?'"

As I returned her stare I realized that the woman in front of me was, at least in part, a stranger. The shy teenager with questionable self esteem had been replaced by this direct, confident, but still beautiful, woman. She held my gaze, refusing to let it go.

I broke first. The growing weakness, warded off till now, had returned and my legs trembled from its force. "Give me a minute," I told her as I slid into the room's desk chair.

"You all right?"

I waved my hand while avoiding her eyes. "How is Mom?"

"Need more time to work on your story? Okay, fine. She's as well as can be expected, all things considered. Started having trouble with her memory a few years ago, and I don't mean her usual difficulty of keeping all her lies straight. We had to move her into the Alzheimer's unit at Anderson Creek Nursing Home, having to hear all the while how you would have done a better job finding a place for her."

"Me?"

"Oh yes. She was angry when you didn't come home, followed by a period of what appeared to be genuine concern for your safety. I couldn't even indulge my own fears because I had to spend all of my time reassuring her that you were all right and would show up one day. I had to wait till I was alone to do my crying." She unclipped her hair, shaking the strands over her shoulders. "Were you alive? Were you dead? Of course, the longer you were gone, the more noble you became. You should hear her go on to her roommate. And I do mean go on, since five minutes after she finishes telling your tale, she'll start right back at the beginning, 'Did I ever tell you about my missing son?' The only good part is that her roommate's memory is even worse, so it's a new story every time for her too."

I studied my hands to avoid Barb's glare. I had thought the pressure of the moment would inspire some brilliant explanation to explain my decades long disappearance. But it had not.

"Do you trust me?" I whispered.

"Absolutely not. You've given me no reason to."

Such a bitter tone. "Maybe it would be better if I just left so you could get back to your wonderful life."

"Fine. Email me again in another thirty years." She stepped to the door and waited, watching me, her hand on the knob.

I remained in my seat, unable to move.

We should go.

"I'm afraid," I whispered.

Her brow furrowed for a moment before she self-consciously wiped it smooth.

Was this fair? My pain was so fresh, hers was almost ancient, though still present. I could see it behind the Cover Girl facade. And here I sat in my self centeredness, forcing her to relive that pain in the hope of some small relief for myself while putting her at Christ only knew what risk.

I was such a selfish asshole.

A scalding thread laced its way down my left cheek, and I could not help but chuckle at the absurdity of the dead knowing tears.

"Oh my God," Barb said in a hushed tone. "Are you crying?"

Embarrassed, I turned away. "It's that damned cigarette. When did you take up smoking?"

"You never cry," she said, ignoring my question. "I remember when mom came out of her bedroom screaming about two dollars missing out of her purse. You were what, nine? She snatched you up off the floor and started beating you with that coat hanger you'd rigged as a TV antenna. Then she threw it across the room and stomped off yelling about how the Lord was going to punish her for raising a goddamned thief. And you never cried. Not even a sniffle."

"No."

"Jesus Christ, why not?"

I lifted my head and met her eyes. "Because I knew you were the one who took it."

Her mouth rounded into an O, and she backed into her chair, slumping into it. "Huh?"

"I saw you coming out of her room, stuffing it in your pocket. I was outside, looking in through the kitchen window."

"Good Lord," my sister said, her voice low. "Why didn't you tell her it was me?"

This time, she was the one who dropped her gaze. "I didn't tell her because she never asked. She just assumed it was me. So if I had cried, if she had beaten one sob out of me, it would have been like admitting she was right."

Barb swallowed. "She whipped your legs bloody," she whispered. "You didn't wear shorts for two weeks, and that was such a hot summer."

I shrugged. "She'd done worse."

"Did you know why I took the money?"

"No."

"Our class was going on a field trip to the Coca-Cola bottling plant," she said, her voice husky and soft. "Mom had given me the money for it the day before, but Joey West and his friends had taken it away from me during recess. They said if I told anyone, they would wait for me after school and get me on the way home. Mom had made a huge deal when she gave it to me and told me that I had goddamned well better not lose it or else. I knew what 'or else' meant, and I was scared. So I stole it out of her purse."

I nodded. "You should have told me. I would have gotten your money back."

"No! You had already been suspended once for fighting, a second time and they might have kicked you out for the year. I didn't think she would miss it, or I wouldn't have done it." She looked at me, her eyes glittering. Then she laughed as she wiped away her unshed tears. "Christ, look at us! Have you ever seen two sadder cases?"

I could not help but return her smile. "A pair of deuces, to be sure."

She laughed at the name our mother had given us, the lowest pair a deck of cards held. "Two of a kind. Better than one of a kind, you always used to say."

"True, but I wasn't very smart."

"Stop it. We both know what a lie that is." She grabbed some tissues from a nearby box and blew her nose. "Okay, back to your tale of woe. How bad is it?" she asked.

I forced myself to meet her eyes. "Who says it's bad?"

"Now you're scaring me." She crumpled the tissues and threw them away. "You're hiding something. Question is, what? And why?"

My mouth opened and closed multiple times. But I could not risk it. "I need for you to trust me," I said. "Can you do that? Just for a while?"

She locked eyes with me. "You were the one constant in my life, the one person I could always count on," she said. "When you disappeared, it felt like the bottom had dropped out of my world. I had felt alone all of my life up until then, but when you disappeared I found out what being alone really meant. If it hadn't been for Penelope and Charles, God only knows what might have become of me. She's gone too, by the way. Or did you already know that?"

The reverent tones she used whenever she spoke Penelope's name made me crazy inside. I did the best I could to suppress my rage. "Yes, I know."

"She never stopped looking for you." Her eyes narrowed again. "Is there a connection? Between your disappearance and hers?"

No, too close. "Not that I know of," I said in as bland a tone as I could manage. "But then, I haven't seen or spoken to Penelope for thirty years. Not since that night."

The expression on her face warned me she was suspicious. "I know something is wrong," she finally said. "But I'm going to make a conscious decision to trust you. For now. Later, well, we'll see."

I exhaled in relief. "Thank you."

"Well, I owe you. Two dollars generates a lot of interest over thirty-nine years, you know?" She stood. "I know we're not huggers, either of us, but this is a special occasion. So come here."

I met her halfway, folding her into my arms while burying my face in her hair. Her heels added to an already imposing height, and I did not have to bend forward much at all.

"God, you're so cold," she murmured.

I pressed my face deeper, my nostrils full of the strawberry scent of her shampoo. I felt the warmth of her skin against mine, and listened to the subterranean rush of her pulse against my cheek.

I heard the shattering of glass as though it came from a great distance, followed by a crash. It felt like being drunk, the blurring of my vision, the dizziness. The river beneath her skin roared in my ears like a cataract, and I wanted nothing more than to lower my face and drink from it forever.

"Are you all right?" she cried.

I looked up from the shards of the glass coffee table, which I had stumbled over after flinging myself away before the madness could overwhelm me. "No . . ."

Terror and confusion fought a war for control just behind her eyes. "Damien? . . ."

"I—I've got to go," I whispered.

She gasped like a dying fish. "No!"

"I've got to go now!" I roared as I ripped open the door, somehow staggering through it. Her scent followed me out, the peppery fragrance of her blood seeping from her pores. Images filled my brain, her desperate squirming to get away, the intoxicating joy of her useless struggle, the liquid taste of her filling my mouth. . . .

Ultimately what stung the most was the lack of surprise on Charles's face when I burst into our room. "Get up!" I snarled. "We have to leave! Right—Goddamned—Now!"

* * *

Hours later I remained curled into the left corner of the Land Cruiser, as far from my driver's infuriating smugness as I could manage. Which failed to silence him, once he finally began speaking. But this time I knew I deserved the abuse.

"You see, this is the reason for the topovar. You all are capable of the greatest atrocities while in the grip of the Hunger. To go without feeding for a week, that's courting disaster. Two weeks? Unadulterated recklessness. But a month, as you just did? Pure insanity."

I did not argue with him, because he was right. My own stiff neck had led me half a breath from committing a crime of unimaginable horror, which I could never have forgiven myself for. As it was, I had terrified my sister beyond reason. And what if she suspected the truth? What danger had I now put her in?

"So are you ready to start listening to me?" Charles said.

I sighed. Again, out of habit, not need. "Yes."

"Good! First damned lick of common sense you've shown thus far. Don't get me wrong, I know you don't trust me, and I understand why. But at some point you are going to have to put your suspicions to the side and give me one iota's worth of credit. Believe me, if I had any desire to do you harm, you would have seen evidence of it by now, right?"

Again, this made sense. Which, of course, is why I mistrusted Charles in the first place. As I stared forward into the darkness of the empty highway, I tried to justify my suspicions, but at this point my reasoning sounded weak, even to myself. If he meant me harm, what did he have to gain by waiting?

The road twisted as we navigated its hairpin curves. Twin headlights appeared suddenly on high beam, making my tender eye tissues flare. Then I realized why. They were in our lane.

"Charles!"

He saw it the moment I did, the oncoming grill of a tractor-trailer rig. But just as we swerved into the left lane, so did it.

As heavy as the Land Cruiser was, the rig slammed it backwards like a toy. Just above and to the right of my head, something exploded, smothering me. Or would have, had I needed to breath.

We were rolling. I dangled by my seat belt for a moment before our momentum flipped us upright to a halt. My head had cracked against something hard, dazing me. Then a sharp whiff hit my nostrils. Gasoline. The tank must have ruptured.

The image of Margaret's head, blinking in the flames, flashed through my brain, and I fought with my seat belt. "Charles?"

No response.

As I struggled, I heard the sound of shoes clopping, accompanied by low voices.

"Alive?"

"We'll see."

The door I had been leaning against suddenly opened, just as I unlocked my seat belt. I tumbled to the ground.

"There!"

"I see him!"

Hands reached down. The truck's headlights made shadows of the forms standing over me.

"Hurry up, for Christ's sake!"

Hands lowered, holding—something. A blade, the length and width of a machete.

"Now! Now!" a voice screamed.

I caught the man's wrists as the edge of his weapon brushed against my throat. My head. He was trying to cut off my head.

"HURRY!"

The animal woke in me and I tried to push back, but could not move the knife away. Weak. So damned weak. . . .

Then I felt its edge parting the flesh of my throat.

You're going to die, just like Margaret. He's going to keep cutting until he hits pavement. Afterwards he'll kick your head into the ditch to keep company with the trash and the filth while your consciousness flickers like a dying candle, and you pray for release before the sun comes up . . .

I struggled desperately while staring at my would-be murderer's face, at the rictus of his grin and the sweat as it dripped from his chin to splash on my face, on my lips . . .

No.

Not sweat.

Blood.

The drops slid over my tongue, now a steady rain from a cut under his eye. It flowed into my throat, burning like hot liquor. And as I swallowed, I saw in his eyes the dawning of uncertainty. Then fear.

New strength flashed through my body like an electric shock. I twisted his left arm to the side, and bit deep. Bone cracked, then splintered, as he screamed.

"Billy!" the other man howled.

I flung Billy to one side, then leaped at his friend, clubbing him to the ground before falling on top of him, my teeth in his throat. He lay unmoving, perhaps dead, as I had my way with him while his friend Billy howled in pain.

But only for a brief time.

When it was over, I stood over their torn and broken bodies. I had not been dainty. Blood covered my shirt, and most likely my face as well. Sane once more (well, relatively speaking), I took in the idling truck cab, and the demolished Land Cruiser.

Charles.

The nose of the SUV had been crushed. The driver's door had buckled and was jammed shut. I smashed the glass, which allowed me a firm grasp on the window frame before I ripped the door from its hinges. Charles's head lolled like a newborn's as he slumped forward, held upright only by his seat belt. Was he dead, or merely unconscious?

I gave him a quick examination. He did not move, but was still breathing.

Now what was I going to do? Use Charles's cell phone to call 911 certainly. Which I did.

What now?

It was close to midnight, according to my Timex. But though it would be some time coming, daylight was inevitable. The 911 dispatcher would send not just an ambulance for Charles, but also police. And what would I tell them? Certainly we were the victims here, but what would they see? Two men in the middle of the road, throats torn out, their blood all over me. How would I explain that?

And for that matter, who were they? Penelope's theoretical enemies came to mind, but was the answer really that simple?

I searched their bodies, the madness of the hunger now gone. No wallets, no identification of any kind.

I made for the tractor-trailer rig, then noticed oncoming lights. A car. Driven by whom?

And in that moment, I panicked. More killers? Perhaps the police? Or no one in particular, just future witnesses to a scene out of a horror movie?

I could not decide who the newcomers were. So I fled.

*   *   *

I ran through the woods as though pursued by flames, my legs carrying me in great leaps and bounds over wide patches of brush and between the moss-laden trunks of trees. And though panic still held what was left of my heart in a desperate clutch, a small part of my fight or flight brain marveled at how clearly my eyes pierced the shadow-strewn gloom. The forest glowed with a pearl-gray light, even the outlines of the leaves were crisp and clear. Small animals, their eyes like tiny lamps, scurried away at my approach.

Slowly my fear ebbed, and was replaced by an overwhelming sense of exhilaration. The blood in my belly burned like strong brandy, and my head swam under its influence.

God, had Penelope felt this way after killing me?

I slowed my pace, the euphoria fading as my mood turned somber, thoughts of death now reoccupying my brain. Why had those men tried to kill us? Fear of being charged with vehicular manslaughter? Engaged in criminal activity and wished to leave no witnesses?

No. They had crossed into our lane, swerving again as Charles fought to avoid the head-on collision. It had not been an accident. They had deliberately rammed into us.

Us? There was no us. They were trying to kill you!

The realization stopped me in mid-stride.

But that made no sense. Charles and I had spent the last four weeks in Penelope's mansion, isolated and alone following the appearance of the hobo arsonist. Had he been one of them? If so, why wait another month before taking action?

Uncertainty. Had the police become involved? Weeks of cautious waiting, and then you left tonight. They watched, then followed. Knew about you. Know about Barb.

The heat in my belly turned cold. Whoever these (supposed) enemies of House Ember were, now they knew for certain that I existed. Or believed it, which amounted to the same thing. And how many of them were there? The two in the truck were not working alone, I felt certain of that. Which meant there were others. And when those 'others' discovered that their associates had failed to kill me, where would they come looking for me?

The mansion.

Which meant I could not go home again.

It's not home. It's where you were murdered.

I shook my head. Irrelevant. It was the safest haven I had. Emphasis being placed on the *had*. No safety there, not anymore.

So where could I go now?

Like being roasted in an oven, Charles had said.

I checked my Timex. Almost midnight. How long until dawn? Six hours? Seven? I could not cut it close, I needed a margin of safety.

So you find someplace to hole up during the day. What then?

I clutched my now throbbing head. I could not risk Barb. God only knew how much danger I had already put her in. Were they coming for her, even now?

No. It's you they want, you they tried to kill. Charles was right about the top-ovar, neither of those men gave him so much as a glance. You were the target.

I touched my throat where the knife had cut me. The skin had closed over, the healing process having already begun.

They will not bother Barb. At least, not yet. They will monitor her, in the hope you give yourself away by contacting her. As long as you keep your distance, she should be safe.

While logical, those thoughts gave me cold comfort. Who said these people were logical? Maybe they'll kidnap her, hoping to ransom her in exchange for me. Or they might use the threat of violence (or worse) against her to draw me out.

That only works if they know how to communicate with you. If they cannot do this, then it makes more sense to leave her alone. For now.

It occurred to me that 'now' could take a considerable amount of time. If Penelope's enemies were other vampires, then they might take that long view Charles had spoken of and settle back to wait, patiently, for me to give myself away.

And why not? I knew I could not return to the mansion, they had to know that as well (though they would certainly watch it anyway, just in case.) Barb could not help me, and I dared not contact her anyway. Where else could I turn? I had no friends. More than at any other time in my life, I realized I was truly alone.

I sat on a nearby stump, miserable now, my fingers stroking the rectangular lump in my jacket. Penelope's journal. I had taken it with me when I met with my sister, unwilling to allow it out of my sight.

Winterfax.

The word sprang to mind as though it had been whispered into my ear. What had Penelope written? That House Ember was sept to House Winterfax?

It had been an unfamiliar word, so I had looked it up. The term in English referred to a clan which was part of a larger clan. And while Penelope's use of the word implied it had greater shades of meaning among the Breed, the essence appeared to hold true in her writings. Houses Ember and Winterfax were connected in a way that implied at the least mutual support of some kind.

And how well it has served Ember in its current crisis.

I grimaced. Perhaps. But perhaps not. And since my list of possible allies was even shorter than my list of options, best not to reject this one out of hand.

But how to contact them? I had read Penelope's journal from cover to cover, more than once, and nowhere within those pages had I found any useful information regarding House Winterfax, other than its name and that of its Visconté. Andracéil, the White Lady.

Charles had shrugged in ignorance when I had repeated the name to him later. Penelope had been not only the center of his universe, but its borders as well. And if he had known little regarding House Winterfax, then who else might?

The Binghams.

I stiffened at my recollection of the name. Arthur and Tracy Bingham. And as I remembered the name, I remembered faces as well. A young couple, hanging on Penelope's every word while standing on a Manhattan sidewalk next to a taxicab's open door. The woman raven-haired and lovely, the man dark with classic features which had reminded me of the statues of Greece. Both dressed as though they had just stepped down from a department store window, each as flawless as an emerald-cut diamond.

Thirty years ago.

The thought laid a damp cloth on the heat I felt even now, that burning sense of inadequacy which for days had eaten at me after seeing them together. Until Penelope's return. Followed by my death.

Probably as ignorant as Charles.

Maybe. But maybe not. Either way, I had no better idea, so this one would have to do until another one came along.

Now, how to get to New York? The Land Cruiser had been destroyed. There were other vehicles at the mansion, but they might as well have been parked on the moon. And even if I found (stole) a car, how long would it take to drive to New York City and find the Binghams who—all things considered—might not wish to be found?

You are an idiot. Forget New York, do you even know where you are right now? Daylight may not be coming in the next five minutes, but it is coming. How long will it take to find a hiding place where you will be safe from the sun and from discovery?

I had no idea. Which meant I had to start looking for one immediately.

Half an hour of putting one foot in front of the other brought me out of the woods and next to another two lane highway. I stared up and down its length. It made sense to head north, but I saw no road signs. How far might I walk before finding one, only to discover I had spent half the precious night going south?

I looked up at the overcast sky. Would I even recognize the North Star if I saw it?

Since I had no idea which direction to take, I returned to habit and picked one, then started walking. Cautious now, I kept as far off the shoulder as I could. At least it was dry, so I did not have to traipse through the mud. I remembered (how long ago it seemed) my last journey on a lonely country road, only to be startled by the blaring horn of a silver Mercedes.

I walked for what felt like hours, not because they dragged but because I knew I had only so many left before sunrise. I had no idea what I was looking for, other than some sort of haven. But nothing I saw looked safe. Trailers, some trashy, others with elaborately-decorated lawns, lay interspersed alongside wood-framed houses with peeling paint and porch steps made from cinderblocks. Nothing to protect me from discovery, much less a cruel sun waiting just over the horizon to bore out my eyes before crisping my flesh like an overdone steak over hot coals.

I did not see it at first. What I saw were twin red reflectors bordering the driveway, its unpaved length stretching into the trees and out of sight. Then I saw it. Bills and catalogues spilled from its open maw. A black mailbox, one of the big ones you often saw out in the country. I stared at it for a moment as my sluggish brain played catch-up with the shiver running down my spine.

No one has picked up the mail, not for a good while. So tell me, genius, what does that mean?

An empty house. Not for long, perhaps. But almost certainly empty now.

Only one way to find out.

Gravel rolled beneath my feet as I made my way up the steep incline. A thick mass of trees bordered the drive on both sides, their dying leaves rustling in the wind. Just ahead a heavy chain hung from two rusting posts. A large padlock held the furthest left link to a metal ring. Enough to block a car, though no barrier to foot traffic. I hopped over and kept walking.

After the highway below had vanished into the distance, I spotted a mound ahead on the ground, a black and white lump. I approached it slowly. As I did, I caught the stink of rotting meat.

A dog, lying on its back, legs splayed and stiff. And in its side a large hole, the edges blurred.

No, not blurred. Moving.

I bent forward. There, crawling in the fur surrounding the blackened flesh. Maggots.

The wink of bright metal at the animal's neck caught my eye. Dog tags.

Not a stray, then. Someone's pet, with a hole in its side large enough to put my fist into. Hunting accident?

Sure. Some local redneck mistook his neighbor's cocker spaniel for a raccoon and shot it in their driveway. Happens all the time.

No business of mine, I thought as I quickened my pace. I only needed someplace dark to hide out for the day and (if fortune smiled on me) a computer with an Internet connection so I could track down the Binghams. Then I would worry about my other problems, like how to get to New York.

The woods thinned and I stepped into a large yard. A log house filled much of the space, its windows shuttered and dark. In front, parked near a large porch, I saw a dark green sedan.

Don't get excited.

I looked inside — no keys — before trying the door. Locked.

Then the scent hit me, and I walked around the vehicle. There, on the ground next to the rear tire. A gas can, resting in a wet circle of spilled fuel. I picked it up, the strong odor stinging my nostrils, and shook it. Empty.

I put the can down and stepped onto the porch. The screen door had been latched, but a hole in the netting allowed me to slip a finger inside just far enough to pop the hook off the eyehole screw lodged into the sill. I twisted the doorknob. Locked, of course.

Well, aren't you the discriminating criminal? A killer who's wracked up a body count of three—so far— and here you are hesitant over a little breaking and entering.

I ground my teeth and twisted. The knob squealed, then snapped, and I stepped inside. After I crossed the threshold, it occurred to me that nothing had prevented me from doing so. In the movies, vampires could not enter one's home uninvited, not to mention cathedrals and other places of worship. God protecting the sanctity of home and church, I always assumed.

Oh well, maybe the people who lived here were atheists.

The sharp stench of gasoline still clung to my nostrils, and I almost missed the odor, peppery and sweet, like cinnamon candy with an aftertaste of salt. Blood.

If I had not fed so recently, I would have caught scent of it sooner. Experience had already taught me that I grew more sensitive to its smell the longer I went without feeding, and the gas stink had masked the odor from outside. But not in the house. Here, the fragrance had grown overpowering.

And then I saw her.

She stood in the doorway, her flannel nightgown stained brown with old blood. Not her own, though I could not have said how I knew that. Her wide blue eyes reflected nothing, like twin mirrors clouded with age. Two years old, three at the most.

I shut my eyes the moment I saw her, but I need not have bothered. Though the hunger stirred lazily within, as though waking to the scent of coffee and bacon in the morning, it turned over with a sleepy shrug and slumbered once more.

But for how long?

"I'm hungry."

My eyes snapped open. "What?"

"I'm hungry," the toddler repeated, in a tone of aggrieved pique. "And Mommy won't get up."

I did not move. "Where's Mommy?" I asked, as casually as I could manage.

The child looked at me as though I was the greatest fool she had ever encountered. "She's in bed with Sissy. Sissy won't get up either."

Twin instincts warred in my head. One screamed for me to run, before someone walked in and caught me here.

The other whispered, something's wrong here. Very wrong.

So what was your first clue, Einstein?

"Will you wake Mommy up?" the child asked, her hand outstretched.

I nodded as I placed my index finger in her palm. She clutched it with surprising strength. "C'mon!" she said, tugging impatiently.

I followed her into the hallway. At its end a faint blueish light spilled out from an open door, along with a chipper voice detailing the expected temperatures for the coming day. I froze, ignoring the toddler as the scent washed over me like a wave at the beach. Blood. And something more.

"Hurry up!" the child cried in a strident and demanding tone. I allowed her to lead me, and together we stepped inside.

A bedroom. Against the right wall, a large television. Not a flatscreen like the one Charles watched his beloved Washington Redskins on, but an old cathode ray model, tuned to the evening news. And against the left wall, a large bed. I stepped towards it, the child releasing my finger as I moved forward.

Two women, one older. She clutched the younger, smaller girl, as though protecting her. Blood clotted the back of her head and her neck. The second one, 'Sissy', lay with her head buried in her mother's chest. The bullet had caught her in the face, shattering her cheek. The scent told me both had been dead for some time. Though again, I could not have said how I knew this.

So where was their murderer?

A wailing started up behind me. Not of grief (the child did not appear to understand that Mommy and Sissy were never getting up again), but the cries of hunger and frustration.

I picked her up, patting her on the back while I left the room, as I remembered doing once upon a time with Barb. As I stroked her back and her hair, her cries wound down into a series of phlegmy sobs interrupted only by the occasional hiccup.

So what now? The murderer was obviously long gone, the scent of the bodies had confirmed that. Old blood had soaked the mattress, as well as the toddler's nightgown when she had tried and failed to wake her mother and her sister.

The child's sobs had the hoarse quality I recognized as coming from a voice strained from constant crying. First things first.

I searched the cabin, making sure there were no other dead bodies (I knew I would have smelled any living ones).

Nothing. We were alone, just the two of us.

I found the kitchen, its sink piled high with unwashed dishes and suffused with a sour odor that reminded me of spoiled milk. Though not necessarily spoiled milk. One thing I had learned since 'waking up' was that many things did not smell quite the same to me as they had when I had been alive. My brain had been rearranging its memory cards, and what scents went with what, for the past month, necessitating caution whenever I encountered anything unfamiliar.

I checked the ancient refrigerator with its high handle far above the reach of little arms. A gallon of milk, half empty, sat on a shelf bare of any other food save for the usual condiments. I remembered how I had made a meal more than once out of loaf bread and ketchup for Barb and myself when there had been no other food in the house and our mother was nowhere to be found.

I searched the cabinets. There, cereal, something with a colorful cartoon character I did not recognize on the front. I found a bowl and a spoon, then sat the child in her high chair. She ate like a starving animal while I pondered my next move.

I checked my watch. Three am. Sunrise came at, what, six am? Maybe earlier? Winter was coming, but not quite here yet.

Best to assume the worst, five am. So whatever else I did, in less than two hours I had to find somewhere to hide until dark. And I could not stay here. But what about the child?

As I watched her fishing in her bowl for the last morsel, the beginnings of a plan formed. Take the car outside, there had to be keys somewhere. Drive to the Virginia border, then call 911. Tell them about the house, about the girl. Let the police come and take care of her.

I shook my head. No. Leave the child alone with the rotting corpses of her mother and sister? It should not have mattered, after all, how long had she been alone with them already? But I could not do it.

Okay, new plan. Get her cleaned up and take her to the border with me. Find someplace with people, maybe one of those all night truck stops. Then flag down a waitress, tell her I had found the child standing outside of the women's restroom, must have gotten away from her mother and I had to go, could she watch the kid for a couple of minutes? Then leave fast, give her no time for an objection. After no one came for the child, she would call the police, who would take it from there.

Yes, much better. I would be seen, true, but so long as no one saw the car, it would not matter. And by the time they found out who she was, I would be long gone and a fading memory to any witnesses. Then find something, an empty barn or abandoned garage where I could hole up for the day.

How far was the Interstate? I had no idea. Maybe the car had a road-map; if not, I would have to stop and get one.

The toddler flung her spoon into the bowl and gave a loud burp. No time to waste. I would clean her up fast, put some clothes on her, then head out. When I picked her up, she yawned.

I stripped her down and washed the blood off, dressed her, then gave her one of the stuffed animals lying around. I went through three before finding one she did not throw away the moment I handed it to her.

It was not until I passed a mirror in the hall that I caught a look at my-self. My white shirt was covered with blood, as were my hands and face. My suitcase was in the now-destroyed Land Cruiser, so I had no clothes. But I could go nowhere like this.

I put the child in front of the living room television and turned it on. Eventually I managed to find something to hold her attention. Once she was quiet and engrossed, I found a bathroom. The blood covering my hands and face had hardened. I scrubbed my skin raw.

After I looked less like a homicidal maniac—*Playing against type, eh?*— I went back into the bedroom. Rummaging through various drawers, along with the closet, I found a t-shirt and a pair of jeans that just barely fit. A relative's leftovers, perhaps. A damp washcloth was good for a quick fix of my belt and shoes.

I searched a purse I found on the dresser. There, car keys, and some money as well. I paused, then shoved it in my pocket. I could make good later, once a later actually existed for me.

I checked my watch. A quarter after four. Less than an hour till a pos-sible sunrise. How the hell was I going to do everything that needed to be done before then?

No idea. But nothing would get done by standing around with my thumb up my ass.

I patted my pockets, had I forgotten anything? No doubt I had, and would remember it later to my regret, but it could not be helped. I crammed my bloodstained clothes into a bag, picked up both child and toy, then turned as I heard the front door opening.

A man stood there, staring at me. He was close to my own height, light brown hair, bit of a paunch. He held a rifle loosely in both hands. The child in my arms squirmed as she squealed. "Daddy!"

Then the rifle came up, his finger already squeezing. I flung the little girl at the sofa just as he fired.

The bullet hit me in the gut. It felt like a sledge hammer had struck me just above the navel. The impact did not send me flying back, which surprised me, a veteran of countless police dramas. My legs went limp, and I collapsed against the wall.

He stood over me, stock against his shoulder, looking down. I tried to slide away, but my legs would not move. In fact, I could feel nothing from the waist down, and I realized the bullet had shattered my spine. I was paralyzed.

So it ends like this, I thought, as I watched the man standing over me, his gun aimed at my chest. Make it the head, I tried to say. Only way to be sure.

The man took a slow, deep breath, then spoke.

"You have to understand," he said, his voice shaky and a bit petulant. "I did it for them. I was protecting them. The money's all gone, there's nothing left. We're destitute. I can live with the shame, I should live with it. My punishment for failing." He coughed, a harsh hack. "But there is no reason for them to suffer for my mistakes."

He shifted his gaze back to the couch. The toddler was not screaming, much to my surprise, just watching her father, her wide blue eyes fixed on his. "And to cap it all off, I was too weak to finish the job. I put Noel in front of the TV, but she kept turning around. It was just going to take more time, I figured."

"Well, it's been two days now. The last of the milk expires tomorrow. Now or never. And the truth is, I still hadn't made up my mind after wandering around out there in the woods for half the night, not even when I got back. And then I saw you through the window."

He shifted the rifle. "So it's okay now. Because no one is going to blame me, you see."

Then he pivoted, the long barrel of his rifle swiveling. Towards the sofa. "They're going to blame you," he said as he squeezed the trigger.

I closed my eyes, and listened to the child's screams, followed by the metallic snap of the gun's hammer on an empty chamber and a whispered "Dammit."

My eyelids snapped open again. I watched as the girl's father searched his pockets for another shell. And my legs still refused to work.

He found another bullet. So small, to do so much damage. He rammed it in, then took aim again. As he did, I slid my hands underneath my numb ass, crouching as best I could. Then, as he let out a shuddery sigh while staring down the barrel's length, I *pushed*.

For a moment, I thought I had still somehow managed to screw up and misjudge the distance. He stood a good six feet away from me, and as I popped off the floor like a champagne cork, his arms were just out of my reach.

So I grabbed the rifle instead.

He clung to it desperately, for which I was grateful. Had he let go, he could have simply grabbed the girl from off the couch and then run out the door. With two non-working legs, and a weapon I had no previous experience using, he could have finished his task outside before returning to finish me off, maybe by setting fire to the house. Which, judging from the spilled gasoline outside, might have been the plan, to cover his traces.

But instinct took over, and the combination of my grip, along with my dead (no pun intended) weight, pulled him down to the floor with me, in range of my own weapon.

My teeth.

Though my lower half was incapable of movement, my upper body retained both motion and strength. I wrestled the rifle out of his grasp, then followed that action by tearing open his throat.

His screams mingled with those of his daughter. Though I had not been hungry a moment before, instinct took over, and I fed. Soon his struggling eased, the hoarse sound of his rapidly diminishing breaths the only sound to be heard.

And at the end a faint whisper, in a squeaky voice almost unrecognizable as his own.

"I . . . *win!*"

Then nothing at all.

The whiskey heat of his blood leaked down my throat and below my navel, where I felt it spread to my legs. I shifted, and discovered I now had feeling in the lower half of my body. But with sensation came its sibling, pain.

I lay there for what felt like hours, unable even to crawl. Eventually, as my wounds healed and my spine mended, the fire in my gut cooled to burning embers. Using my arms, I dragged myself to the sofa, uncertain what I would find there.

The toddler lay, eyes closed, but still breathing. Fainted? In shock? I rolled onto my back and shut my eyes, focusing on the half of me which still could not move, as if through sheer will I could speed up the healing process.

Finally, a twitch. Not much of one, but better than nothing.

I continued to lie there, focused on the growing sensations traveling down the length of my body, as though my nerves were hot wires. When I could finally move my legs a bit, I opened my eyes. The first thing I noticed was a lightening of the darkness. I checked my watch. Both the minute and hour hands were clasped as though in prayer, meeting at the '6'.

Six thirty.

I rolled over and saw it piercing the curtains, a thin pale ray, inches from my face.

Terror and instinct took over. I crawled back towards the bedroom where mother and eldest daughter lay still. The closet door yawned open, I had not closed it. As cobalt blue warmed to a pinkish glow outside the transparent curtains, I dragged my uncooperative body into the closet and closed the door behind me, hoping desperately that there were no cracks in the oh-so-thin cheap wood.

Cramming my seventy-six inches into the tiny space, I folded my legs and arms into some nightmare version of Twister. The stench of fresh mothballs clawed at my nostrils, so I expelled the last wisp of air from my lungs and stopped breathing. Linen skirts and silken gowns covered the hardwood floor like a pallet, empty wire hangers rattled overhead. And though the air was cold, I could feel the sun's growing warmth on the wall at my back. There was precious little room in the cabin's limited floor plan for extras, and the closet had been squeezed between an outer corner and the master bath. No protective layer of sheetrock covered the log walls, and my skin prickled as I sensed the sun's rays fingering the crevices for access through a loose chink or tiny pinhole.

Then I saw it.

The sunbeam cut through the air above me like a laser beam, dust motes dancing along its molten edges. Not from the back wall, as I had feared, but through the narrow gap between door and sill. In my haste, as well as my monumental stupidity, I had neglected to close the bedroom's window shades.

I stared at the beam of light with the fascination normally reserved by a mouse for a snake as — inch by snail's pace inch — it crept down the back wall.

Then panic set in. I reached up and began shoving garments between that golden knife blade and myself. It moved slowly and steadily, now just above the closet's antique glass doorknob, placing it level with my face. I caught myself praying (even though I had no faith in God left) that it would not slide low enough to hit the crystal and scatter, prism-like, falling on my defenseless eyes. I remembered Penelope's mansion, Charles ripping down the curtains, the sunlight piercing the flesh of my hands like microwaves, grilling my eyes in their sockets.

I rifled through the hanging wardrobe as though it was a deck of cards, panic melting into sheer terror when I realized through touch how thin the dresses and blouses were. Summer clothing, put away for the coming winter, the translucent cloth as useful a barrier as stained glass to whatever property sunlight possessed which made it so dangerous to them—me. Us.

Then I found a long coat of thick wool which had been pushed to the far side. Reaching under the light, I managed to pinch its hem, just barely within fingertip's reach. I moved it gently, ever so gently, towards me. Despite my lack of breath I smelled the hairs of my arm crisping as they brushed the sunbeam. Had I retained a beating heart, it would have been pounding.

I slid the garment along the upper rod, hoping against hope it would not fall. Free space was at a minimum, and should the coat catch on something before I could get a firm grip on it, I would have had no choice but to cross the ray's path with my naked arms in order to retrieve it.

Finally I succeeded and wrapped myself in protective darkness, grateful that the comatose toddler's dead mother had been such a tall woman.

Huddling inside the dense folds, I closed my eyes. The world drifted out of reach, like a helium balloon, and I heard familiar voices whispering from within a silver cloud, the words barely registering as such. I listened to their tinkling sounds, like windchimes, as I floated, almost a cloud myself. And as I surrendered to their song, I could almost understand it. . . .

Then my eyes opened, and I realized I had fallen asleep for the first time since my 'awakening'.

The door creaked as I opened it, a sound as loud as gunfire. The curtains of the open window swayed in the evening breeze. Outside, darkness.

The tang of corruption had grown stronger. And the child?

I found her motionless on the couch, her eyes closed, as though still asleep. I placed my ear next to her tiny rosebud of a mouth, listening to her short, quick breaths. Alive. But she had not moved, so far as I could tell.

It was only then that it occurred to me to examine my own injuries, or rather, the lack of same. A puckered scar made an exclamation point of my navel. The wound was sensitive to the touch, but I felt no real pain. At least, not anymore.

I worked quickly, ignoring the sprawling corpse of the father on the floor, his arm stretched over the rifle in a lover's embrace. Nothing had been disturbed, the duffle bag remained where I had left it. I loaded the car, cleaned myself once again, then found more clothing, another pair of jeans and a black shirt feminine enough to make me uncomfortable, but not so discomfited that I would have preferred running around bare-chested. Unfortunately it was the only remaining garment I could find that would fit me.

Then I stood over the child.

One phone call is all it will take. The police would be here within the hour. The world is full of misery, and she has had more than her share, not to mention she will be in greater danger with you than being left here.

I picked her up, knowing as I did that there was nothing noble about my actions. I was simply being myself, and that person could not leave the child alone and surrounded by corpses. Had I taken the time, I knew I could have parsed the selfishness of my actions. But the night grew older with each breath she took, and hours of driving lay ahead.

With the aid of a map in the glove compartment and the registration card, I figured out where I was, not far from Interstate 40. From here I could head east to I-85, then cross over into Virginia to merge with I-95, which would take me to New York. But first, the child.

After the events of the previous night, the final resolution felt anti-climatic. I found my all-night truck stop. She never made a sound during the drive, but lay quiet and still.

I carried her inside, hidden between my chest and duffle bag. More people than I had expected, which actually worked to my advantage, making me less conspicuous. I found a table off to one side, and when no one was watching, I slid her into the seat, out of immediate sight. I almost left then, but a sudden image of the toddler being found and carried off by a stranger with questionable intentions took me to the counter where I mentioned the child to the waitress, a woman of indeterminate age and a hard look I recognized from my own life, spent in many of the South's poorer trailer parks. Perhaps this would make her sympathetic to someone else's bad luck. Or so I told myself.

Then I left and — as best I could — put Noel out of my mind. Her story and mine had now parted ways, and I had other matters to attend to.

Finding the cabin, though, had given me an idea. When I reached the outer belt line of Washington DC, I pulled off and found a subdivision with two things I desperately needed from the local real estate; a 'For Sale' marker in the front yard and a garage. Risky, I knew, so I looked for a sign faded from prolonged exposure in front of an expensive house designed by someone with questionable taste. The search took longer than I would have thought, but eventually I found the perfect place, a two story monstrosity of surpassing ugliness. The foundation was already showing signs of decay, though the house itself could not have been more than ten years old. And not one, but two garage doors, one large enough to admit a city bus.

A sticker in the window advertising the manor's security system was a concern, but I gambled that such were cheaper than the service itself, which turned out to be the case (though I parked two blocks away before breaking in, just to be sure). I found a switch to open the garage, then went back for the car. It helped that it was almost four in the morning by this time, and I did not need headlights in order to see.

I spent an anxious day hiding in that hideous faux pas of a mansion after going to ground in the windowless basement the owners had been thoughtful enough to include, my every muscle rigid with tension, and ears straining at the slightest of creaks. A local newspaper picked up from a nearby driveway warned me when to expect both sunrise and sunset.

Once night fell, I was free to continue. But first, I had to make a call.

While the recently deceased rifleman had been a familicidal maniac, he had been conscientious enough to keep up his cell phone payments. Unfortunately, according to information, Arthur Binghams's phone number was unlisted.

I thumbed through Penelope's journal looking for something—anything—that might help, and found what I was looking for scribbled in the back on an otherwise blank page, the letter 'B' and a phone number. It might have been anything, but maybe. . . .

One ring. Two. A third.

Then a click. "Hello?"

I cleared my throat. "Ms. Bingham?"

A pause. "Who is this? How did you get this number?"

I had rehearsed the opening of this conversation for some time. It took a moment to remember it. "I'm calling from the Ember household. Is this Ms. Bingham?"

Another pause, more prolonged. "This is Miss Bingham. Who am I speaking with?"

Miss? "Tracy Bingham?"

"No, that's my mother. I'm Moira. My mom—isn't here right now."

I cleared my throat again. "May I speak with your father?" I asked in the deepest and most mature voice I could manage.

"Dad's not here either." A short pause. "Is this Charles?"

So she had at least some knowledge of the Embers. "No. Charles was in a car accident a couple of days ago."

"Oh my God! Is he okay?"

Good question. "He was stable the last time I saw him," I responded truthfully.

Another pause. "And you are? . . ."

This part I had not forgotten. "My name is Eugene. I'm sort of a — ward of Penelope's. If you know what I mean."

When she did not respond, I began to worry. "Moira, are you — um — a member of the Family?"

"Huh? Oh, yes, yes. From the day I turned sixteen."

Something inside of me ground against stone. Sixteen? Well, at least Penelope had waited until the girl was properly weaned. "Moira, we are having a bit of a Family emergency, and I really need to talk to one of your parents."

"Mom and Dad are at the retreat, and I can't discuss that over the telephone. You do understand, right?"

No, I did not understand at all, but clearly from the tone of her voice she expected me to. "Do you know when they will be back?"

"No, but if there is a Family emergency, then I'm supposed to act on their behalf. What do you need?"

She sounded willing, even eager, to be of assistance. "I need a place to stay," I said slowly.

"Absolutely not a problem. Something had been scheduled for this weekend, but I'll cancel it. Where are you?"

"Washington," I said, adding, "DC, not the state."

"Will you have any trouble getting to Manhattan?"

I checked my roadmap. "I should be able to make it," I said, trying to sound confident.

"Just you? You don't have a driver?"

Idiot. Penelope always *had someone driving her about.*

"No," I told her. I never had been very good at lying, and instinct told me that it would be safest to stick as closely to the truth as possible. "I said this was an emergency, remember? It's just me, no one else."

Silence again. This might have concerned me, but one thing Penelope had stated in her journal more than once was that topovar did not lie to Family. In fact, the implication was that they could not, though she had not elaborated.

"I would offer to come meet you, so you didn't have to drive yourself," Moira said, "But there have been a couple of suspicious incidents, and my parents think we're being watched. Here I'm not terribly concerned, this is a very exclusive and expensive building, and I have total confidence in our security. Outside of these walls, I can't make any promises."

I nodded, then realized how ridiculous the gesture was, since she could not see it. "Give me your address."

"Have you ever been to Manhattan before?"

"Once," I replied. "Thirty years or so ago."

"Wow; you don't sound much older than me. Okay, our building overlooks Central Park . . ."

She assured me there would be no problems once I arrived, that she would speak to the staff and that I should simply give my name to anyone who questioned me. No, I did not require parking arrangements, since I planned to abandon the sedan once I reached the city and walk the rest of the way.

The drive proved uneventful, though I did experience an anxious few moments as I neared the city limits when I realized that the fuel gauge had apparently been sitting on 'E' for some time. Fortunately, due to the late hour, traffic was surprisingly light. I did not want to run out of gasoline in the middle of the street, so as soon as I crossed over the bridge I found an empty parking space with a list of restrictions to put the Ten Commandments to shame. This concerned me not at all, since I had no intentions of ever driving the vehicle again. I wiped over any surfaces I had or might have touched, then left, with the keys still in the ignition. If Fortune smiled on me, someone would be both foolish enough and unlucky enough to 'borrow' it, and be justly rewarded if they were stopped by the police and the license number checked.

Making my way through the city posed no difficulties. I had been here before, after all, and was familiar with the simple grid network of streets and avenues. What did surprise me, since my memories of New York City were so recent and clear, were the lack of fleshpots and other sexually-oriented establishments. Bright neon burned like faerie fire throughout Times Square, with massive signs peddling the most mundane of wares: soft drinks, perfumes, electronics and an endless variety of jeans. I did receive the occasional questioning look from passersby, as though being evaluated for God only knew what. This did not bother me. I simply met the eyes of anyone who sought mine and opened my soul to all and sundry. To a man (and woman) they quickly found something else more interesting to look at as they continued walking, perhaps a bit faster than before.

I reached the address Moira had given me. An ancient building of stone blocks, it squatted on its lot like a querulous old man on a park bench. A word to the doorman and I was escorted inside, then directed to the elevators.

A large man in a gray uniform with the word 'Security' above his pocket watched me while pretending to stare at the opposite wall. The elevator was smaller than I would have thought, but expensive looking, all polished dark woods accented with brass. I pressed the dark circle haloed in light which read simply 'P'. The doors closed with the hushed whisper of a mother to her newborn, then the slightest of bumps told me I was rising.

When the doors opened, I found myself staring down a long hallway which duplicated the look and mood of the elevator. At the far end two double doors faced me. Large enough for a cathedral, each sported a rectangular metal plate with the letter 'B' in an elegant font etched deeply within.

I crossed the distance, my feet gliding noiselessly over the thick gray carpet. At the door a golden button rested in a hub of the same rich metal. I pressed it, half expecting the sonorous clanging of church bells. But I heard nothing.

Someone had, though. I heard a clacking, followed by a rattling. Then the right door opened.

She poked her head through the slim gap with the inquisitive stare of a nervous Chihuahua. I could not see much of her, but what I saw was striking. Luminous sapphire-blue eyes took me in before moving past me to the hallway beyond. Jet black hair cut as short as a boy's accented a pale face framed by sharp cheekbones. The pink of her lipstick matched her nail polish. After scanning the hallway, she returned her attention to me.

"Please come in," she said while stepping back, head slightly bowed, her eyes lowered. A tension in her neck and shoulders implied that I was staring, so I broke gaze and walked past her into a short hallway with a door on either side. Listening to the clicks as she secured the locks again, I made my way down the hall into a room of startling size.

What little I knew of apartments had not prepared me for this. A blonde hardwood floor led me in. To my left a fireplace of glossy black stone dominated the side wall. At the rear a series of windows stretched from the floor to what had to be at least a twelve foot ceiling. Through the glass I saw the city's lights, as thick as the Milky Way on a cold winter's night. In the center of the room two white leather sofas with metal frames faced each another over a coffee table large enough to serve dinner for six, Japanese-style. Rectangular chairs perfectly matching the couches filled the leftover space, while end tables dotted the corners of the square. Despite this, the setting left considerable space to circle the room, which I did. A broad spiral staircase led up to a second level. Photographs in black lacquered frames formed a large rectangle on the wall to the right of the entryway. The pictures were of people, singly and in groups. I recognized two of them. Their photos formed a collection, some of just the couple, a few with the daughter, and others with what appeared to be family members. The Binghams.

But what drew me hung over the fireplace, its gas logs hissing. The portrait had to have been seven feet high, illuminated by a light fixture the color of antique bronze. Her eyes stared into a distance just above the viewer's head, her upper body shadowed by the tumbling waterfall of her auburn hair falling in waves over her naked shoulders and bare arms. She sat on a chair as elaborate as a throne, upholstered in a velvet as dark as blood. Her elaborate green and gold gown, accented with hints of violet, spilled down the length of her body, parting at her cleavage before coming to a rest just above her slim, crossed ankles.

Penelope.

Within the confines of the portrait, just over her head, hung a shield device like a coat of arms. On a background of enameled black a silvery crescent moon dominated the upper left alongside an eight-pointed star. And in the lower right, a constellation of still more stars, perhaps a rose. Or possibly a sword, the sweeping arc of its blade curling down and to the center of the bottom's point. The flower (or pommel) was noticeably larger than the other stars, followed by twin leaves/thorns/a hilt of lesser—but still respectable—size. Smaller stars formed the stem/blade as it tapered to a point. There was no other ornamentation.

Footsteps sounded on the hardwood floor behind me. "She's so beautiful," Moira said in a hushed voice that would have sounded more at home in the front pew of an ancient church. "Don't you think?"

I nodded as I swallowed past the swollen lump in my throat. "Yes."

"I think I was six the first time I met her. Mother made a huge production of it, like being introduced to a queen. Did she sire you?"

Heat washed over my face. "I—yes. Yes, I suppose she did."

She lowered her eyes. "I'm sorry, forgive me. It's not my place to pry."

My stomach tightened at her hushed, reverent tones, and I fought down a wave of revulsion. "Don't concern yourself."

"Thank you. Are you—I mean—have you? . . ."

Revulsion spilled over into nausea as I realized what she was trying to ask. "I am—fasting," "I said through clenched teeth."

"Of course," she replied, her confused tone a contrast to her words. "I had just sat down to eat when the doorbell rang. May I? . . ."

She had the look of a whipped dog who knows it has done wrong, just not what precisely. For the first time I felt sorry for her. "Go ahead. I didn't mean to interrupt."

She gave me a timid smile and walked away, shoulders hunched as though expecting a blow. Not having anything better to do, I followed her. No small pleasure, that. She wore thin gray cotton shorts cut so high that I could see the swell of her buttocks just below them, and a tank top of a similar, stretchy material. The spaghetti shoulder straps bared her upper back, exposing shoulder blades as defined as an angel's wings. She looked over her shoulder at me, and a blush spread from her face to her neck. She quickened her pace, and I focused instead on her small bare feet, their nails painted the same delicate pink as those of her hands.

She led me into a kitchen which could have serviced a restaurant. Cabinets of light wood crowded against stainless steel appliances, there was no wasted space. Bundles of fresh herbs hung like plants over the counter-tops. They looked familiar, though I recognized neither their appearance nor their scent.

Their scent! I could not recall ever smelling such a fragrance! It reminded me of the girl's perfume, a rich odor of earth and spices intermingled with a sweetness like rich honey. My head spun. "What is that?" I asked, sniffing.

Moira looked around as she hopped onto a barstool at the counter, a plate of half-eaten spaghetti in front of her. "Rosemary? Mother likes to grow her own herbs."

I shook my head and took a nearby stool. "I wouldn't know what rosemary smells like. If it didn't come out of a can or a box in my house, you went hungry."

Moira gave me another puzzled look as she twirled her fork. Then she leaned forward. I fought not to stare into the gap between her top and her breasts. "Were you sired recently?" she asked.

An image swam before me, of Moira spread atop the white Carrara marble countertop, her eyes half-lidded, her breath a bit fast, as she turned her face to offer me whatever I might wish to take from her.

The picture made me dizzy, and I shifted in my seat. Her breath was sweet with the same intoxicating odor saturating the air. "That depends on how one measures time," I said. A pleasant buzzing filled my head.

She lifted her chin, her smile now a flirtatious grin that traveled from her mouth to her dark blue eyes. "And how do you measure time, sir?" she whispered. I could barely hear her, so I leaned further forward, and promptly fell off my seat.

The ridiculousness of my situation made me laugh. "I'm sorry," I said as I lay sprawled on the tessellated floor. "I must be more tired than I thought."

"Are you?" she said, her tone cool and distant.

I twisted my head to look up at her. That small effort took all of my strength. "You. . . ."

She slid from her seat and kneeled beside me. The scent of her breath caressed my face like a honeysuckle breeze. "I've been told it smells differently to us than it does to you."

I tried to lift my arms. It felt as though I lay under an impossible weight, crushing my chest. "Wha-? . . ."

"The garlic. Like the sweetest perfume, Jerome told me. He assured me you were unlikely to recognize its fragrance, or its effect. Like being drunk. Even holding your breath doesn't help. Works through the pores, or so they speculate. Affects the nervous system. God only knows what eating it would do to you. But I've been force-feeding myself all evening, just in case. Almost a shame you didn't attack me, it would have been interesting to see what effect a mouthful of garlic-saturated blood might have had on you."

The concrete burying my body had overflowed into my head. "But . . . I . . . You're . . . Family."

She nodded. "True, I am a member of the Family." Her lips drew so close I could feel her breath in my ear.

"Just not a member of yours."

* * *

Moira tied a rough damp cloth over my face, blinding me. A washcloth, or perhaps a dish towel. Probably still dirty.

Whether she did this to protect my eyes (which I could not close) or to protect herself, I had no idea. After revealing she was not a member of House Ember, she never spoke to me again. I did hear her voice once at a distance, but could not distinguish the words. She would pause occasionally, then speak again, but there was no reply. Telephone, I assumed.

I had my choice of terrors, but what frightened me most was that even though I had all the mobility of a slab of raw meat I could still feel the cold tile underneath my back, the chill of air conditioning from a nearby floor vent. A familiar situation. At any moment I expected to feel the prickle of tiny legs clambering over my skin, inside my clothing. Exploring, feeling. Tasting. . . .

I heard the rustling of a bag as Moira packed more of the hateful garlic around my shoulders and head. Even prone on the floor, and as stable as it is possible to be, the scent made me dizzy, like bed spins. Reality grew fuzzy. Sounds echoed with the unpleasant buzzing of a cheap alarm clock. A metallic taste saturated my mouth, as though I had been trying to chew aluminum foil.

Minutes crept like hours. Sometimes my frustration grew intolerable, and I would fight to move something, anything. An arm, a finger, even an eyelid. But nothing worked. I was completely paralyzed.

Then, after an eternity and from somewhere far away, came the sound of footsteps.

Panic took over. I struggled once more to knot muscles as responsive as wet sandbags. Nothing. The steps grew louder. Finally they paused, still some distance away.

Two voices began speaking, Moira and one other. Despite the fog in my brain, I could tell they were not speaking English. Occasionally what sounded like a question would be directed at Moira, who responded using what sounded like the same language, if not so fluid.

Then twin sets of arms lifted me as though I was a body pillow, carrying me, then dumping me into some kind of rectangular box. I could tell its shape because my hands and feet banged the sides as I was dropped inside with little thought and less care.

Still blinded by the cloth, I heard the rattling of wood on wood just above my face. Then the hammering began.

At that moment, I screamed. Granted, it was a soundless scream, since my throat was as paralyzed as the rest of me, but it was a scream all the same. An image flickered through my mind from an old black and white horror movie, and I imagined the next sound to come, the thump and rattle of dirt clods.

Then I heard a voice. The unfamiliar one Moira had been speaking with, but now just a short distance away. Male, with a thick, unplaceable accent, now using English.

"If you should suddenly recover some power of movement or speech, unlikely as that might be, you may be tempted to some foolish display. I encourage you to resist. For if you fail to do so, then our curiosity might suddenly find itself warring with more practical concerns, and you could find yourself resting at the bottom of some ocean trench, still paralyzed, with only the creatures of the sea for company and an infinite amount of time in which to ponder your situation. I hope I have made myself clear."

I lay in my coffin (whether real or imagined), resting in a bed of the despicable garlic, and silently replied, "For now, yes."

More shifting, followed by movement. A growing stupor enveloped my brain. Not quite unconsciousness, more like the sensation of blind drunkenness. By now I could feel the absence of the wet cloth from my face (it had slide off after a sudden jar), but it made no difference, I could see nothing. Then a sharp series of thumps, followed by a barely discernible vibration. A vehicle.

As time passed my senses grew still duller, reality less real. Whether it was psychological or simply the garlic, I slid in and out of awareness. Occasionally there would be more jostling (once I was thrown so violently against the side of my 'coffin' I could not believe it remained intact), followed by more transporting. Then I heard what sounded like jet engines. The one thing I never heard was another human voice.

During a rare lucid moment, as I played Hide and Seek with my sanity, I realized everything had grown still, and had been so for some time. Pain like the cold iron chisel of the world's greatest hangover split my brain, and even though I could still feel the press of the garlic buds, I could no longer smell them. Odor fatigue? Or had whatever toxic properties they possessed faded during my journey? I still could not move yet, though. Perhaps the effect took time to wear off?

Then the sound of crowbars, of nails squealing, and then light. Too much light. I screamed silently again.

"Cover his eyes," a voice ordered. Then someone slipped what felt like an elastic blindfold over my face. The inside felt slick and cool. The burning ceased, and if I could have inhaled, I would have sighed with relief.

My crate was flipped, and I rolled onto what felt like cold stone. Then a strange voice said, "Strip him. then hose him down."

The water was frigid, the stream forceful enough to push me across the floor into a nearby wall. It played over me, soaking me completely. At some point, long after my skin had grown numb, it ceased, followed by more hands, toweling me (mostly) dry before dressing me again. Hands fluttered over my wrists and ankles, and I heard the metallic click of locks being engaged.

Then a familiar voice whispered into my ear, its accent even thicker than before.

"You will soon be able to move. When that happens, you might wish to test your bonds. I recommend you resist that temptation. Their lightness is deceptive. They are silver wire. I do not know if you have ever been injured by such metal, but the sensation has been likened to that of alcohol on an open wound. In addition, wounds caused by silver to one such as yourself do not heal like other wounds. At best, you would retain permanent scars. At worst? . . ."

Even blind, I could see the shrug.

"Now," he continued, "Our Lady, she wishes to question you. For this reason, you are not to speak, not to me, not to anyone, until she chooses to address you. Answer any question she puts to you, and always be respectful. Do otherwise, or disobey her in any way, and the consequences shall be both unpleasant and immediate. When you can move, nod your head to indicate you understand what I have said."

I had watched this scene in how many different movies? The captured hero, the villainous host. This was the part where I was supposed to display my courage with witty banter. Or it would have been, if my lungs had been working. Not to mention that I could not think of anything to say.

The reality of the situation was that every instinct I owned was screaming "Danger, Will Robinson!". I had the sensation of balancing on a wire strung between the roofs of two skyscrapers while looking down at Matchbox cars and people smaller than ants. One single moment of carelessness was all it would take.

So when I discovered I could move my fingers, I struggled until I could nod yes. First job, get out of this alive. The second job would have to take care of itself.

Twin sets of hands lifted me to my feet, bracing me when my knees buckled. When my legs finally appeared capable of supporting the lion's share of my weight, I was led forward.

We navigated what appeared to be various rooms, halls and staircases. I listened to the sound of keys in locks and distant murmurs. Feet scurried right and left, clearing a path for us. We were still inside, but my god, how large was the building? By the time we came to a final halt, my muscles were trembling with fatigue.

Then that same voice again. "I am going to remove your blindfold. Dark as the room is, it will still take time for your eyes to adjust. Close them, and take your time opening them. Say nothing, do nothing else."

A hand pulled the blindfold away, and I was glad I had not hesitated to shut my eyes, because it was quickly yanked off, and even then I could feel tears flowing. Dancing smears of red and yellow light flickered through my lids. After a while, the glow grew less painful, and I could finally see.

I stood in a room like something out of a medieval castle. Paintings and tapestries hung from walls at least thirty feet high. Filling the gaps between the art was a selection of weapons; swords, maces, and some I did not recognize. And on the wall in front of me, a coat of arms that looked familiar, with a golden crescent moon and eight-pointed star on an emerald field, but centered in the shield instead of filling the upper left, and missing the rose/sword combination on the one above Penelope's head in the Bingham's oil painting.

Below the shield, seated in a massive chair of wood gilded with gold, its cushions a bright green silk, sat a familiar figure.

She looked much like her portrait. I could not discern so much as a single altered detail. Her pale hair fell like a snowdrift over porcelain shoulders. An artist's brush had sketched eyebrows like hoarfrost over eyes the same shade of blue found in deep ice. Colorless nails glittered as she ran one beneath the glowing ruby red of her lower lip. Her painting hung in the foyer of the Ember mansion, and I knew I had read her name in Penelope's journal.

Andracéil, the White Lady. Visconté of the greatest, as well as the oldest, of the Breed's noble families, House Winterfax.

In my peripheral vision I saw others. Far to the right stood a giant of a man with thick brown hair, a square jaw, and the physique of an Olympic athlete. A few feet behind him stood another familiar face. Moira. She wore an bright green gown trimmed in gold and a turquoise blue, the cloth shimmering in the sea of tapers that lit the room with a buttery yellow glow.

To my left, I saw a youngish-looking man, with spiky blonde hair, dressed so flamboyantly, I could not help but do a double take. He looked as though he belonged on a stage with an electric guitar in his hands. A grin played with the corners of his mouth as he stared at me with frank curiosity from a seat near the White Lady's dais.

There were many others, standing in shadows too dim for my weakened eyes to penetrate. I returned my focus to the Lady, and noticed something mounted above her head within easy reach, an enormous pole ax. Dark stains tarnished the wicked edges of its crescent blades.

The Lady peered down at me, then spoke in a whisper like the tinkling of icicles chiming against one other in a frozen breeze. "What is your name?"

I swallowed once, then again, trying to clear my throat. An unreasonable burst of terror washed through my gut at the thought of giving her my true name. "My sister calls me Damien," I said.

She cocked her head, bird-like, as she regarded me. "You are a man of faith?" she asked. Her voice was barely discernible, but I could tell from her accent that English was not her native language.

"I—ah, I'm not sure. That is. . . ."

"With your permission, my Lady?" said the man with the spiked hair. She did not take her eyes away from me, but gave the briefest of nods.

"In popular American film culture, Damien is a name more often associated with the Satanic due to its use as an appellation some years ago for the Anti-Christ in a series of increasingly pedestrian horror films," he said. "For this reason, it is a name considered synonymous with the devil."

"How odd," the Lady breathed. "For I have known many priests with that name." She stroked the point of her chin with one slim finger. "Interesting. Thank you, Jester."

The man bowed his head, as if to say, 'You're welcome'.

The Lady tilted her head to the right in the direction of the tall, brown-haired man. "Jerome?"

Suddenly a streak of fire on my upper back drove me to my knees. I cried out in surprise as well as shock as I collapsed beneath the lash of an expertly wielded whip.

"In the future, I will expect you to answer the questions I have asked," the Lady said. "I did not inquire about the name given you by your sibling, but the name by which you are known. Which would be? . . ."

I stared up from the floor, fear warring with defiance. Finally I said through gritted teeth, "Eugene."

She looked confused. "What a curious name." She focused on me as though I was some unfamiliar species of insect she had found in her flower garden.

"Now," she continued, "Let us get to the brain of the matter."

"Heart, my Lady," Jester said, his head lowered submissively. "The heart of the matter."

"Say you so? I would have thought the source of identity a more crucial hub than a simple pump, though I must admit there is a certain logic to it, even discounting the common use of the term as a literary device. But then English is young, as languages go."

The Lady returned her attention to me. I fought to ignore the hot coil of pain running from my left shoulder to my right hip, and met her cool gaze.

"Who sired you?" she asked.

Had I not heard Moira use the term in her penthouse apartment, I might not have understood her question. "Penelope Ember," I replied.

If the single stroke from before had taken my voice, what followed almost ripped the lungs from my chest. Despite my rage, I could not stoically bear the lashing. Instead I rolled on the floor, hating myself as each blow wrung a howl from me. Finally the Lady lifted her hand and the blows ceased.

"Youngling, if you insist on lying to us, then I must have Jerome bring out the special whip, the one with silver wire threaded into the leather. And those wounds shall heal neither quickly nor properly. So I ask you again; who sired you?"

My face burned with tears of fear and rage. "If you don't believe me," I spat, "Then just go ahead and kill me now, because I don't know enough to tell a convincing lie, and this is the only story I have."

She listened, then nodded. "Very well. Jerome, grant him his wish."

"My Lady," the one called Jester said, "May I interject here?"

"If it does not take long," she replied. "I do have other matters to attend to."

"As I well understand," Jester began, "And I am quite sympathetic, since those matters are of direct concern to me. But while you and I do not understand why this one persists in holding to a clearly impossible story, there may be something to be gleaned from hearing his tale. At worst, we shall be amused. At best?" He shrugged.

The Lady sighed. "Not for myself, but for you, my Jester, I will indulge." She looked down on me. "Withhold your lash, Jerome, until his story is done. Now — what was it again? — Eugene? Answer me this. In what year were you sired?"

I shifted, trying to adjust my wrists. I felt the beginning of a burn, and wondered if during my thrashing I had cut myself on the silver wire with which I was bound. "Nineteen seventy-nine," I managed to choke out.

"I see. Hold, Jerome. Do you understand why this cannot be?"

I shook my head.

"In our culture, which you appear to know nothing of, when a new Family member is welcomed, it is traditional for such sirelings to be fostered to another House for at least a year's time, longer if reason exists. Like marriages among the ancient nobility of humans, such exchanges strengthen House bonds."

"Houses may foster sirelings one to another for diverse reasons," she continued, "But no lesser House would ever offer a new Breed first to any but the greater House to which it holds fealty. To do otherwise would be an unspeakable, and unforgivable, insult.

"My dear Penelope, whom I sired myself and gave to House Ember as its Visconté, disappeared almost a year ago. And you, little one, have the scent of the newly reborn. But not only that, you claim to be older still, to have been turned almost thirty years before the Lady Ember's disappearance, which damns you as a greater liar than I had already assumed. For once Penelope had shared her blood with you, you would have been brought to these halls, to complete your rebirth within the bosom of Winterfax.

"So, if your tale is true, then explain to me why one — whom I loved as a mother loves her daughter — would keep you from my side for nigh onto three decades before vanishing into the aether, whereupon you waited one year more before seeking out your own kind?"

Well, this is it. This is how it ends. Fine. The hell with all of you.

"First of all," I said, "I was not 'sired', or 'turned', or any of these other friendly little terms you have. I was murdered. Penelope Ember gave me a cup of tea mixed with her blood, and then she killed me."

The White Lady looked at me, her face so still even her eyelashes did not move. "Unconventional, to be sure. Though not unknown. And certainly within her rights. Jester, have you heard of such in recent times?"

The bony scarecrow focused his stare on me with the intensity of a cat staring at a mouse hole. "I know of no living Breed who has been sired in such a manner, other than in our ancient tales. Then typically by accident, rarely deliberately. And I must say, I cannot imagine why any civilized member of our culture would deliberately do such a thing, take such an obvious risk, even if it did not fly in the face of every tradition we hold sacred." He bent forward, his gaze fixed on me to the exclusion of all.

"Quite so," the Lady said in that whisper of hers which forced me to give her speech my full attention. Which was, perhaps, the point. "Penelope Ember is, or was, a great respecter of tradition. So tell me, newborn, before Jerome decorates one of my finest rugs with your bodily fluids, why would the Visconté of House Ember — charged with the practice and preservation of her culture — make use of such an unconventional, as well as untraditional, method of adding to her Household?"

Part of me wanted to just spit in her general direction and hasten what I was convinced was a predetermined end. But the other part, that raged against the injustice of both my treatment and my situation, demanded to be heard.

"She said I was her — as she put it — ace in the hold. Members of House Ember were disappearing, she had no idea why, or who was responsible. So she killed me and put me in her basement, where I was supposed to rise later."

"How . . . odd. Jester?" the Lady said. "You know, or knew, Penelope better than anyone here, save myself. What say you?"

He nodded. "We spoke once of the destruction of Ember's hearth, of a number of her family members perishing when it burned to the ground many years ago. A terrible tragedy, yes. But deliberate, premeditated? If she believed such, she never so implied. At least, not to me."

"But then, it must be also be said," he continued, "That if anyone would keep such concerns a secret, it would be her. Penelope Ember was a garrulous sort, but to confess family weakness? Or fear? She would rather have stood in the charred ruins of Ember Manor, ankle deep in its glowing coals, and said in that charming accent of hers, 'What ashes?', rather than admit she faced an enemy she could not overcome."

"You speak truly," the Lady said, returning her full attention to me, "So, let us assume you have so far spoken the truth. You have not, but for amusement's sake, we will pretend you have. Penelope gave you some of her blood, which initiated the transformation. Then she drained you, killing you, which would hasten it, so that which would have taken thirty days would instead—or so our tales say—have required but one. When you rose that next evening, what then?"

Well, this is it. Fuck you all. And good riddance.

"I was eighteen when Penelope Ember murdered me," I said. "Then I laid in that basement dead, or whatever you want to call it, for thirty years before I, as you put it, 'rose.'"

You never notice true silence until there is a complete absence of sound. No one moved, no one spoke. Even the flickering candles seemed to make no noise.

Then Jester leaned forward in his chair, his eyes wide, his grin wider. "The Sleeper has awakened," he murmured.

"Prove this," the White Lady said to me, her eyes bright with something that reminded me of madness. "Prove this now, or I will take your life myself. And be assured, I will not be half so gentle as Jerome."

Prove it? How? "Charles was there," I said, trying not to sound as desperate as I felt. "She had told him to watch over me."

"Jerome?"

The giant turned. "Moira?"

The small girl grew even smaller, if such were possible. "I made some calls," she said, "Before my Lord Jerome arrived. Charles is being held in an intensive care unit at UNC-Memorial Hospital in Chapel Hill, North Carolina. He's in a coma. Car accident. He's not expected to survive."

"How convenient," Jerome said as he turned back to us. "And of course there is no one else who can verify your tale?" he said, truly looking at me for perhaps the first time.

"Yes," I said. "There is one other person."

"And who might that be?" asked the White Lady.

I met her look, and did not turn away. "Penelope Ember."

"Of course," the Lady replied. "And even more convenient that your remaining witness is herself missing. No doubt when she reappears near the end of Act Five . . . Or is it Act Three? What is the modern convention, Jester? Oh, no matter. Stay your hand, Jerome. As I said, I will finish this."

I watched her rise, to place her hand on the polearm overhead. I cried out, "Here!"

"Here what?" the Lady said, displaying emotion for the first time. Boredom.

"In my pocket."

Her brow crinkled. "Jester?"

The blonde rake of a man unfolded himself from his seat and stepped next to me. His polished black boots gleamed as he bent forward and rummaged through my jeans.

"Back pocket," I said.

He gave me one of his odd looks, then slipped his hand into my Levi's, a puzzled look on his face as he removed its contents. Penelope's journal.

"Curiouser and curiouser," Jester said as he stepped forward to hand the thin volume to the White Lady.

"You would know better than I," he said, "But I must confess the handwriting does look familiar."

"It does indeed," she breathed while flipping through the pages. Something caught her eye, and she paused to read.

She scanned the pages, turning from one to the next with agonizing slowness. Then, finally, she looked up.

"This is indeed her hand," said the White Lady. "And it appears an error has been made. Nathan, release our guest."

A second figure, who had been lurking behind Jerome, moved forward. His hands moved quickly over my wrists and feet, unlocking my bonds. Suddenly I was free. I stood, back on fire, and foolish though I knew it to be, lifted my eyes and met the Lady's frank gaze.

"Perhaps someone can explain," she whispered, even softer than before, "Why a more proper, not to mention thorough, search was not made of our guest?"

Jerome lowered his head. "The fault is mine, my Lady. I did search him, but though I speak English, I do not read it. It appeared to be nothing more than a simple notebook. Still, if there is blame, then it falls upon my head. I await my Lady's justice."

"There is no need to wait," she said. Her eyes moved to Moira. "A favorite, is she not?"

Jerome nodded. "Yes, my Lady."

"No longer. Now she belongs to him," the Lady said, nodding in my direction.

Moira looked from Jerome to me, then screamed, a cry of such pain and deprivation as I had ever heard, before collapsing to sob on the cold stone floor.

My lips were already forming the words, "No, I do not want her!" when Jester caught my eye, followed by a tiny, but definite shake of the head.

Then his gaze shifted, and I followed his glance to the ax above the Lady's seat. My skin itched, and somehow I knew those twin blades were tarnished silver.

Andracéil, Visconté of House Winterfax, got up from her throne, then stood before me, her hands folded, waiting for me to respond.

This is a game, and you do not know the rules, my inner voice hissed. *If you are going to be defiant, then let it be on a day of your choosing. Not theirs.*

So instead of telling her that I would rather die than breath the same air as that of the second woman to betray me, I lowered my head. "As you wish, my Lady."

A smile like wet sleet brushed the corners of her mouth. "Then bear witness, children of Winterfax. For on this eve I open House and Hearth to our newest fosterling, sole scion of House Ember . . ."

Then she paused before turning to Jester. "He must have a new name. I cannot abide 'Eugene', it rolls off the tongue like a stone. You shall be his Mentor, so tell us, what shall he be called?"

Jester looked at me, his manic grin stretched across his face. "We shall call him as his sister once did. Damien." Then he leaned forward, teeth bared in a vicious smile. "This shall be your name in House and Hearth, known to your family alone. But you must choose the name which we will call you openly. And that will be? . . ."

It came to me as a memory, whispered with Penelope's lilting voice, later penned by her ivory fingers, and I said, "Call me Mordant."

*   *   *

I have never been comfortable as the center of attention. Wishing to be such is not the same thing. In our daydreams, we are the suns of our own little solar systems, the centers of gravity, and everything revolves around us. We always say the right things and do the right things while basking in the radiance of our own reflected (and imaginary) glory.

But to be the focus of all eyes, and not know why? That is to unsettling what plunging off a mile-high bridge is to tripping over one's feet.

My skin prickled from the heat of their glowing orbs as the hidden and visible alike watched me, silently, without breathing.

Then the White Lady swept the room with her gaze, a chill wind blowing past and through me, and everyone's attention refocused on her. "Prepare him," she whispered to Jester before she turned and disappeared through a doorway, a small retinue trailing in her wake like the hem of a wedding gown.

Jester stepped next to me. "May I have your shirt?" he asked, his voice low and intense. When I hesitated, he grabbed the front of it and pulled. Buttons flew in all directions, and I stood dumb as he yanked the black garment down my back and arms, then walked off with it.

"Jerome!" he called.

The creature stood well away from Andracéil's silken throne, his brow knitted in what appeared to be furious concentration. Moira stood nearby, shifting her weight from one dainty foot to the other. "Yes?" the vampire said.

"As the young lady is no longer a member of your *Usoleté*," Jester said, "It is neither proper nor fitting that she continue to wear its colors. Therefore I have brought her temporary attire, until something more suitable can be arranged."

Jerome met Jester's eyes, then nodded before turning to Moira, whose own eyes had grown large and damp.

"No," she whispered. "Please!"

"The Lady's *chantéque* is correct," Jerome said in a voice like cold stone. "It is not — fitting. Remove my colors, and accept your new ones."

Moira stared at her feet. "But underneath, I'm not—I . . ."

"Now!" Jerome said.

I could not turn away as the girl, eyes brimming, pulled the dress over her shoulders, allowing the green and gold silk gown to puddle at her feet as she covered her nakedness with her hands as best she could. It was the least erotic sight I had ever seen.

Very good. You're learning how to lie. Try to tell a more convincing one next time, though.

I ignored the voice in my head, along with its mocking laughter, as Jester handed the girl my shirt. She put it on, her face a mask of misery as she stood there shaking, her hands clutching the buttonless front to keep it closed.

"This way," Jester said as he crooked a finger and walked away. I followed him, Moira trailing us, her head down.

The thin blonde vampire led us to a door dark from years of oiling. "In here. No!" he said to Moira as she made to follow us. "You curl up at the threshold like a good little lapdog, and one of us will call you if any boots require licking." He did not wait for a response, instead shutting the door firmly in her face.

A great deal of anger still boiled in my gut at Moira's treachery, but much to my own surprise I could not keep silent. "Did you have to treat her like that?" I said.

"Yes. I could explain why, but frankly there are far more important matters to discuss," Jester said. "Though if I thought you possessed even the slightest glimmer of an understanding of human psychology, I might spend some of our valuable and limited time explaining what anyone else here would have both immediately and intuitively understood. But you don't, so I can't. Now, sit."

I looked around. We were in a large room, lined floor to ceiling with bookshelves and their contents, multiple volumes covered — like the furniture — in a rich burgundy leather. I prayed it was of animal origin. A desk occupied one corner, along with a number of cabinets and other furniture. I stood there, consciously and uncomfortably aware of my still healing back.

Jester sprawled into one of two well-padded armchairs near the room's large fireplace, in which glowing coals nestled among small tongues of flame. He nodded at a matching chair opposite his own. I sat cautiously.

He rested his sharp chin on steepled fingers. "You are a conundrum of an impossible sort. Where to begin?" He stared at me, and I grew uncomfortable beneath his scrutiny.

"My mind is boiling with questions," he began. "But let us start at the beginning. Your beginning. I heard what you said, but I want to ensure there has been no misunderstanding on either of our parts. You say that you were never trained as a topovar; that, in fact, you were created after being drained and, as a result, dying at the hands of our dear — and most likely deceased — Lady Ember?"

I considered elaborating, but did not want to involve my sister in any way. "Yes."

"And she expected you to rise the following night," he said, more to himself than to me. "And when you did not, and the years passed . . . Did she wonder? . . ."

"What did you mean, the sleeper has awakened?" I asked.

"Aware of your surroundings, were you, despite the distractions? Perhaps Penelope did see something extraordinary in you." Jester leaned back, reminding me of a snake at rest.

"You are impossibly ignorant," he finally said. "Despite this," and threw Penelope's journal to me. I caught it and shoved it into the back pocket of my Levi's.

"When I realized what that little item was, I concluded that our dear Penelope had gone quite mad," Jester said, half to himself. "Committing our history to written form, risking the chance it might fall into human hands? But now, having seen it for myself, I realize I did not give Ember's fiery Visconté sufficient credit."

"Why do you say that?" I asked, interested despite myself.

"Because she wrote that document in *sinégar* ink."

"What's that?"

"A rare and precious artifact. And in limited supply, since the plant whose fruit was used to make it has long been extinct. When properly processed, the juice of *sinégar* berries creates a stain visible only to the eyes of the Breed."

"What did you mean, the sleeper has awakened?" I repeated, determined not to be put off.

"Persistent." Jester chuckled. "To answer your question, I was referencing a popular science fiction novel. Do not read any more into my comment than that."

"To continue (and do not interrupt me again unless you require clarification), there is a great deal you must learn, and our Lady has assigned to me the tedious and thankless job of educating you. In order to do that, I must educate myself. So," he said, leaning forward, "How many humans have you killed thus far?"

The question startled me. "Who said I killed anybody?"

"Reply to my questions with a question once more, and I shall ask my Lady as a personal favor to pass you off to Jerome. She would do it, and I am confident you would not care for his particular brand of tutorial discipline. Now, answer me."

My jaw clenched, requiring me to speak through gritted teeth. "I've killed four people. But it was in self defense, or defending someone else. I did not murder anyone."

"What does that matter? Of greater concern is the fact that you undoubtedly drained them. Which will almost certainly require damage control. Understand this, for our purposes there are two kinds of humans, bonded and unbonded. Bonded are the topovar, or those who are being considered for such a status. Unbonded are all others. To kill another's topovar without good reason is a property crime, judged by the House Valyar or Visconté. What one does with one's own property is, of course, one's own business.

"To slay a unbonded human in such a fashion as to invite unwanted speculation regarding the existence of our kind, that is considered an act of criminal stupidity. We go to extraordinary lengths to insure our anonymity, and should you wish a permanent death, there is no quicker way to obtain one. To be sure, mistakes occur. We are, after all, predators by blood and by nature. If an 'accident' takes place, you would be expected to clean up after yourself. There is no greater admonition than this, never bring suspicion of our existence to the unbonded. Can I make myself any clearer?"

I met his level gaze with one of my own. "I hear you."

He stared at me, his lips slightly parted. "You have not reconciled yourself to your new life, have you?" He tilted his face towards the fire. "This raises a difficult question."

I opened my mouth, then closed it again. Twin arguments warred inside my brain. Part of me hated being the monster I had become, and would have been happy to see it all come to an end, freeing my soul for whatever transition might await it.

But there was another part, the part which recognized it had been given a second chance at life. Not a life like the one I had planned, but life nonetheless. Should I throw it away a second time?

Or was I just rationalizing?

"You say I don't have to kill anyone?" I asked.

"Have to? No more than any human must."

I turned to the fire and stared at the glowing coals. "But I have to drink human blood to survive."

"Yes. In modern popular culture, various writers have populated their tales with all manner of bastardized versions of our kind who feed on animal blood, synthetic blood, and Christ knows what else. I wait for a vegetarian vampire who subsists entirely on a diet of tomato juice. He will, no doubt, be the soul of sensitivity and self-deprecating to a fault. But you can only sustain your life on human blood. And fresh blood at that. Which is why we require the topovar. And before you ask (since I can see the question in your eyes), blood is not wine, to improve with age. It must be consumed in the same moment as it is shed. Coagulation, or simple age, destroys its life-sustaining properties. And no, we have yet to understand why this is so."

"Why would anyone do this? Willingly?"

"I assume you are referring to the topovar." Jester settled himself into his chair. "Various reasons. Money, for one. We hold little in our own names, the risks of exposure are too great. Our topovar are our trustees, managing our interests. Periodically our wealth grows so vast that it becomes necessary to divest some of it. As Einstein was supposedly quoted, 'The greatest power in the universe is compound interest.' Take the one now huddling outside our doorway. To see her now, she appears a pitiful sight in her torn shirt and nothing else. But in her natural habitat you would scarcely recognize her, a socialite of nigh unmatched wealth and social status who, with a word, could ruin any number of her lessers. And, I have little doubt, has already done so, likely more than once.

"But there is yet another reason, which you may not have witnessed for yourself if your feedings thus far have been (or so you have implied) violent. Our bite induces a state of unmatched euphoria in humans. Take one's throat in your mouth, and you may then do with him or her as you please."

I felt a surge run the length of my body at his words, and I recalled any number of mental images which had flooded my brain for the past few weeks. The effort required was substantial, but I forced them away.

Jester observed my struggle with what appeared to be amusement before he leaned forward.

"What you have, many outside of this room long for passionately, while understanding that few will be chosen. Unlike humankind, which hastens to overwhelm its limited natural resources at a suicidal rate, we practice an unbending form of population control. From within the topovar only a tiny number shall cross over to take their place among us. All know it, and accept it. We are discriminating to a fault when we create a new sireling. There can be no misplaced trust. Our numbers are deliberately kept small, to better disguise our existence."

"I'm surprised you haven't tried to take over the world," I said.

"For what purpose? As Stanley Lieber once said, 'With great power comes great responsibility.' Ruling the world would be a dull and thankless job, with no end of political complications and pointless power struggles. Oh, should we wish to do so, no doubt we could, though I hardly see the point of it. One might as well wish to become King of the Mayflies!"

"But now, on to more serious matters," Jester said, his tone and intensity reflected in his words. "For in you, as I have said, we have a conundrum. You are one of us, yet not one of us. I see the struggle inside of you. There are unanswered questions regarding your existence, which is why you still live. However, the moment the risks of keeping you alive outweigh the possible benefits. . . ." He raised his hands. "Well, then the choice shall be made for you. Now, which shall it be?"

As I stared into his eyes, as dark and glittering as black opals, I felt the sincerity of his words. If I could not be in spirit what I was now in flesh, then they would destroy me out of fear I might betray their existence to humanity, either deliberately or by accident. So I had to make a choice. Live as a monster, or die a human being.

Part of me insisted there could be no choice. While I had come to doubt the existence of any kind of a God, what about the voices of my dreams as I lay dead in Penelope's basement? So many times I had struggled to sift through those half-heard whispers, to remember something clear and unambiguous. But I could not.

So what now?

Once again I felt the anger. I had been murdered. While Penelope might have hoped my death would not be permanent, it was merely a hope, not a certainty. How many people throughout human history had died at the hands of others, for the basest or blandest of reasons? And how many of those victims had been offered such a chance? How could I disparage something so many (including myself, I recalled bitterly) had wished for so deeply, another chance at life, while watching their own slip away?

No. I would not die again. Not a second time. There had to be a reason why this had happened to me, and I swore I would find out what it was.

"I want to live," I said in a low, but determined, voice.

"Hmm?" Jester shook his head and smiled. "Perhaps you misunderstood me, young Mordant. My question was purely rhetorical. Whether you live or die is not a choice you shall make; rather, it is a choice which shall be made for you."

"But until then," Jester continued, "I will perform my duties as the Lady's *chantéque*. And my first duty is to make certain you are not going to run about Winterfax Manor slaughtering someone's favorite because you are too squeamish (or too noble, which amounts to the same thing) to feed until you are driven mad with hunger. Moira!"

My fingers locked down on the arms of my chair. I knew what he expected of me now, just as I knew that to refuse would mean my end. I heard the door open. "Yes?" a frightened voice husked.

"The time has come, the walrus said, to talk of many things," Jester sang to her. "First, we are going to teach young Mordant here how to open a bottle without breaking it. Come now, do not linger, I can smell you have not been uncorked in some time. Now, Mordant, you are going to learn the first lesson a sireling is taught, how to milk the cow without killing it. Stay, girl."

I looked at Moira from the corner of my eye. She stood nearby, white with fear. I felt my rage at her lessen, though it did not fade altogether.

Jester casually pulled her to the floor between us. I tried not to stare at her near nakedness.

"Before you feed, you should calm your vessel. Some will not need such soothing, and will be anxious for your kiss, but always assume your meal is a knot of frozen terror. Much like this one. Now, when you do finally bite, fill your mouth with saliva so that it mingles with the blood. This causes the euphoria. Pain will surrender to pleasure, and this is the most dangerous time. For once your vessel has slipped into this state, he or she will feel neither discomfort nor fear, and will happily allow you to feed until their heart literally stops beating. This is a concern because, when the hunger is upon you, sating it will be your sole priority. Now, girl, into his lap. And no flinching, for if he misses his mark and strikes a major artery, then I might have to join in. You know how the Lady despises waste."

Moira, her every muscle trembling, crawled into the chair with me. She closed her eyes as she leaned forward, her face buried into my shoulder, her arm against my chest, her neck taunt and exposed.

Now I trembled. I could smell the blood underneath her warm skin, hear the shush-shush of it circulating. A moment before, the idea of my teeth in her flesh had repulsed me. Now I could think of nothing else.

Despite my growing need, I had no idea where to bite. I did not want to pierce her and unleash a fountain. My confusion must have been obvious, because Jester sighed with exasperation and—reaching forward—placed two fingertips on her exposed throat before leaning back to watch. I met his eyes again, and suddenly knew what he was thinking. He *expected* me to fail, believed that, once I began, I would not be able to stop.

And yet he wanted me to continue.

As I realized this, with Moira's body pressed against mine, her muscles still vibrating uncontrollably, I felt a hatred for him as strong as anything I had ever felt for Penelope. Maybe he had always wanted Moira for himself, and resented that she belonged to Jerome. Maybe she had offended him somehow. No matter. I determined at that moment that whatever I had to do, she would not die in my arms. Not tonight.

My bravado weakened as I turned my gaze back to her pale throat, her skin flushed pink with the rich oxygenated blood whispering just below the surface.

And I knew, just as Jester did, that I was going to kill her.

I would not do it intentionally, but that did not matter. Once I tasted her, the hunger would gain a life of its own, and I would be lost in its madness. It did not matter how strong I was, or thought I was. It would prove stronger.

Then I knew what I had to do.

I bent forward, taking her neck into my mouth. I remembered what Jester had said, though he need not have bothered, for my mouth watered already. I shifted in place, sliding my foot to the side while angling my body just so. Then I bit.

The sensation was indescribable, like popping a ripe berry in one's mouth. I heard her whimper, and tasted salt from the tears flowing down her cheek into my lips. My own eyes watered as the taste and the smell of her, a sweet peppery richness laced with the acrid tang of fear, flooded my senses. I swallowed, time and time again, listening as her moans of pain softened into something else, just as primal, just as elemental. I experienced a brief moment of clarity, a recognition of conscious thought swaying in the balance, before the taste of her overwhelmed my senses, and I gorged on her.

In that time, nothing mattered. I felt her breathing as it grew shallow, it moved me not at all. Her strong heartbeat slowed to a sluggish thump, and still I continued to drain her. She moaned again, pushing herself at me with the last of her fading strength.

Then the pain began.

I registered it in the beginning as a distant annoyance, like a persistent alarm clock intruding on the outer edges of a warm, deep sleep. Then it grew more insistent, more demanding, until it wrestled with the hunger like a living thing. Finally I could endure it no longer and, with a cry of rage and agony coupled with still unsatisfied need, I rolled Moira from my lap to the floor before twisting away from the hearth, tears scalding my eyes as I bent to examine my injury.

The sneaker continued to smolder. The canvas upper had burned clear through from where I had shoved my foot almost into the flames. Smoke rose from the sock as well, or what remained of it. The exposed flesh had turned black, with a raw red showing through the cracks in the flesh. I recalled reading once that such charring destroyed the nerves. Not so, at least in my case. Sobs forced their way through my clenched teeth, and I met Jester's astonished eyes with a challenge in my own.

"He shall know your ways as if born to them," he muttered in a distracted tone, before focusing on me once again.

"I am tempted to ask where you learned that little trick, except that I know it has never been committed to paper in any journal or text I have ever read. Conquering the *rhejmar*, the hunger, is a rite of passage for all our kind. To do so under these circumstances. . . ." He shook his head as he stood. "The Lady will certainly wish to know of this."

"In the meantime, I will arrange accommodations for you and your new vessel. Even as quickly as our kind heals, that burn will take time. Remain here, and I will send members of my own hashna. They will show you how to care for one who has been so deeply drained. Your pain, of course, must be endured until the healing is complete. Until they arrive, remain here." Then he turned and left.

I crawled next to Moira, and searched for a pulse. Finally I found it, weak and thready, but present. I suppressed the desire to curl next to her to share a non-existent warmth. Instead I folded the floor's rug over her pale, motionless form. Then I rolled onto my back to wait.

*   *   *

Jester's hashna came, as he had said it would. There were four of them, two women and two men, all young, though not as young as myself. Or rather, as young as I felt. And all handsome, all beautiful, like everyone else I had seen within these walls.

They saw to Moira first, pouring orange juice down her throat before wrapping her in a thick blanket and checking her vitals.

By now the pain in my foot had lessened, and I could stand. Walking, though, that was another matter. When they were ready to escort the two of us out, one of the men tucked himself under my left shoulder to act as a living cane. We followed the leader, a woman who carried a modern-looking piece of luggage, as we navigated a series of hallways as extensive and complex as a corn maze before pausing outside a set of heavy double-doors made of thick timbers bound with bronze.

"These apartments belong to our Lord," the woman said. "You are to consider yourself his honored guest." She opened the doors and preceded us inside.

Or rather, preceded me. The two carrying Moira continued down the hallway. I turned to look after them.

"She will require more care before she will be healthy enough to resume her duties," the woman said. I examined her more closely. She had an exotic look, as though she had been conjured by one of Scheherazade's dreams. A gown of green and deep gold with indigo accents followed her body's curves down to her ankles. Jeweled sandals encased her slim feet. Her nose was slightly humped, and a bit long. Hair fell past her waist like an evening river of watered silk, and her eyes were the green of fresh mint leaves. She flushed under my examination.

"My name is Candide," she said. "My horshno is Robert. Until your hashnaid can nourish you once more, we have been instructed to provide for your needs, whatever they might be."

I removed my arm from Robert's shoulders and shuffled to a nearby chair. "I have no needs, thank you," I replied as I lowered myself to the cushions.

I heard the doors close with a solid thud and looked up. Robert had gone, but Candide remained.

I did my best to ignore her, focusing instead on the room. After what I had seen of the castle (though palace might have been a more apt description), this room appeared almost cozy by comparison. A canopy bed of black wrought iron, its gauzy curtains obscuring its interior, filled the far wall. The furniture was delicate and ornate, the chairs more ornamental than functional. A fireplace, empty and cold, filled half the space on the wall closest to the bed. In the corner a washbasin and stone pitcher served in place of the nonexistent bathroom.

"This part of the manor has not been fully modernized," Candide said. "There is electricity, but no plumbing as of yet. You, of course, have no need of a water closet, but should your guests require one, they should turn right as they leave and go to the last door at the end of the hallway."

She placed the bag, a green valise decorated with small fleur-de-lis, on the bed. "Our Lord has asked that you be provided with more suitable clothing. Should you require anything else, please let me know."

I nodded without looking at her, focusing instead on my injured foot. Sections of the blackened skin had begun to slough away, leaving behind skin the color of white marble. I bent forward to remove what was left of my sneaker.

Almost in the same moment, Candide knelt at my feet. "Allow me," she murmured as she plucked at the laces. "Some places heal more quickly than others, and you may open a fresh wound unwittingly."

I looked down on her as she worked at my shoe. "How old are you?" I asked.

Though her hair obscured her face like a curtain, I caught a glimpse of a smile between the strands. "Is it not considered impolite, even in America, to ask a lady's age?"

"I—yes—that is . . ." I shook my head. "You look young, but you sound, um—older."

She chuckled. "Let us say that the shadow of middle age lengthens to cross my path."

"You're almost thirty?"

Now she laughed. "I will be forty-seven upon my next birthday."

"But—that's impossible! You look so, so—"

"Young?" With a deft twist, she freed my foot from the charred remains of my sneaker. I hissed as it peeled away from my instep.

"Your pardon!" Candide cried in genuine distress. "Let me see!"

I leaned back as she examined me, her touch light and soothing. "It is well," she said in obvious relief. "Some skin, but no blood."

I nodded, embarrassed by my display. "You cannot be that old," I said, hoping to distract her.

"Why, thank you, sir," she said with what appeared to be a proud smile. "My Lord nourishes himself upon me regularly."

So many questions occurred to me. But I did not want to appear ignorant. That is, any more ignorant than I felt. "You don't age if they, I mean he, feeds on you?"

"Oh, we do, just not as quickly as we would otherwise." She placed the sneaker to one side and began working on what remained of the sock. "You are young?"

I nodded. "Very young."

Candide nodded as well. "It is very difficult for such. Our Lord has trained many, it is said. You are fortunate to have been given over to him." She peeled the damaged sock from my foot. Her touch was almost maternal. Though not quite, I thought as I looked down into the plunging neckline of her gown, and felt something flooding my cheeks. Not exactly heat, but something.

More like freezer burn, my inner voice tittered. I ignored it.

"I do not know the customs of your House," she said. "But in Winterfax the Family feeds in private. If that was not so in your House, it will not be allowed here unless Lord Gilliad declares otherwise."

"Lord Gilliad?"

She smiled. "His House name. Outside he is Jester. As within *coffeyar* we were told you are Lord Damien, but outside we are to refer to you as Mordant."

I sat there, thoughts spinning in my brain like debris in a funnel cloud. Candide's long, slim fingers kneaded my foot. "And how long since you first rose and took your place among the Breed, my Lord?"

Her question took a moment to penetrate the cloud inside my head. "Four weeks? No, five by now, I believe."

Her hands stopped moving. "Weeks?"

"More or less." I focused on her again. She trembled like a mouse trapped by a cat's paws. "What's wrong?"

She did not answer me right away, and when she did, terror filled her voice. "How have I displeased you, my Lord?" she gasped. "In what way have I offended you?"

"Huh? You haven't offended me," I said. Though as soon as the words left my mouth, I realized that she had not been speaking to me, but to the absent Jester.

Her hands slipped away, and she literally crawled backwards. "If my Lord truly has no need of my services, as he has said, then I shall not impose upon him any further." And with those words, she sprang to her feet and fled through the door.

I stared after her in confusion. It could not be fear I might attack her, she knew I had just fed. But if not that, then what had frightened her so?

More questions, I thought as I lifted my foot to rest it on the couch. But maybe soon there would be answers to go with them.

*　　*　　*

Even though I could not see the sun, I felt its presence outside of the thick limestone walls. But dimmer than I had yet experienced, almost ignorable. The sensation had never felt this indistinct, and with that came a sense of relief, almost of comfort.

Which only lasted until I tried to open my room's door. Locked. I tested its strength, but I might as well have tried to force my way through the stone walls. With no other options available, I lay on the bed to think.

During that time no one disturbed me. I could hear distant voices and footfalls, though. No doubt a place this size demanded a great deal of effort to maintain, and I wondered again where I was. Candide had said "even in America", which led me to believe my captors might have crossed the ocean. Europe, perhaps?

As I felt the sun's rise, so I felt its setting as well. Soon after the door opened and Jester strode in.

I looked at him from where I lay on the enormous bed. "With all your obsessions with tradition and etiquette, I would have thought you'd have learned to knock before entering. I might have been jerking off."

He stared at me, not with anger, but in confusion. Then he laughed. "Such odd notions your people have."

"Where I come from," I said, "Entering the room of your guest is considered rude."

"Indeed? We have a similar custom, and if you were my guest, you would perhaps have, if not the right, then at least a pretext for being offended."

I sat up. "Your juice boxes told me I was to consider myself your 'honored guest'."

"You may consider yourself to be anything you like," Jester said before his jaws parted in a gaping yawn. "What you are, that is another matter."

"So what am I then? A prisoner?" I said while getting off the bed.

He smiled. "Your status, such as it is, is undetermined. The Visconté has declared that for now you are to be treated as the legitimate Valyar of House Ember, by default. And Visconté as well, an amusing notion. However, your only claim to either title rests in your being (apparently) its sole surviving member. Should one or more members of your House be discovered, then tradition shall determine the rightful heir to that title which, absent other mitigating factors, would be determined by age. Under those circumstances, your claim to either would be tenuous at best."

"Speaking of age," I said, "Your hashnaid appeared surprised to learn I was only four weeks risen."

"Indeed?" Jester fell into a chair which looked as though it could barely hold his weight. He flung one long, thin leg over its arm as he faced me.

"'Surprised' comes close. 'Terrified' would be a better fit."

He threw his head back and laughed. "That one has grown just a bit presumptuous," he said finally. "One can never allow a topovar to believe it has curried a lasting favor. What would there be left to strive for then, I ask you?"

I crossed the room to stand opposite him. "She thought I might attack her. Kill her, maybe."

Jester gave me the self-satisfied smile of a cat with a mouse's tail dangling from its lips. "And did you?"

I shifted, pushing unbidden thoughts out of mind. "Of course not."

"Fascinating," he murmured. "The newly risen for the first year of their existence are never allowed to be alone with a human. They are ravenous, and must learn to control their appetites." He smiled. "All of them."

I remembered the people I had killed, how they had screamed. "So why did you leave me alone with her?"

"You presume. I did not leave you alone with Candide, she allowed herself to be left alone with you. A bit of carelessness I doubt will be repeated anytime soon." His smile grew wider.

I maintained focus on him. "So what now?"

Jester leaned back in his chair, his arms cradling his head. "Now you answer my questions. To begin with, you will tell me your story. All of it."

I took my own seat opposite him. "I was born the son of a poor share-cropper . . ."

"Droll. Let us bypass the no doubt tedious narrative of your deprived upbringing. Begin with how you met Penelope."

I began. The story came hard. I provided little embellishment, which led to frequent questions and interruptions from Jester. I said nothing about my reunion with my sister, implying instead that Charles and I had been heading for New York when the 'accident' occurred, as well as the second attempted murder of my person (the first could not be called 'attempted', since it had been quite successful). That part of the story elicited the darkest frown I had yet seen from him. I also told him about the cabin, and the man who had slaughtered his family.

"Such tales have grown increasingly commonplace," he said. "Someone loses his or her mind—though the offender is frequently male—then slaughters family members, co-workers, and/or friends, only to take his own life in the end. Such a waste."

I did not respond, since I knew very well what Jester believed was being 'wasted'. All I could see were the widening eyes of Noel's father, just before he died, as though he had seen something surprising. I hoped it had been the doors of Hell opening wide to welcome him home.

Jester rested the point of his chin on his knotted fingers. "These 'disappearances' of the various Embers confuse me," he murmured. "We are a passionate and violent species, which is why we place such store on custom, etiquette, and tradition, as an aid in the restraint of our more volatile impulses. There have been frequent conflicts among the great Houses in the past, as well as occasional battles, even the odd war or two in the days since the *Coloque*. But such hostilities have typically been covert, never overt. To be sure, we remain in a state of constant conflict, struggling for power and influence, primarily through the human realm. But such matters nowadays are conducted with a delicate touch, and the actual killing of our kind, much less the deliberate destruction of a House and its members, is heavy-handed and blatant, inviting a repeat of the wars of old. It would be insane."

I wanted to appear bored and disinterested, but could not manage the lie. "Did Penelope—I mean, House Ember—have enemies?"

Jester frowned. "Not in the sense you mean. Human conflict as a rule is based on a struggle for limited resources while employing their propensities for racial, national, or cultural prejudices, which are then used to motivate the sheep whose bodily fluids are the ones which are actually spilled in the service of those in power. Hardly a difficult task, such a story practically writes itself. Our only limited resource is the blood we require to sustain our existence, and the topovar supply that. Our wealth provides us with everything else we need, or might need. And our topovar are groomed to occupy positions of great power and influence in the human realm, which they are then expected to utilize for our benefit, should it prove necessary. We select only the most deserving of them to elevate, keeping our numbers small to minimize risk of discovery, while continuing to wield power and influence over humanity from the shadows."

I shrugged. "Someone has to benefit from the destruction of House Ember. If not, why do it?"

Jester's frown deepened. "This is what disturbs me. While our Houses engage in social and political machinations to make Machiavelli look like a dewy-eyed ingénue by comparison, there is nothing I can imagine to be gained by such an act of obvious aggression. Such a House would find itself under siege by those Families bound to the offended, a risky proposition. Humans know nothing of our true existence, and if any of them were to suggest we were more than tales for cheap cinema and vapid erotica, such a person would be regarded as insane by his fellows. Were we to engage in indiscriminate slaughter, that would draw undesired and unwelcome attention, but we do not. At least, not often enough to matter. The topovar worship us, and we so dominate their minds that the notion any of them would act against us is inconceivable."

"That did not stop Moira," I said dryly.

"She was not of your House, at least not at the time. No," Jester said, flicking a nail against his sharp, white teeth, "There is something—wrong here."

Jester had me repeat my story from the beginning, then repeat it again. He probed me with constant questions, some of which I had no answers for.

Then he asked the question I had feared the most. "Does anyone else know you still live?"

I did not know which answer would prove worse, a lie or the truth. "My sister knows," I finally said. "But only that I am 'alive'. Nothing else."

Jester leaned back. "And if I asked for her name, would you give it to me? The true one, that is."

I shrugged. "You might be able to torture it out of me. Eventually."

He laughed. "More and more, I see in you what Penelope must have," he said. "And you are quite right, we could indeed torture it out of you. Eventually," he amended, sighing as he placed his hands behind his head. "But for now, we shall let matters stand. One may always break an egg, but restoring it afterwards is a tedious and difficult chore." He got up as if to leave.

An image flickered through my brain, of Jester (or one of his 'family') stalking Barb along a dark and narrow street. A sudden violent surge rose in me, and I clenched my fists and jaw in an effort to keep from leaping on him, ripping open that pale, slim throat and watching the blood as it poured from his wounds and clotted on the floor.

"How long am I going to be kept a prisoner in this room?" I asked.

He turned, and smiled. "Let us say I am working on that," he said as he left. I listened to the clicks and rattles of various devices as he locked me in once again.

*   *   *

During the days that followed, Jester came to my rooms (or rather, his rooms) for what was fast becoming an endless interrogation. I was never allowed outside those four walls during that time. Sometimes Candide would enter, trembling from head to toe, to stand at the doorway and wait for whatever use I might wish to put her to. And though I knew it was stupid to do so, I continued to send her away untouched. Jester was using me to punish her, or so I assumed, and I refused to oblige him. Instead I spoke to her calmly, asking her questions about her life. She would then grow silent, and ultimately request permission to leave when it became obvious I would not feed on her. And though I felt the hunger growing like a tumor in my gut, my equally fierce stubbornness refused to bend. I knew this could not continue, a fact Jester must have been counting upon when he entered my room one day with someone I had never seen before.

"Good evening, brother," he said as he entered. "We have a visitor whom you simply must meet."

His exaggerated joviality set my defenses on high alert, and I watched with suspicion as he escorted a young woman into the room.

There appeared to be nothing extraordinary about her. She was small, somewhat pretty, though sharp featured. Her light brown hair fell past her shoulders, and her eyes were the rich color of hot chocolate. A draft from the open door blew past the two of them in my direction, and I caught her bloodscent, a spicy fragrance that sent a tremor through me.

"This is—well, names are not important, since you will not have much time to get to know one another. Your asceticism has impressed me, Mordant, and others as well. For this reason, and to provide you with guilt-less sustenance, I have—at great personal sacrifice—decided to offer you this marvelous little confection."

I turned my back on them both and stepped to the fireplace, taking the poker in hand and stirring the fading coals. "Please leave," I said, barely able to force the words past my lips.

"We encountered one another in an unusual—what do they call it?— chat room, catering to individuals with the most exotic tastes. This one particularly intrigued me. She has the kind of fantasy which comes along once in a lifetime. I say once, because its satisfaction does not allow for a repeat performance, if you understand me."

I did understand him. The scent of her need flooded my senses, and I felt a sudden dizziness, as if I was about to step off the rooftops of sanity and plunge into madness.

Though it took all of my fading strength to make the plea, I somehow managed it, the words coming out as a whisper. "Don't."

"Enjoy!" Jester said cheerfully before I heard him open, and then close, the doors. Leaving me alone with . . . her.

For the next few minutes, there was no sound except that of the girl's own breathing.

Finally she spoke. "You think I'm crazy, don't you?"

"You flatter yourself," I said through gritted teeth as I continued to focus on the flames.

Her dress make a rustling noise as she moved closer, her heart pounding like a bass drum in her chest. "I remember watching some god-awful movie on late night TV. Pay cable. The girl had been bound and chained to a table. Then he took a sheet off a counter, and there were all these devices. Knives, and worse. They kept the camera there as the music got louder and louder, and you could hear her screaming."

She paused. "I can't tell you what that did to me. No one had to tell me I was different. I knew it. Just as I knew no one else would ever understand."

"You're crazy," I whispered.

Her hair made a hissing sound as she shook her head. "I've thought that. Many times. Even the people I got to know, the ones into S&M and all of that safe, sane and consensual stuff. When I hinted that my greatest fantasy was to be killed, to be tortured to death, I could tell even they thought something was seriously wrong with me."

"But there isn't," she said with a childish defiance. "I'm not depressed, and I'm not crazy, or at least no crazier than anyone else. All of the things that matter to other people: marriage, children, growing old, none of that has any meaning for me."

Her feet shushed on the rug as she stepped behind me. "I want what has obsessed me for years. I want to die. And not just die. I want to be murdered. I want to be killed horribly, in pain, with cruelty and malice aforethought."

"I know you think I'm insane. I know it makes no sense. What I know is that I need this. For most of my life it's been all I can think about. The one who brought me in here, he promised me. He said you would give me all this, and more."

I shook uncontrollably as I felt the touch of her breath on my ear. "I don't know how long I can be brave," she whispered. "Please."

Then I fell on her.

She screamed, of course. Perhaps in terror, possibly in ecstasy. I did not care. Every need I had been suppressing for so very long filled me, and then overflowed. I tore off her clothing, the better to expose the soft flesh underneath. I bit her, in several places, her blood filling my mouth like the juice from a overripe peach. I used none of Jester's tricks of soothing calm followed by overwhelming pleasure. Instead I fed viciously on her, as Penelope had on me, and when she did finally began to scream "No!" I laughed at her.

Eventually her struggles grew weaker, her breath more and more shallow. She bled from any number of places; her throat, her breasts, the soft juncture of her thighs. Blood matted her hair, what little I had allowed to spill unused, and as her pulse grow faint, her breathing shallow, she twisted her neck in a painful and almost impossible angle as she whispered a phrase into my ear, delivered in a familiar tone with a recognizable cadence.

"I —win!"

The words flowed down my spine like ice water. For a moment that stretched into an eternity, I listened to their familiar echo while teetering between sanity and surrender.

Then, with a wail like a demented banshee, I flung her away a moment before plunging my fist into the burning coals of the fireplace. She fell back against the entryway, and for a moment something in her face wavered. There was no real change, no sudden transformation, only a simple distortion, like a reflection in an antique mirror. And yet I felt overwhelmed by the sense that I was staring into the face of someone, or something, alien. Something — displeased.

Then the moment passed, so quickly I could not have said it had happened at all, and there was only the girl, sobbing, a bubble of snot quivering in one nostril.

I turned away, closing my eyes. Then I heard the doors open, and the slapping of leather on stone. "Get her out of here!" I cried. "Now, goddammit!"

There was the quick stepping of feet and the rustling of movements, followed by the slamming of a door, and I was once again alone. When I felt sure of this, I yanked my hand from the coals, howling with suppressed and unfulfilled need. I slammed my injured fist into the floor, then beat my head against the stone walls, injuring myself in any number of ways. But nothing worked. I wanted only to finish what I had begun.

And when it truly hit me that I was to be frustrated in that desire, I collapsed into a corner with my burned hand, pleading for God to show some fucking mercy and, if I could not take the girl's life, would He at least have the common decency to take my own?

*   *   *

When next I saw Jester, he could not look at me and control his mirth, but instead laughed with complete abandon. Unwilling to allow him the satisfaction of even the appearance of discomfit, I maintained a solemn and expressionless dignity. Which only served to further increase his amusement at my expense.

Though I did burn with humiliation over my lapse of control, there were two silver linings to my situation. The first was that the tale had obviously spread amongst the Winterfax topovar, who no longer avoided me as though I was a wild animal who might turn on them at any moment. And though she wet herself the first time I fed on her, Candide did offer her throat without the fatalistic attitude of the condemned mounting the gallows. True, I still could not trust myself when slaking my hunger, so I fed always within reach of the fireplace and its glowing embers. And with the passing of time, my self control grew stronger.

The second benefit was even more welcome. From the day I flung that suicidal lunatic out of my room, the doors to my apartment were never locked, giving me (albeit limited) access to the manor.

The rules were simple, I could enter any room lacking a door. There were many such, open to Breed and topovar alike, brimming with massive works of art as ancient as anything one might find in a museum. Portraits hung high in gilded frames from which their life-sized subjects could look down upon their assumed admirers. And there were statues as well, also life-sized, sculpted in a variety of noble, even erotic poses, some carved from stone, others cast in bronze.

But the room in which I spent the most time was the one where I had found myself upon my initial arrival. Unlike that first evening it was rarely occupied, its emerald green throne with the golden frame now sitting empty. I spent hours there, studying the tapestries encircling the enormous space, which appeared to tell the story of the founding of House Winterfax.

I could see, both by the garments of their subjects as well as the antiquity of the settings, how ancient the oldest must have been. I often lost myself in them, repulsed by the content but mesmerized by the intricate details, and how the weaver used them in a narrative without words.

One in particular held my attention, and I stood before it the longest. For there she stood (perhaps a third of the way into the tale), dressed only in moonlight, her bare feet leaving no mark of her passage upon the snowy trail on which she trod, her fingertips caressing the bowed and exposed neck of some faceless subject. Andracéil, the White Lady.

But the most remarkable creation I encountered during this time could only be defined as a work in progress. Her name was Argenta, and she was the essence of art. That is, beautiful beyond reason and — in equal measure — quite insane.

I entered what I had come to regard as the Throne Room and saw her in a corner just behind the dais, staring at a web in which a small spider, pale as a skull, busied itself making a package of a future meal. Every now and then the cocoon twitched, and both spider and woman (obviously no topovar) shuddered with suppressed ecstasy.

"It knows," she murmured in a voice surprisingly deep and throaty for such a delicate creature. She was small and reed slender, with large, luminous eyes the color of a tropical sea. Her hair, a gleaming coal black bound in a thick braid, flowed down her back to just below her knees. She wore a simple dress of watered silk, as red as a candy apple, and soft shoes of the same material. She angled her head, not looking at me, but still conveying the expectation of a response.

"That its life is over?" I said, suppressing the absurd and pointless impulse to smash both predator and prey.

"That balance yet holds sway," she replied, sounding more as if reminding herself of something she had forgotten rather than conversing with me. "Though Chaos stands but a breath away. But when the walls grow thin, the Sleeper shall dream no more." She turned and looked in my direction, as if seeing me for the first time. "Who are you?"

I recalled Jester's lessons and responded formally. "I am Mordant, of House Ember."

She stared so long past my shoulder that I wondered if she had forgotten I was there. "No," she finally said.

"I beg your pardon?"

"You are the sudden breeze that announces the storm." She turned back to the web, stretching one slim, bone-white finger to its denizen, who crawled over her dark red nail, then paused on her knuckle. "My sister knew you well," she said, eyes fixed on her arachnid companion as though engaged in a staring contest. "Soon the curtain shall split, exposing the proscenium to an audience surprised to discover that it now occupies the stage."

She glanced back at me, smiling. "I am Argenta," she said. Then, with a flick of her tongue, the spider vanished.

Somehow I suppressed a shudder, instead watching as she turned to regard the double-bladed poleax hanging just above the green throne. I studied it with her. The wood of its shaft had dark stains where it had been frequently gripped. Thick tassels, just below the business end, formed a circle, their purpose obvious, to keep the haft from getting slippery with blood. Both they and the heavy silver blades were discolored, from what I had to assume were multiple uses.

"Filthy metal," she said, as she regarded the weapon. "And that is its secret. For it has a voice too, you know. All things do. But the unrepentant blade strikes pure, and you must welcome its kiss if you are to prove her savior." She giggled as she lifted a slender hand, running her fingers over the weapon's shaft. My shoulders stiffened in cautious anticipation and I stepped to the left, placing distance between us.

She lowered her hand before facing me with a smile. "We will speak again soon," she said as she floated away on feet which barely appeared to make contact with the floor.

I turned on my heel, not willing to allow her behind me, then watched as she glided into the distance, her gown shimmering like candlefire.

A gentle cough behind me announced the presence of my Instructor. "I see you have met Argenta," Jester said with a barely suppressed chuckle.

I watched the darkness consume her before turning away. "Has she always been a lunatic?" I said.

"Careful," he replied with a smile, holding a finger to his lips. "She is the Lady's favorite, and almost as ancient, though — as you have so studiously observed — as crazy as it is possible to be without being a danger to one's self. To others, though. . . ." He shrugged.

I slid to one side in order to keep both Jester and the shadows into which Argenta had vanished in sight. "You didn't answer my question."

Again he shrugged. "Argenta has been as she is for as long as I have known her, though those much older than I say she was different once. The story is that she and her sister were the most favored of the White Lady's blood harem before Argenta was turned, in part because of claims she could hear the voices of the dead. Then (as it was told to me) someone — or something — unseen whispered into her ear. No one claims to know what was said to her, but soon after she lost her mind and has been this way ever since. In many ways she is a danger to the Family: unpredictable, wildly impulsive, at times out of control, which is why she is never allowed outside these walls without an escort. Yet the White Lady will hear no ill of her." Jester stared down the hallway. "She believes Argenta heard something, or possibly saw something, so terrible that it shattered her mind, and our Visconté hopes to learn what it was. So she keeps Argenta close at hand, hoping one day for a moment of sanity protracted enough to allow her visions to be shared."

I could not help but stare at the darkness into which Argenta had disappeared. "She has a sister?"

"Had. A twin. Her sibling, however, was found . . . wanting."

"What happened to her?" I asked.

Jester (I could never think of him by his House name, Gilliad) waved a careless hand. "To witness her sister elevated, and not herself, left a bitter taste. The tale is that after Argenta was chosen her twin approached the Lady to ask after her own prospects, a vastly presumptuous act. Whatever the news, it could not have been pleasant, for later she approached the White Lady's throne and asked for permission to die. It was granted. Andracéil herself buried her, I was told."

Jester turned on his heel and walked away. Having nothing better to do, I followed him. "Why are there separate Houses?" I asked.

"There were not, not in the beginning," he replied. "There are many tales of our origins, but all share one commonality; our ancestors all came from one place. But over time, differences of opinion regarding how the Breed should interact with humans separated the families. In those days we were worshipped, but our vulnerabilities were exploited by our enemies. In the ensuing wars, the Breed almost came to an end."

"From those ashes rose a council of twelve, who debated and then agreed upon the only laws all Houses hold in common, the foundation of *Coloque*, the Separation. From that day forward, the Breed would not practice war, either with humanity or among ourselves. And while there have been rare instances of those who defied *Coloque*, all other Houses have always joined together and risen against them, erasing such outlaws and their names from the face of the earth. The first precept of the Separation is that no human was to be reminded or (much later) made aware of our existence, and as the centuries have passed our kind now exists only in tales of myth and legend."

"Except for the topovar," I said.

"Not all of the Breed keep topovar," Jester said. "House Bremen, for example. Their members live apart from one another, reasoning that what does not cluster together cannot be easily extinguished. They live among humans, even (some claim) marry them. And in exchange they are protected by them."

"And Winterfax prefers to treat humans as animals," I muttered.

"Not at all," Jester replied, undisturbed by my resentful tone. "We treat them as favored servants. And as a consequence, they enjoy great power and wealth, as well as the hope of possible elevation, in exchange for providing us with sustenance, as well as unconditional obedience."

"How fortunate for them," I replied sarcastically.

"They think so," Jester said, again undisturbed. "I take it you are unfamiliar with Bushido?"

The word sounded familiar. "I've heard of it," I said cautiously.

"A concept practiced by the Samurai of medieval Japan. It demanded complete loyalty to one's Master, even to surrendering one's life if called upon, and was a crucial element of the culture."

I shrugged. "So?"

"Human beings do not practice that which is incompatible with their natures," Jester said. "The topovar serve us, offer themselves to us, even worship us in their fashion, not because they fear for their lives, but because it is in their nature to do so."

I stiffened. "Not everyone thinks like that."

"Indeed. But so long as *Coloque* is practiced, I could care less what other Houses do, Malakhar among them."

"Who are they?"

"House Malakhar truly does regard humans as animals. That is, prey. Or such is the gossip, I myself have yet to meet a member of that Family. Though it has been said that the occasional Winterfax horshno or hashnaid, after giving evidence that their trustworthiness could be called into

134

question, has had the singular opportunity to experience the Great Hunt. Whenever there is an unexplained disappearance, the gossip among the topovar is that the missing offender was offered to Malakhar, as one might offer a bottle of wine to a distant relative."

My fingers knotted. "Are these 'tales' true?"

"Which time?" Jester lifted his hand. "You must excuse me, I was on my way to break my fast when I saw you with Argenta."

I remained behind as Jester took his leave.

Three days later, the White Lady summoned me.

*　　*　　*

When I entered Andracéil's chambers, followed by Jerome only a step or two behind, I cannot recall that I had any conscious expectations. Despite this, I still felt surprised.

The room was smaller than I had thought it might be, though still enormous by comparison with the guest quarters Jester continued to make available. A fire blazed inside a stone fireplace large enough to accommodate the length of a human body. White furs of various sizes and species formed a low bed before the hearth. There were, of course, no windows.

The White Lady reclined on the pallet, her colorless flesh almost blending in amongst the furs, like ice on snow, and I realized she was naked.

Lying in front of her, blood droplets decorating his throat like rubies, sprawled a young man. He stood out in vivid contrast to the Lady's paleness, with his dark skin and coarse black hair. Pupils like pinpoints revealed he was still in the grip of what Jester had identified as *Som na Idilque*, the Ecstasy. His chest barely rose and fell.

"Your pardon, Visconté," Jerome said from behind me in a voice that spoke of a lowered head and averted eyes. "I was given to understand you were available."

"It is no matter," she said in that voice like the hiss of falling snow on pane glass. "I was done long ago. Take this one, and then leave me with our guest."

Jerome stepped by to pick up the Lady's most recent meal. The man's head lolled like an infant's as Jerome carried him through the doorway, pausing only to glare at me before exiting.

When I turned back, the Lady had begun wrapping herself in a silk gown that reached from her neck to the floor. Beneath the pearl gleam of her skin I detected a warm flush, like dawn on a frozen lake. "So many unknowns, I scarce know where to begin. Come," she said as she waved me towards a low couch. "Sit with me."

The thought of being within arm's reach of that monster had turned my legs to stone, so it was only with great effort that I forced myself into motion and took my seat.

"Above all else, understand this," she said in that throaty whisper one had to devote full attention to in order to make out the words. "I am quite old, and experienced in the ways of liars." She ran one lone nail, hard as the tip of a paring knife, down the length of my upper arm, leaving behind a thin white line. "Do not frustrate me with pointless attempts at deception. It would be . . . unwise."

Her fingertip found its way beneath the hinge of my jaw line, pressing so hard I expected at any moment to feel blood trickling down my nape. "Jester says you learn your lessons well," she said, her eyes lidded and somnolent. "Now tell me, for what purpose?"

Her finger did not move. A vivid image of my throat opening with a sudden slash kept me focused despite the terror inspired by her emotionless words. "At your command?" I said, feeling this was not the answer she sought, but still unsure what question had actually been asked.

The edge of her nail dug deeper. "You are a violent disruption to the natural order of things," she murmured. "And under any other circumstances, there would be no question as to your fate. But whatever that fate is to be, I am convinced that this is not the time for it. Which begs the question, what are we to do with you?"

"There have always been strong bonds between Ember and Winterfax," she continued. "I am still puzzled why your lady kept so closely her recent troubles, though I do understand her fear of showing weakness. Like myself, Penelope learned from the past." She shook her head, a twitch of a movement. "But that cannot be the all of it."

"You walk in a fog, young Mordant," she added. "I sense around you the shadows of unseen presences. So until that fog has been lifted, we shall respect the wishes of Lady Ember. You," and here she poked me hard in the very same spot I had so recently bitten Candide, "You are to undertake the reconstruction of House Ember. This is the task I set before you. Your House has unseen enemies, and since I find myself blind as to the proper disposition of the mystery you present, we shall allow events to take their natural course. Either you shall succeed, and in the process strengthen our own House, or you shall share the fate of your family and be erased from the earth."

They are not my family, I wanted to scream. And on the heels of that suppressed remark I heard the echoes of my sister in our shared youth who, as we commiserated over our own familial situation, had said, "You can choose your friends, but you can't choose your relatives."

How would Mike Brady have handled this?

Andracéil's eyes grew unfocused and — more from a nervous desire to fill the sudden silence than from a need to converse with this creature — I heard myself say, "So you think one of the other Houses has declared war on Ember?"

Her eyes refocused on me. I struggled with the sudden impulse to drop my gaze. "There has only been one reply to those foolish enough, or desperate enough, to violate *Coloque.*"

I leaned back, hoping — unsuccessfully — to relieve the dagger-tip pressure of Andracéil's nail at my throat. "So who then?"

"You misunderstand," she said, eyes wide as she appeared to study my every pore. "I only speculate on how another House might profit. Though there is an unfamiliar taste to this banquet, or so it seems to me." She finally removed her hand from my flesh. "And if this is so, are you the hors d'oeuvre, the entrée, or the dessert?"

My head hurt from trying to follow the bizarre thread of her conversation. "What do you want from me?" I asked.

She leaned towards me so quickly, I could not help but draw back in alarm. "I want to know your role," she hissed. "Are you a bit player or major character? Hero or villain? Secret catalyst or unwitting dupe?" She gripped my wrist with fingers like cold steel, her pupils dilating until the whites vanished. I flashed back to the last time I had seen such a thing — in the moments before Penelope had taken my life — and my belly froze with terror. "What are you, my dear young Mordant?"

She held my gaze, truly held it, for I could not look away. "I don't know what I am," I said, as honestly as I knew how.

She pinned me with that black stare until, though the knowledge of it shamed me, I knew I was about to lose control and begin screaming, unable to stop.

Then she pulled back.

"Even so," she whispered. "You do have a part to play, young sireling, though you know it not. Argenta has seen it, I believe. And I will learn what it is. Leave now. I will summon you again after I have thought more on these matters. Until then, you are charged with the proper ordering of your House. Now go."

I stood and retreated through the open door, unwilling to turn my face away, though she now paid me no mind at all, instead busying herself with some small object close at hand.

That was the last time I saw the White Lady until the day of my execution.

*　　*　　*

As I closed her chamber door, a sudden movement to my right startled me. I stepped back against the sill as Argenta, eyes fixed wide, leaned in close to whisper into my ear.

The Sleeper has awakened, hear the call!
Houses, witness the breaking of the seal.
To part his flesh, the edge of doom shall fall,
And spill his blood, his purpose to reveal.

Then she giggled while sliding by, pressing her slim body — glacier-cold — against me as she continued on her way.

The days passed slowly. I continued to meet with Jester in what I had come to think of as the Study for my lessons, mostly dealing with the ancient history of the Breed. Little time was spent on my own House, and even less on Winterfax. Once I asked about the strange language the surrounding books were written in, and was told that this tongue was unavailable to the recently sired. Advanced studies, and I was not yet deemed worthy of the time and energy involved in its instruction. Perhaps one day, Jester said with a smirk which I translated as, 'Two days after Hell has frozen over.'

When we were not buried in that room, I continued my exploration of the castle. I discovered that there was a reason for the lack of windows, for the Winterfax family occupied a series of basements in the lower levels of a truly massive structure. The upper floors, those above ground, were maintained by the ruling family of whatever country we were in. They were Winterfax topovar and had been for many generations, belonging (for I could think of no more suitable term) to Andracéil. And while it would have been fascinating to have spoken with one of them — assuming any of them spoke English — I suspected that none of the topovar I saw were included in that family. I say suspected because no one within House Winterfax, Breed or topovar, willingly revealed anything more about themselves than necessary.

Which made me curious, exactly how many of the Breed were there here? I had met only five I was certain of: Jester, Argenta, Jerome, Nathan (whom I rarely saw), and the White Lady herself. There had to be others, but if I ever did see them, it was at such a distance that I took them for more topovar, of which there was a good number. Blood flowed freely in that place, I gathered, though the closest I ever came to witnessing a feeding had been during my interview with Andracéil.

After a time, Moira was returned to me. I knew that I would be expected to feed on her, but kept putting it off as Jester's hashnaids continued to make themselves available to me, more comfortably now than before. I could not feed from the horshnos, the act was far too intimate for me to feel comfortable satisfying my hunger with a male, though doing so might have made things easier in other ways. I ached during a feeding, my every nerve strained from the need to indulge other appetites. But I did not believe I could trust myself. Had I done so, I knew that I might have lost control and taken everything.

But despite the fear of what I might do (and perhaps for one or two, because of it), the women came to me willingly, hungry for the Ecstasy. Moira, however, was sullen, still bitter over having been taken from Jerome and given to me. And for my part, I still harbored a deep resentment over her betrayal, though I knew from her standpoint that it was no such thing. After all, she had belonged to Winterfax, not Ember. And what role might

I have played in Penelope's disappearance? She knew otherwise now, of course, but had not at the time.

This gradual realization as the days passed softened my rage and my resentment, and during a rare time when we were alone together, I tried to have a civil conversation with her.

"When we first spoke on the phone," I began, "You said that your parents were away, as though you expected me to know where they were."

She did not reply, nodding instead.

I persisted. "So where had they gone?"

She sighed, as though conversation with me was the least desirable of her options, but obediently replied nonetheless. "Socializing with Outsiders constantly is stressful. You have to guard so much of yourself, who you are, what really matters to you. And only the most trustworthy are honored with the exclusionary status of membership in a blood harem, and then only after prolonged service. Winterfax reserves hashnas for potential candidates for elevation. The rest of us float in our outer orbits of wealth and privilege, lacking for nothing, wanting so much more, but unable to ask because it is forbidden. To do so automatically relegates you to the outermost circles, where you will remain for the rest of your life."

"Those of us who serve, but who are not members of a hashna, do not enjoy the regular company of others like ourselves," she continued. "So, periodically, we arrange retreats. Opportunities for unguarded speech with others who understand. That's where my parents are. Charles was this year's organizer, but my mother had to take over for him after the accident." She played with the hem of my buttonless shirt, which she still wore, the only garment she now owned here in this place.

As I watched her constant efforts to cover her nakedness, I suddenly felt an inexplicable sensation. Regret.

"You believed that Jerome was about to bring you into his blood harem, didn't you?" I said.

Moira did not reply, nor did she nod her head. She simply lowered her face, tears streaming down her cheeks.

I felt conflicting emotions in that moment. Anger and disgust, for how could anyone subjugate herself to being an occasional Happy Meal for a creature who considered her not even on the same level as himself? But at the same time I also felt something unfamiliar, something which shocked me the moment I identified the unfamiliar emotion.

Envy.

I had to clear my throat twice before I trusted myself to speak. "At least he wanted you."

Moira lifted her face and stared at me. "But you are here," she said, obviously confused.

I clenched my jaw. "But I might not have been."

Now Moira stared at me in frank and open wonder. "Yes, so you told the Lady." She studied the ceiling before bringing her gaze back to me. "So she sired you. At eighteen, and without an apprenticeship, sharing her blood with you. Elevating you."

Her tone irritated me, making it seem as though my murder had been some great honor. "That's one way to look at it," I snorted.

My sarcasm flew over her head (or perhaps beneath her contempt) as she shook her head, dazed.

"How did you impress her so?" she finally said. "What was there about you to inspire such trust?"

I opened my mouth, prepared to let her know in no uncertain terms what I thought of Penelope's 'elevation', then closed my jaw again. Arguing with her would be pointless, we saw this from two completely different perspectives. Being turned into one of these creatures was something Moira had been actively working for, and hoping for, the majority of her life. And from her viewpoint, it must appear desirable. After all, her parents were topovar, and had been for over thirty years. No doubt they nursed the same ambitions, which of course they would have passed on to their child, after sharing their secret life with her.

How had that happened, I wondered? Had it been an accident, with a young Moira walking in unexpectedly to see something which on the surface would have been terrifying, something which would have required an explanation?

Or had they sat her down one day to explain it to her, reviewing its potential benefits, parents recruiting their high school child like boosters on the merits of the college they themselves attended?

I emerged from my revelry to find Moira still staring at me in wonder, and with a little bit of fear.

"What are you?" she whispered, echoing the White Lady's words.

*   *   *

The next day Moira attended me during yet one more of Jester's lessons, this one a dry recitation of the duties of a House Valyar. It might have been more interesting were it not for his codicil that neither Winterfax nor Ember had had a Valyar in centuries. Understandable, since the primary responsibility of a House Valyar was to serve as a kind of general in case of open warfare versus human or Breed, and there had not been an instance of either for a very long time.

With no warning, Jester tossed Moira the book he had been using as his text. She almost dropped it, requiring one hand to keep closed that still-buttonless shirt. The only other garments in that place suitable for a woman were gowns, and all of them were made from fabrics in Winterfax's House colors, which she was not now allowed to wear.

I watched her as she crossed the length of the room, her head lowered as she searched for the book's proper place.

"What are the House colors of Ember?" I asked Jester in a voice I hoped was low enough not to carry.

"Very dull," he replied. "Black and gray, though some might call it silver. Or would, if not for the obvious connotations. Your House device features them properly. You do know what it looks like, don't you?"

I tried to remember. "Black. With some stars, and a moon, right?"

Jester expelled the sigh of the long suffering. "What abomination has Penelope wrought, that the last of her House cannot identify its blazon?" He sighed yet again. "Perhaps I should have remained quiet and allowed Jerome to undress you with that bullwhip of his. Lapdog!" he cried out to Moira, who flew back to us as though she wore Mercury's sandals.

"Yes, my Lord?" she asked.

"Go to the Armorial room and retrieve Ember's device. And if your eyes linger where they have no business, I will know it. Quickly now. And no barking along the way."

"Why are you so cruel to her?" I said after Moira, head lowered once more, fled the room, the torn front of my shirt clasped in her left hand, her bare feet slapping against the stone floor.

"I would ask you the same question, if it were not for the fact that you remain a hopeless imbecile where these matters are concerned."

I clenched my fist, saying nothing, instead thinking on his words and trying to make sense of them.

"Is there anyone here who can make a dress?" I asked Jester without looking at him.

He shrugged. "There are a few seamstresses who are not without talent," he said while studying his nails. "Though little cloth in colors other than Winterfax green and gold, although each *Usoleté* has its own shade which is used to accent the House colors, and which for this reason would never be made available to you. My own is indigo. It might be possible to locate a bit of spare cloth, however, and I suppose some clever use of dyes could suffice to reproduce Ember's colors. With the proper motivation, that is," he said with an airy wave of his hand.

I nodded. "What do you want?"

"What do you have?"

I shrugged. "Nothing. At least, nothing here."

Jester reproduced another of his endless sighs. "I do so despise the indigent, they are such a burden. However, I might be persuaded to stretch my generosity this one time, in exchange for a future consideration."

"Such as?" I asked, immediately suspicious.

"How will I know until that day arrives?" he replied. "Of course, you do have the option of continuing to allow your topovar to run about the halls like a street urchin from a Charles Dickens novel. As you will."

Moira chose that moment to enter, her breath labored as she struggled with the weight of the massive shield. "Shoes as well," I said, voice low.

"But of course. Ah!" he said as Moira staggered to a halt at our table, "Finally she sees fit to grace us with her presence!"

"I beg your pardon for my tardiness, I came as quickly as I was able," she said between gasps.

"Your Lord should exercise you more often. Now hold that upright, just so. Mordant, what do you see?"

I examined the coat-of-arms. The background was black, the stars and crescent moon a silvery gray. "This looks familiar." I said, pointing to the moon and the star occupying the upper left portion of the shield.

Jester snorted. "It should, it only adorns the wall above the Lady's throne. That is the emblem of Winterfax."

"Why is it on Ember's device?"

"It represents Ember's fealty to our House. Ember is young, as Houses go. Only the oldest families have no such additions delineating an alliance with an older, more established House. It is the rose that distinguishes it," he said, pointing to the stars in the lower right portion that did resemble a flower. "Or the sword, if you will."

"Which is it?" I asked.

"Penelope once told me it is both, depending on need." He turned back to Moira. "You may cease your impersonation of a pack mule and return to your canine duties once more, as soon as you have returned your burden to its proper place."

She did not speak, instead simply nodding before taking her leave, wrestling desperately with the shield in an effort not to drop it.

"All devices of the Breed are based on the objects found in the night sky," Jester said as he removed a book from a pile sitting on a nearby chair. "Though some say that Bremen cheated." He opened the massive volume in front of him to show me a shield in blue with a large golden circle at its center. "It is, supposedly, the full moon. But there are those who claim that it is in fact the sun, encouraged no doubt by the background which calls to mind the day sky. But Bremen has always danced to its own insane tunes."

I looked at the others. One showed what appeared to be a comet, another the corona of a new moon. Or perhaps an eclipse. "Which one is that?" I asked, since I still could not read a word of the Breed's strange language, which Jester referred to as *Dalavar*.

"House Malakhar. Though some call them House Carnifex'" he said with a small smile.

I examined the device more closely. "What does Carnifex mean?"

"It is Latin for 'Executioner'. Though 'Butcher' would serve just as well."

I remembered Jester's earlier description of House Malakhar, the hunters of humans. "Why do you call them that?"

"Malakhar has no blood harems," Jester said with a flip of his fingers. "Though they do have topovar. They are predators, not herdsmen, to use their own phraseology. Their topovar serve as procurers, collecting potential prey for the 'Great Hunt'."

I shook my head. "Why do you allow this?"

"They do not ask for our permission. And to answer what must surely be the next question on your lips, yes, their actions do expose the Breed to greater risk of discovery, though they would argue that it is Houses such as ours which pose the greater threat, by allowing humans to know of us and yet live. Points of contention, which I do not believe will ever be resolved to anyone's satisfaction. The only alternative would be open conflict, thereby all but ensuring discovery of our existence. And Malakhar has a reputation for covering their tracks with extraordinary efficiency. Great Hunts are carried out far from inhabited areas. For the most part, that is," he finished with a clearing of his throat.

I turned my gaze on the returning Moira. She noticed, and a flush ran the length of her as I felt the *rhejmar* clawing at my gut. From the corner of my eye I caught Jester's amused gaze. He had recently taken to making comments about the strain being placed on his generosity, and I knew I could no longer continue to feed on his hashna when I had a topovar of my own.

"With your permission?" I said to Jester, my voice thick with need. He smiled and waved me away. I left, forcing myself to maintain a slow pace as Moira followed two steps behind, Jester's mocking laughter echoing after us all the way.

* * *

The hashnaids fluttered around Moira like butterflies, tugging here, tucking there. I watched in curious bemusement.

The gown was far more modern in cut and style than those worn by the rest of the women belonging to Winterfax's blood harems. It clung to Moira's slim body, accentuating a bust and hips smaller than those of the typical hashnaids I had come to know during my stay. The black made her look very pale, though that might have been the result of the blood I had taken from her three days prior. Now it would be weeks before I could safely feed on her again. The thought led me to wonder how much longer would Winterfax continue to extend its generosity to me, and gave me a greater appreciation for the logistics of satisfying their needs.

The women parted, giving me full access. The gown's hem fell to just above her ankles, where slippers of the same ebony shade, accompanied by silvery buckles, adorned her small feet. I wondered if they really were silver. If Jester had had a hand in their choosing, they almost certainly were.

She smiled, then spun in place, eyes sparkling for the first time since she had been made a present to me, and I felt the stirrings of a hunger for something other than blood.

"Beautiful, is she not, my Lord?" said one of the hashnaids, who reminded me of a blonde serving girl I had once seen on the label of a bottle of very dark beer.

I nodded, jaw clenched. "Jester expects me soon," I told Moira. "Go ahead. Let him know I will be on my way shortly."

Moira's shoulders slumped a bit, and the rest of the women looked deflated. "At your command, my Lord." Moira whispered before turning to leave. The rest of the hashnaids followed her, similarly subdued.

The dulling of their mood confused me, but I put it out of mind, having other things to think about.

Returning my attention to the fireplace, I stared into the flames. Since coming to Winterfax, all of my attention had been devoted to the narrow tightrope I had been walking for the past several weeks. Now that a sudden and painful death appeared slightly less likely, unanswered questions were now bubbling to the surface of my brain.

Starting with the men who had run Charles and I off the road. Who were they? Topovar from another House feuding with Ember?

But if the elimination of the Ember family was linked to the attempt on my own life, then it could only be considered a declaration of war. This might have seemed more credible if it were not for the alliance with House Winterfax, which Jester had all but stated was bound by duty and honor alike to respond in kind. And Winterfax was — supposedly — both the oldest and the strongest of the twelve Houses. Who would risk angering them? What was there to gain?

I wrung the arm of my chair with enough force to make the thick wood groan. Blind. I was flying blind. What I needed was information, and the most accessible source I knew was sitting in a nearby dark room, waiting for me.

I left the room at a brisk pace. For once, Jester was going to spend one of our sessions answering questions, not asking them.

I had barely left the suite when I heard my name, like a child singing a nursery rhyme.

"Mordant . . ."

I paused, looking around, then up. So little light, the ceiling a cloud of shadows.

"Moordannt . . ."

A low laugh. Behind me . . .

I spun, and there she stood, perhaps fifty feet away, the long pale fingers of her left hand wrapped around the throat of Moira, who fought desperately for breath.

Argenta.

"Promises have been made. Promises must be kept." The raven-haired Breed giggled. "To save us all, soon doom must fall." Her fingers tightened, wringing a hoarse gasp from her captive.

I inched forward. "Is it me you want?" I said as calmly as I could manage. The insane vampire's eyes were wide and wild, and I knew she was strong enough to instantly snap Moira's neck like a number two pencil.

Then, in one smooth motion, she lifted Moira over her head and cried out to me, "Catch!"

Then she leaped.

Straight up.

I watched, stunned, as she vanished into the darkness overhead, Moira flung over her shoulders like a sack.

"Catch us! Catch us! Catch us if you can!" she cried, her taunting laughter disappearing as quickly as she did, as she scurried like a cockroach into a small window just below the ceiling.

I leaped after her, but fell short. I landed hard, and badly, cursing at the pain shooting through my right ankle. I knew it would heal, but by the time it did, Argenta would be long gone. Goddammit, where was she taking Moira? Perhaps to some dark hole, where she would eat the girl like a spider?

I had to get to her. But my ankle would not bear enough of my weight to allow me to jump after them. I smashed my fist against the wall in frustration.

Then I realized that the answer was right in front of me.

I kicked my left shoe from my foot. The right would not matter, since I could not use that foot anyway, but I kicked off that shoe just the same. I gripped the stones, forcing the nails of my fingers and left toes into the crevices between the rough stonework.

Then I began to climb.

I could not move as quickly as Argenta with my injury, but unlike her I was unburdened. I hoped the difference would favor me.

The window opened into a horizontal shaft, thick with dust and cobwebs, and little room to spare. I crawled as quickly as the close quarters would allow. When I came to a splitting of the ways, I swore, then caught a scent from the right passage.

Blood. Moira's blood.

I pushed myself, ignoring the sharp edges beneath my hands and knees. The searing pain in my ankle had lessened a bit, allowing me to move faster. The floor sloped upwards. Now I could smell my own blood, seeping from my palms, worn raw on unpolished stone.

There! An opening.

I forced myself to slow down. What if Moira was simply bait, a carrot to lure me to a deserted wing of the manor for who knew what reasons?

The ceiling of the crawlspace was a bit higher here at the end, though still far too low for anyone but a small child to stand. I crouched, feet beneath me, in case I had to make a sudden charge, then crawled on hands and knees to the opening and looked down.

Twenty feet below I could see the floor, crowded with boxes and crates of every size, most all stacked atop one another, forming streets and alleyways. A storeroom of some kind and, to judge by a thick layer of dust, rarely visited.

There, down below. Movement in a far corner. A pale upturned face, smile broad, eyes gleaming with madness. Argenta, with Moira's hair in her fist, her high, brittle voice an echo in the huge space.

He comes and goes,
His doom to share
But does not know
Fate knows no pair.

Then, quick as a cat with a mouse in its jaws, she dashed through an open archway, dragging a now upright Moira, whose breath was ragged from keeping pace with the lunatic or else risk having her arm pulled out of its socket.

Suppressing my first impulse, to leap across the intervening space and give chase, instead I turned and — gripping the edge of the opening — hung for a moment before dropping. My ankle snarled in pain, but held firm. Hobbling a bit, I sprinted as quickly as my injury would allow through the archway, which opened into a stairway leading up. The steps were deep and high, the walls far enough apart to allow six men to walk abreast. I took them two at a time, while keeping my right hand on the wall to steady myself. On and on it went, and I wondered how far it could possibly go.

There, just ahead. An opening, black as velvet and sprinkled with a multitude of twinkling lights.

Stars.

I plunged recklessly ahead, gripped by a fierce combination of terror and exhilaration. No longer willing to be cautious, I shot through the doorway full speed, leaping up and around to cover every possible angle. There, on the ground, chest heaving in counterpoint to the stillness of my own. Moira.

But no sign of Argenta.

I hit the ground in a crouch, fists knotted, adrenaline (or its equivalent) blinding me to the pain in my ankle, ready for whatever might come. Nothing did, so I sped to Moira's side. She looked up at me, fighting for her breath after the mad footrace Argenta had led us on. I grabbed her by the shoulders while trying to look in every direction at once. "Where is she?" I demanded.

Moira shook her head as she struggled to speak, while at the same time trying to push me away. "Gah!" she finally choked out.

I continued to scan the grounds. We were outside in some sort of flower garden. Bushes and shrubbery, any of which could have concealed the diminutive maniac, filled the space. I sniffed the air, but caught nothing of Argenta's scent.

Moira, breast heaving, grabbed me by the front of my shirt and pulled herself close. "Go—back!" she finally managed to gasp out.

Then I heard the laughter, low and almost sane. I turned.

She stood, one broad-beamed door in each hand, her hair a mane, her eyes almost glowing as she began to sing.

What's done is done,
Winterfax doors do yawn!

Witness his destiny to fulfill!
For we have won
Now with the dawn
Comes the breaking of the seal!

Then, still laughing, she slammed the doors shut.

As I listened to the rattling of what sounded like heavy locks being secured, a sense of icy terror flowed down my spine. With the echoes of her words still ringing in my head, I turned away from the door and saw it, a blush of warm pink on the horizon.

The sun. The sun was coming up.

*　*　*

I must have gone a little crazy myself, because moments after seeing that glow saturating the eastern clouds, I found myself pounding on that ironbound portal, beating my knuckles bloody. There was a howling in my ears, and for a moment I though it was my own voice. Then two hands grabbed me, and it was all I could do not to rip the arms they were attached to from the shoulder sockets of their owner. Instead I looked down into Moira's eyes, as wide with panic as my own must have been.

"My Lord Ember!" she screamed into my face, "We must leave! Now!"

Leave? And go where? The walls of the castle were blank stone, with not so much as a cubbyhole for shelter. A desperate scan of the grounds revealed no protective structures, not even so much as a garden shed. I looked over Moira's head at the sky as it turned from pink to an angry red. Someone moaned. It might have been me.

"There is no time!" she cried as she pulled on my arm. "Hurry! You have to trust me!"

I almost pushed her away then. Trust her?

Then stay where you are, my inner voice said with a chuckle. *Lots of alternatives, if you stop and think about it. Aren't there?*

Shuddering, too terrified to do otherwise, I allowed her to drag me away from the door.

Once we started moving, she burst into a sprint. I matched her slow pace, fighting the urge to pick her up and carry her, since I had not the first idea where she was taking me.

We ran alongside the wall, its blank facade mocking me with its lack of protection. There were windows, though, and for a moment I considered leaping through one. Only a stray moment of sanity kept me alive, as I realized their taunting safety was only an illusion, for the windows were huge and would expose the entirety of the rooms behind them to that swiftly rising orb, leaving me blind and stumbling while allowing me just enough time to contemplate how long I would remain conscious while burning alive.

Drowning in my own fear, I let Moira continue to lead me. During our mad dash, images flickered past my eyes like the pumping of a View Master. The mountain the castle stood upon, its massive base anchored in granite, honeycombed God only knew how far below by the rooms and halls of Winterfax. High, high walls of gray-green limestone, dotted only intermittently by the odd window. Towers capped with conical roofs, their apexes crowned by flags and pennants. A stone bridge spanning a protective gap as we neared the structure's corner.

Finally we reached the end of the wall. "This—way!" Moira choked out as she fought for breath.

We circled around to a concrete parking lot. There were several vehicles, including a large white truck with lettering in a language I could not read. The rear door was open, its boxed contents bleeding white vapor. I felt the cold as we neared it.

"Inside!" she said. "Hurry!"

The bed was high. It took a moment to brace my bare left foot on the ice-slick bumper, the right still throbbing from my ill-timed landing earlier.

Then my injured ankle caught fire.

I did not see the sunbeam hitting me, but I could smell the charring flesh. Screaming, I staggered against the truck's rear. The muscles in my body turned to water, and I knew I did not have the strength to pull myself inside.

Then, with a howl I would not have believed such a slight body could possibly have contained, Moira got her shoulder beneath me and through sheer force of will rolled me into the truck before leaping to catch the door strap. The rising sun cast a brick red halo around her, its heat washing over me with a blast furnace roar before her ninety-eight pounds won out and the rolling door slammed shut.

I curled into a ball on the corrugated metal floor, covered by a thick layer of frost. Stacks of frozen perishables in cardboard boxes surrounded me, their cold forming a blessed counterpoint to the angry heat I felt radiating from my flesh like sun poisoning. I pressed my streaming eyes to the frigid metal, wondering if the hot droplets flowing down my face were not tears, but blood.

Then the floor jerked beneath me. The truck was moving.

Over the length of our journey my seared flesh healed, though slowly, a numbing lassitude replacing the pain as my blood-starved body rebuilt itself. I could tell my energy resources were low, the *rhejmar* chewed at my gut like a starving wolverine. Eventually it would devour my resolve and then segue into an unreasoning madness. How long could I hold out?

After an eternity the truck shuddered to a stop. Moments later I heard footsteps come to a halt at the rear door.

A pause. "Are you in control?" I heard Moira say.

Was I? Unconsciously I had gone into a crouch at the sound of her approach, my mouth painfully dry, legs coiled beneath me. I forced myself into a sitting position. "Yes."

The door opened with a loud rattle. I remained in place, looking about.

We were in an underground garage. Moira had parked the utility truck near a large green bin, some kind of dumpster. There were no windows anywhere. Banks of fluorescent lights lit the cavernous interior. There were few cars, the closest a sleek sedan with an odd symbol I did not recognize on its hood.

Moira stepped away from the vehicle. I noticed she kept a wary eye on me, her body tensed for any sudden movements on my part.

I exited the truck on the side furthest away from her, my muscles trembling with weariness and fatigue.

She continued to keep her distance. "What now, my Lord?"

What now, indeed? "Argenta wanted to get rid of me, why I don't know. And Andracéil said I was not to leave the grounds for any reason." I focused my bleary eyes on Moira. "You know these people better than I do. If I were to go back, after dark, what would happen?"

Moira shifted uncomfortably. "Are you one of those who blames the messenger for her bad news?"

Despite the grimness of our circumstances, I could not suppress a smile. "I can't shoot you. Good lapdogs are hard to come by."

She returned my smile with a thin one of her own, which quickly faded. "The word of the White Lady is law. While I can't say for certain what she would do, based on what I have observed in the past, she might well demand the Final Death."

I could hear the capital letters in that last part. "Even though leaving was not my idea?"

"It will not matter. If Argenta denied tricking you, then it will be her word against yours, and you must know how that will end. Anything I say will mean less than nothing, it will be assumed I am lying to protect the Lord of my House. And even if you were believed, or if Argenta did not bother to deny what she did, it still would not matter. She is Winterfax, and a favorite of the White Lady. You are neither."

There was no denying the truth in her words, and with that realization came a calming sense of relief. If Winterfax captured me again, I would die. It was just that simple.

But I would not make it easy for them. No, not easy at all.

I looked at Moira, my topovar.

Mine.

But one would not be enough.

And not only that, I had other concerns. While none of the Winterfax Breed could leave their protective catacombs until sundown, the same would not apply to their topovar.

"Tell me where I am," I said. "Then tell me what you know about the people who live in that fortress we just left," I said.

She sat on the truck's bumper, apparently this was going to take a bit of 'splaining. "To answer your first question, we are in Livoire se Andolé. It's a small country on the westernmost edge of Russia, bordering the sea south of Finland. Very tiny, as countries go, and completely surrounded by mountains, with only one easy way in by land."

"As for your second question, you must understand that Winterfax is very old, as are their blood harems. The Valdelords, whose castle you are referring to, are the ruling family here, their members are the White Lady's personal hashna. They trace their lineage as far back as the twelfth century.

Sometime during the fourteenth, they pledged themselves to Andracéil. They are wealthy beyond reason, mostly due to their banking interests. For centuries they have financed the governments of Europe in war and peace. Over time several members of their family have been elevated." She hesitated. "The last was Jerome."

I nodded. "How concerned should I be about the Valdelords, or any other Winterfax topovar, trying to recapture me?"

She was quiet for a moment. "I would say unlikely," she finally said. "If the Valdelords, or those who work for them, become aware of you it's more likely they'll monitor you, so you can be found once the sun goes down. Winterfax does not place its topovar in jeopardy unnecessarily. So long as you don't become violent, it's unlikely they will either."

My brow furrowed as I pondered the logistics of my situation. "The retreat you mentioned, where your parents are. Is it still going on?"

She nodded. "They typically last for several weeks, sometimes longer."

"How many of the Ember topovar do you think might be there?"

"I cannot say. My parents spoke no more of their House matters than I would of my own, it was none of my business. But if I had to make a guess, I would say perhaps as many as thirty, possibly forty."

I nodded. At least thirty Ember topovar. And none with an ruler (owner?), a *Teregar,* of their own. Not anymore.

"We have to get to them," I said. "Does anyone at Winterfax know about this retreat?"

Moira shook her head. "Not that I'm aware of. Had Jerome asked me, I would have told him, of course. But he never did. He had no reason to care, after all."

Of course not. "I need for you to get us wherever they are, as soon as possible."

Her head bobbed once in acquiescence. "As you wish. The trip will be too long for my Lord as a normal passenger, so I will make arrangements for you to be flown in a coffin, as before. I have an apartment here in this building, I use it whenever I come to the city, so if you would, please follow me. I'll need some things, including my passport. Then we should go to a hotel, for safety's sake, where I can make arrangements for our flight."

"Where are we going?" I asked as I got up to follow her.

She replied without turning around. "Alaska."

*   *   *

The trunk of Moira's sedan had that new car smell. Most likely a rental. I folded myself into it, then tried not to panic after she shut me in. I sank my nails into the nap of the carpet as the car jostled and bounced on what felt like very rough roads, my fingers digging in even deeper as I felt the heat of the sun warming the small space. All it would take was one careless driver running a stoplight, broadsiding us, popping the trunk open. . . .

Finally we slowed to a halt. I heard the engine shut off, then listened to Moira's diminishing footsteps as she walked away. When I heard her approach once again, I relaxed. Then came the thud of a hand on the trunk.

"Any luggage, ma'am?" a young male voice asked in thickly accented English.

"No!" she said, as if anticipating what I was already visualizing. "The airline lost it, they will have it delivered once they track it down. All I have is my carry-on."

I listened to her turn down a separate offer to park her car before hearing the door slam and the engine turn over. I literally felt the sun vanish as the heat diminished, but still jumped when Moira opened the boot.

We were in another underground parking garage. "What now?" I asked, looking around nervously.

"I've reserved a room for us. You are not the only one of the Breed to ever stay here. The Valdelords own this hotel, among others, and made certain it included special windowless rooms during the original construction. But there was an incident about thirty years ago, a near exposure."

"What happened?"

"All I know is that someone from a House other than Winterfax was almost taken prisoner here by some foreign group. The Breed has avoided this place like the plague ever since. Please follow me."

Moira led me to an elevator with no buttons, only a slot in a brass plate. She removed a card from her purse and inserted it. The doors opened with a hiss of cool air. We entered, and I was startled to discover the elevator going down, not up.

"Basement suite," she said in reply to my questioning look.

The doors opened not to a hallway, but to the rooms themselves, their beige walls filled with furniture made from a pale blonde wood.

Moira tossed her small bag onto a long sofa upholstered in a stone-white suede, then turned back to face me with a critical eye. "You're going to need clothing. Let's see, thirty-two inches in the waist, thirty-four length, I'm guessing. Shirt shouldn't be a problem, something in a large tall. Shoes, what, size thirteen?"

"Fourteen," I said, not entirely comfortable with her close scrutiny.

She nodded again. "Height's throwing me off. Okay, I'm going to call Berluigi's, best selection of men's wear here in the city. Then I have a few other calls to make. Coffin shouldn't be a problem, I know the right people to contact."

Moira turned to go. As she did, I reached out and took her by the arm. She twisted in my grip to stare up at me, eyes wide with a sudden terror before they lowered in a servile acquiescence that did not ring completely true.

"Why are you doing this?" I asked, unable to keep my fears and my suspicions to myself any longer.

She looked at me, then turned away. "My parents have belonged to House Ember since before I was born." She sighed. "Now so do I. If there is one thing we have drilled into our heads from the moment we become topovar, it is that our loyalty is to our *Teregar* first, our House second."

"Won't they be angry with you for helping me?"

"Why? Didn't you just hear me? I'm doing what I'm supposed to be doing. It's a dog's duty to defend its Master." She smiled ruefully. "Even we lapdogs."

I shook my head. I knew I would never understand Moira (or any of the topovar, for that matter), but since their strange loyalties were working to my advantage, they did not bear much in the way of close examination.

"Do I wish things were different?" she continued. "Of course. I wish I still belonged to Jerome, and consequently to the oldest and most powerful House of the Breed, instead of — well, this one." She sighed again, choking off a sob which I believed, had she let it out, would have swollen into a crying fit. But she maintained her composure.

"I'm going to be on the phone for a while," she said. "There's a computer with an Internet connection in the bedroom if you wish to make use of it."

I did. As I thought about it, I realized that I did not even know what day it was. All I felt certain of was that fall had segued into winter, this based on the blanket of snow I had seen covering the grounds of the Winterfax castle. Though that might be normal summer weather here, for all I knew.

I booted the desktop PC, then brought up Google. First I did a search for my sister, no news there. Then I did another for Charles. Nothing, not even a mention of the accident. I did find several articles on the cabin killings, though. The father was being considered one of the victims. Recent speculation was that some transient had broken in and gotten his hands on the rifle of the man, who — the consensus seemed to be — had died defending his family. No one knew why little Noel had been found in a Virginia Denny's, though. One journalist speculated that perhaps the toddler had been kidnapped, then escaped from the murderer, who fled the scene. I spent a considerable amount of time checking articles, blogs, and forums for any information on the child, but only learned that she had been placed in foster care, since there were no living relatives.

After spending some time chasing fruitless leads, I went back into the main room, where I found Moira curled up in a very modern looking chair (and by 'modern', I mean 'uncomfortable'), a small black device in her lap.

I sat across from her on the couch. The peppery-sweet scent of the blood underneath her skin filled the space between us. "What is that?"

"My iPad." Her thumbs flew furiously over the object's glass screen. "I've made all the arrangements. Our plane leaves at 4pm. Later than I would like, but there's no help for it. We take the local airline to London, from there fly out on Virgin, arriving in Newark around noon tomorrow, then take Alaska Airlines to the Juneau International Airport. The retreat's being held at Wicker, a small town near the border of British Columbia. Caters mostly to hunting tourists. A popular site for the gatherings, when I was a child my parents would take me with them. Very isolated, and at this time of year not much daylight, sunrises a bit before nine am and sets a little after three." She made to get up.

"Bathroom break?" I asked.

She shook her head. "I need coffee, I just brewed a pot."

"Stay there, I'll get it for you."

I could tell the offer made her uncomfortable, which concerned me not at all. After I returned from the suite's small kitchenette, I looked over her shoulder while placing the mug in front of her. "I don't know anything about Juneau," I said, staring at the screen of her device.

"It's on the Gastineau Channel in the Alaska panhandle at the base of Mount Juneau, right across from Douglas Island." I watched as she took a long sip from the cup. "The capital's a lot like the rest of Alaska, huge land area with a tiny population. You could fit Delaware inside of Juneau's borders, with enough room left over for Rhode Island if you had a big enough shoehorn. Just imagine a cooler, wetter version of Seattle."

I opened my mouth to say I had never been to Seattle either, then thought better of it. Outside of my two trips to Manhattan, taken thirty years apart, I really had not been anywhere to speak of. Yet here I was, hovering over a wealthy and beautiful world-traveling socialite whose only acknowledgement — had we passed one another as strangers in broad daylight — would have been a dismissive glance, had she bothered to notice me at all.

I retook a seat opposite her, then leaned my head back and closed my eyes, wondering if Argenta suspected I might still be alive, and if so, had she told anyone what she had done. What kind of uproar would my disappearance cause?

Stupid question, and one I already knew the answer to. Once they knew I was gone, recapturing me would become their first priority. Moira had to know this. Yet here she was doing all she could to help me escape.

Unless this is all some sort of elaborate trick. She could be their spy, making plans to hand you over one more time, just when you least expect it.

I shook my head, hard. I would not travel down that road again, not without something to go on other than paranoia. I had few illusions, though. Winterfax would never stop searching for me. Of that I had no doubt.

"Who handles business affairs for House Ember, do you know?" I asked Moira.

Her brow furrowed. "Under normal circumstances that would be Charles. But since he's in the hospital, and probably still in a coma, responsibility for financial affairs would fall to his backup. Which would be my mother."

I nodded, mulling over what I knew.

Winterfax's Breed would be coming after me soon, assuming the hunt had not already begun. But they could do little during the daylight hours, and our flight was scheduled to depart well before sunset. While they might have sent their most trusted after me, which most likely would have meant the Valdelords, I found myself doubting this. Too great a risk of unwelcome public attention. It was possible, perhaps even probable, that some of the White Lady's children had already reached the city. But a search by them could only take place after sundown.

Should we even be going to Alaska? I considered changing destinations, heading back to North Carolina and Penelope's mansion, but quickly discarded that idea.

I also had to assume that even if no one within Winterfax knew about the Alaska retreat, they would manage — eventually — to track us there. Our sole advantage was time. It would take time to discover our destination, and still more time to make plans to retrieve me and to do so in such a way as to avoid raising too many awkward questions. Safety lay in staying one step ahead of them, moving quickly from place to place, losing ourselves within the vast North American continent.

What to do then, I had no idea. But I would cross that drawbridge when I came to it.

*   *   *

Knuckles rapped on the lid of my coffin in a familiar cadence. *Shave and a haircut, two bits.*

I blinked. What had happened? I remembered the arrival of the coffin at the hotel room, and I remembered clambering into it, the snap of metal as Moira secured the lid. Then the buzz of the room's intercom shortly thereafter, male voices asking for directions, a gentle swaying as I was lifted and carried . . .

Then nothing. Until now.

Not even the whispers?

The rapping began again, harder this time and sans the Bugs Bunny sound effects. "My Lord?"

I fairly burst out of my confinement, causing Moira to jump back with a startled squeak. I stared around, fingers curled into talons, expecting the worst.

I lay inside my coffin in the open bed of a pickup truck. Stars twinkled in the frosty sky, and it hit me that I could have emerged into broad daylight. The thought froze me in place, and I shuddered despite myself.

Moira approached me surreptitiously. "Sir, are you well?"

Was I? Hard to say. All I did know was that I could not account for . . . how long had it been?

"What happened?" I asked, my voice a harsh croak.

She shrugged. "Nothing unexpected. We landed several hours ago. I rented this truck in town, rather than use the services at the airport. More trouble to track us, I figured. I would have preferred an SUV, but strapping the coffin to the hood would have looked odd, to say the least, so I settled for an F-150 with four wheel drive." She stepped up for a closer look. "Is something wrong?"

Yes, I did not say, something is very wrong. Once again I could not account for at least a full day. Or had it been two? The last time that had happened was at the cabin, where I had hidden inside the closet while little Noel lay either asleep or unconscious on the sofa, as the dead bodies of her family rotted all around us.

The Sleeper has awakened.

I looked around. We were parked in the middle of a gravel road bordered by twin shallow ditches. Trees crowded the narrow space, huge Sitka spruces at least eight feet around mingling with western hemlocks and red cedars.

And how do you know what kind of trees they are? I heard a voice inside my head say with a chuckle.

I suppressed a shiver. More and more often I found myself in possession of knowledge I could not account for. "Let's get the hell out of here," I told Moira.

"I can drive," she said, "But if you would prefer? . . ."

I shook my head. "No, I need some time to think."

She did not speak, instead nodding her head and getting into the cab. I followed her shortly thereafter, but not before giving the spaces between the trees a close examination.

"How far?" I asked after getting in.

She looked over at me, as if to ask me to buckle my seat belt, then thought better of it. "We've been on the road for a while. Shouldn't be too much further. I haven't been up this way since the summer I turned eleven."

"And how long ago was that?" I asked while staring ahead.

She hesitated. "Fifteen years."

We traveled in silence for a short while. Then she turned and asked, in the voice one uses when fearing an unpleasant answer, "Are you still in control, sir?"

For a moment, I did not know what she was talking about. Then I remembered. "The *rhejmar?*"

She shrank into her seat. "Yes."

I realized then that, yes, I was very much in control. Which surprised me. I remembered waking (if you can call it that) at the cabin, and experiencing the same thing, a cessation of the Hunger. At the time, I had attributed it to having fed recently on the drivers who had rammed their truck into Charles and myself. Now I wondered.

We drove once more in silence, then Moira spoke again. "I ask, sir, because when we arrive, there will be some nervousness from the others, so if you needed to feed before our arrival? . . ."

Her hesitant offer of sacrifice, after having recently given herself to me, rang odd. Then it hit me.

She's afraid you might lose control in front of her parents.

I could not even blame her for her concern. She had much more experience with these matters than I did, and from her standpoint there was reason to be worried.

I wondered if this was analogous to starving, where after having gone without food for an interminable amount of time, one simply loses one's appetite. "I'll be fine," I assured her.

We passed a fork in the road, taking the one which looked less traveled by. I considered making a Robert Frost reference, then discarded the notion as too pretentious. "I thought we were going to Wicker?" I asked, noting that the town sign pointed in the other direction.

"Wicker's the closest town, but our site is a good thirty miles outside of the city limits. The retreat is used primarily by Ember topovar, but it's not unknown for actual family members to come here. Which requires privacy. There's a large basement underneath the main house. Very secure."

We drove again in silence. I spent the time considering what questions I should be asking, since I expected an uproar when these people discovered that a member of House Ember still lived. Which would not be much longer, I realized, spotting the lights of a house glowing in the distance ahead.

I turned towards Moira and said, "So tell me . . ."

That was when the bullet hit her.

It all happened at once. The firecracker *pop,* the crisp quick sound made by the windshield as it spider-webbed around the small hole, the hoarse intake of breath as the impact slammed Moira back in her seat. The truck's sudden swerve flung me into the floorboard, and I saw her foot stabbing unsuccessfully for the brake just before the moment of impact.

There was no give when we hit the tree. The force of the crash slammed my head against the underside of the dashboard. Blood sprayed over me from the hole in the right side of Moira's chest.

I looked up. Her eyes, wide and unfocused, rolled in her head. Then her gaze met mine. Her lips moved soundlessly. She wheezed, fighting for speech, blood pumping from her wound.

Then the *rhejmar*, quiescent up until that moment, consumed me.

I lay mouth to breast like a newborn infant. My chin dug into her chest so hard I could feel the ribs beneath the flesh, and it was only with the greatest of efforts that I resisted the urge to worry the hole open even further. Instinct took over, and I found myself dragging her down below windshield level after ripping the seatbelt away. With my right ear pressed against her body, I heard the now-thready *thump-thump* of her heart as each beat filled my mouth with liquid ecstasy. I watched the light in her eyes grow dim the moment before she lost consciousness.

The damp sound of feet in mud pierced the bubble of my distraction. With an effort, I forced my mouth from her blood-soaked flesh, then cracked the door open and slipped out of the vehicle, sliding into the darkness beneath the trees.

The chill of the outside air melted as the heat from Moira's blood spread throughout my body like an electrical charge. My earlier lassitude vanished, and the dark grew paler as my eyes adjusted. I scanned the road ahead and spotted two figures, both dressed in some sort of black military garb. Each man shouldered a rifle, and each wore a chunky set of metallic goggles. From the way they moved their heads from side to side, I guessed the devices were some sort of night-vision aids.

As I watched them approach the truck, each selecting a side, a fury roared through me, as hot as the blood in my mouth. They had shot my hashnaid. *My* hashnaid!

And now they would pay.

Neither appeared to have noticed my exit from the truck. I slid from the trees on all fours, belly close to the ground, head swiveling from one to the other as I analyzed my prey. I longed to bring down and then linger over each one, ripping out their throats and taking what I craved. But a deeper instinct warned me against such luxuries. Their weapons looked to be military issue, and while I did not know how much damage they could do to me, my experience with the father at the cabin had taught me that even if I could not be easily killed, I could be disabled, at least for a time.

And Moira was still inside the cab.

Divide and conquer, instinct said as I crept behind the first one, staying low to the ground in case he suddenly turned.

This is no time for self-indulgence, I told myself as the *rhejmar* gnawed at my insides. You have to be fast.

So I was.

He must have heard me, he had started to turn. I leaped at him, hitting him low, tearing the rifle from his hands. His finger must have been on the trigger, for there was a loud *pop* as I wrenched the gun out of his hands, taking the aforementioned digit with it. He howled in pain the moment before my fist slammed into his skull, the bones softening beneath the impact. He fell to the ground and did not move.

I heard the clop of booted feet circling the truck from the far side. Once again surrendering to instinct, I rolled underneath the chassis. Knowing it would take only a moment before my remaining assailant figured out where I was, I crouched, then leaped over the cab. He did not spot me until my descent, and by then it was too late.

I raked his face, watching the blood spurt as my nails ripped away his goggles, followed by his face. He screamed as he released his weapon, clutching at his now-useless eyes. I dropped low, slashing at his ankles, hamstringing him.

He collapsed, then tried to crawl away, pleading for mercy. I remained in a crouch, suddenly understanding in the most intimate of ways what it must feel like to be a cat with a mouse between its paws.

Then I remembered Moira.

I fell on him, strangling his cries with my teeth, then — once he lay still — turning to his companion, who offered no objections at all.

My hashnaid lay sprawled over the front seat. She did not move, did not even appear to breath. I put my ear to her chest and listened.

There, a noise. Faint, but persistent.

I gathered her in my arms, then turned towards the house. While running, I scanned the nearby woods, searching for more men like the ones I had just killed. No one.

Which did not mean there might not be more inside. I reached the house, edging my way to the windows, only now wondering who the two cooling corpses had been. Guards, of course. Told to shoot first, ask questions later.

I peered in. The room was large. An enormous fireplace made from river stones filled a third of the rear wall. The furniture was rustic, though expensive-looking. I half-expected to see human heads hanging on the walls, but all I saw was a large bearskin. A roughly hewn bar occupied the space to the left, where an old man stood, as dark and wooden as the logs making up the house. He was mixing a drink. Half a dozen others sat almost in a circle, their heads down. I searched one face after another.

There. Sitting next to one another on a brown leather sofa, their heads close together. It had been thirty years, and though they had aged somewhat, they remained handsome and beautiful still, leading me to wonder (as I had about Charles since my conversations with Candide) how old they really were. Arthur and Tracey Bingham, holding hands, their faces worn and sorrowful.

I did not see anyone armed. Which meant little, but if someone carried a concealed weapon, they would not have time to draw it before I was upon them. So long as I gave them no time.

With that in mind, and Moira in my arms, I kicked the front door open and stepped inside.

All heads rose. Arthur pulled his wife close, the rest shrank back in their seats. The man at the bar sloshed his drink, though he did not drop it. Instead he stared at me, as did the others, mouths agape.

I took them all in. "Who here has any medical training?"

All heads turned towards the Binghams. "I do," Arthur said, after a moment's hesitation. "But . . ."

Then he recognized the body in my arms.

"Moira," he breathed.

The mother let out a small scream as her husband ran forward. I allowed him to take her out of my arms, then watched him carry her to the couch as Tracy stood up, hands over her mouth, to make room. The father opened Moira's blouse, then turned to face me. "Shot?"

I nodded. "The guards outside."

"They were shooting at you?" Tracy said as her husband asked the man at the bar to get his bag. The fellow looked at the three of us for a moment before turning wordlessly to leave the room.

"Yes," I said, smiling the kind of smile that bares the teeth. "I must apologize, though, as your men won't be shooting at anyone else ever again." I spared a glance for the others, two men and two women, who stared at me as though I had just popped out of their worst nightmare.

One of the females, gray-haired and as regal as a queen, said in a confused tone of voice, "*Our* men?"

"Weren't they?" I watched as the bar man returned with a black satchel. He gave it to Arthur, then turned to face me, a large pistol in his hand.

I looked at the gun, then looked at him. "Put that away," I said in a voice I hoped conveyed a lack of concern over whether or not he planned to use it.

The queen stood. "Do as she says, George." She stepped closer. "I don't think he's one of them."

"One of who?" I said, still keeping an eye on George in case his trigger finger showed any signs of tightening, in which case I planned to strip him of his weapon, and the hand as well should he prove reluctant to surrender his gun.

Tracy Bingham sat beside her daughter's head, her hand resting on the girl's pale brow. "Who are you?" she said.

I fixed my eye on her, one half of the couple who (or so I once believed) had supplanted me in Penelope's affections. "Your former mistress used to call me Ace," I said in as cool a voice as I could manage. "My name is Mordant, and I am — to the best of my knowledge, at least — all that is left of House Ember."

No one spoke. Even Arthur Bingham paused to glance at me, before returning to his work.

The youngest female, who looked to be close to my sister's age, and with the same honey-colored hair, stood and then ran to me. I almost slashed her face, but held back as she buried her face in my chest.

"*Khompah*," she said, the word catching in her throat as she embraced me.

I stared over her head at the others, hoping desperately that none of them intended to follow her example. None did, lowering their eyes instead, a submissive gesture apparently intended to convey respect. Discomfited by the sobbing woman, and with no idea how to react, I patted her back clumsily.

"So that is what she meant," the Queen said.

"Excuse me?" I said, while trying to figure out a good way to remove the blonde's death grip on me.

"The Hidden Hope, she told me, when last I saw Lady Ember," the Queen said before offering me a curtsy. "Your pardon, my Lord, we have not been properly introduced." She gestured to herself. "My name is Melanie Scarsdale. The young lady at your breast," she continued while pulling the woman in question away, "is Constance Wingate." She gestured to the others in turn. "This is Horace Fowler, and his companion, William Sinclair."

Something about the emphasis she placed on the word 'companion' gave me pause, but I let an explanation go by for later.

"The gentleman with the pistol, who I suggest consider lowering it, is our good sergeant, George Tanner," Melanie said.

"Sergeant?" I said, still ignoring the gun.

"Retired, from the 82nd airborne," George said as he lowered his weapon. "And begging your pardon, Mel, but we don't have more than a claim that this person is who he says he is. He might be one of them, after all."

I ignored George for the moment. "No need to introduce the Binghams," I told Melanie. "We go back many years."

Tracy stared at me in confusion. "Sir, please pardon me, but I cannot recall ever having met you."

"That's because we haven't. Met, I mean." I stepped to the couch. "How is she?" I asked the father.

He shook his head. "Bullet went straight through. Doesn't seem to have hit any vital organs, but we have to get her to a hospital. She's remarkably stable, however,." He looked up at me. "You fed on her?"

Despite everything that I knew, that these people would have acknowledged my right to have done so, I still felt the heat of embarrassment, even if I could not actually blush. "I did," I said roughly.

Arthur nodded. "Probably what saved her." He stroked his daughter's face.

The tenderness of his gesture made me uncomfortable. "Explain to me what is going on," I said, sweeping the room with what I hoped was an intimidating gaze.

Now all eyes shifted uneasily from one to the other. "You mean you did not come here to rescue us?" Constance said with a growing panic that threatened to escalate into hysteria.

"Moira brought me here. I know nothing about anyone needing to be rescued." I turned to George. "Tell me what's going on," I demanded. "I was told you were here for a retreat."

The old man sagged. "We're being hunted."

Hunted? "By who?"

He lowered himself into a chair before placing his pistol on a nearby end table. "House Malakhar."

*   *   *

The conversation did not flow smoothly, but the gist of it was as follows.

After hearing nothing from Charles, and being unable to contact him, Tracy Bingham had done some research and found out what had happened. She had flown to Raleigh-Durham airport, then driven to Chapel Hill. After checking on a still-comatose Charles, she had questioned the police about the accident, an ongoing investigation. While the circumstances were unusual, they did not appear suspicious beyond the ordinary, or so she was told. A detective informed her that there had been a head-on collision, and that the two men in the other vehicle had died from their injuries. The investigator hoped to learn more when Charles regained consciousness, if he ever did.

With Charles in the hospital, Tracy assumed responsibility for the final arrangements for the retreat, after providing contact numbers to the hospital and the police. No one even considered canceling, since this was to be no ordinary event. No one had heard for a year from Penelope, and there was much anxiety over what to do. Tracy had discussed the situation with her husband, and the two of them had decided to broach the idea with the remaining Ember topovar of having Moira approach House Winterfax for assistance, or at least guidance. That they were willing to do this, violating a well-established protocol delineating how such matters were to be conducted, showed how desperate they were.

The first indication of a problem had occurred when, after a unanimous vote in favor of the Bingham's idea, Tracy had tried to phone her daughter, but her cell phone would not work. No one else's would either, some kind of interference. Then they tried the landline. Dead.

Despite this, panic did not set in until George tried to leave. As soon as he set foot outside, a bullet splintered the door frame an inch from his head. He ran back inside, then called out, trying to learn who their assailants were.

No one answered. But if anyone tried to leave the house, there was more gunfire, driving them back inside.

Then night fell. And with the darkness, *they* came.

"They never identified themselves," George said as he retrieved his drink. "But we've all heard the stories. They stood outside of the lights, telling us that the bravest among us could chose to make the run, one per night, with an hour's head start. The ones who could make it to Wicker, then they would live, so long as they stayed quiet." He shrugged. "None of us believed a word of it, but the alternative was that they would come inside and drag us out at random, and that one would be given a five minute lead. The first option seemed best, all things considered."

I looked around. "Where are they?"

"Come and gone already for the night," George said, finishing his drink, then getting up to mix another. "That was Bethany."

From the sorrowful glances everyone exchanged, I gathered that Bethany had been a favorite. "How did you? . . ."

"We drew straws," George continued, when no one else appeared inclined to speak.

I nodded. "How many?"

"There were forty-two of us," Melanie said after George remained silent. "So we have lost thirty-five of our number. So far."

I ground my teeth. "How many of them are there?"

All eyes went back to George. "I would guess three Breed, but there's no way to be sure."

I tilted my head towards the front of the house. "And the ones outside?"

George pursed his lips as though he was about to spit. "Nightwings. Mercenary outfit. Saw a lot of them during the years I was in the service, chatting up soldiers on the verge of mustering out. Had an eye for certain types, they did, men who frequently got into trouble over their dealings with civilians. They've been around a long time." He tipped his head back and downed his liquor. "Now I know why."

"How many?" I asked.

"Six, I think. Running eight hour shifts in pairs."

Melanie looked at me, as did the others, with the exception of Arthur, who still fussed over his daughter. "So my Lord, what now?" she said.

I suppressed an instinctive 'Why are you asking me?' I knew very well why.

"Give me your opinion of the situation," I told George.

He let out a prolonged exhale. "We can't stay here. The Three have left for the night, but relief for those two outside will be here sometime just before sunrise. There'll be no help for them from Malakhar, not until sunset. That's the good news. The bad news, sunset will be happening around three p.m."

I nodded, looking down at Moira. "Any working vehicles?" I asked, knowing that the rental was a lost cause.

George shook his head. "Disabled, all of them. Patty wasted most of her hour that second night trying to get one of them to start."

"That was a foolish thing to do," the one introduced as Horace said bitterly. "Don't get me wrong, I loved her too. But she had to know it wasn't going to be that easy."

"And what difference would it have made if she'd just run?" argued the one named William. "We all know the truth of it, even if we try to tell ourselves otherwise. None of them made it. We've all heard the screams." He lowered his head.

"That woman ran the Boston Marathon three times!" Horace said, in what sounded like the continuation of a long-running argument. "She would have had the best chance."

I cleared my throat and raised my voice. "Enough!"

Everyone lifted their heads to look at me. Even Arthur.

"You two," I said to the Binghams, "Are going to head for Wicker, along with these three." I pointed at Horace, William and Constance.

"Sir," Tracy said while raising her hand, as though she was still in grade school. "What about our daughter?"

"Unless your husband can come up with a way to get her safely to town, she stays here." I looked at Arthur, who turned to his wife and shook his head.

169

"What about us, my Lord?" Melanie said, including George with a gesture.

I stared at the two of them in turn. They were the oldest of the remaining seven by close to twenty years, and traveling with them would be as great a liability for the remaining topovar as Moira would have been.

"You two are staying behind with me," I said. "I'm, ah, going to need your help. When the guards' relief shows up, that is. We'll follow afterwards." They visibly hesitated, then nodded.

Plans were quickly made. The Binghams took charge of the small troop. After dressing against the cold, and collecting supplies to see them on their way, I met with them one last time.

"How long will it take you to get to town?" I asked.

"Couple of days, I'm guessing," William said as he fussed oddly over the straps of Horace's backpack.

"Why so long? I thought it was only around thirty miles or so."

"That's as the crow flies," he replied. "Can't take the road, we'd be too visible. Cross country's better, through the forest. Slow going though, especially having to watch out for muskeg."

"What's that?"

"Peat bog," Horace jumped in and said. The two of them reminded me of an old married couple. "You can tell where they are by the little pine trees. There's one about a hundred feet in back of the main house. As bad as quicksand, like walking on wet sponges. Hence the flashlights," he said, waving one.

There were no parting words. Truthfully, I had no idea what I would have said to them in any case.

After they were gone, I walked back inside to face the remaining two. They returned my stare, stoic.

I walked to the bar and prepared a couple of drinks, then handed one to each of them.

"We're not going to be helping you with those two guards, are we?" George said as he accepted his glass.

"No," I said, shaking my head.

He sighed. "Knew it would most likely end this way," he said, staring into his tumbler. "Always though it would be her Ladyship, though."

They asked a few questions, which I answered as briefly and succinctly as I could. Then I had Melanie face the wall, to spare her the sight of what would soon be coming for her.

I showed more mercy than Penelope. Neither of them had to run.

*   *   *

Still much left to do.

I carried Melanie's and George's lifeless bodies downstairs into the protected basement with its hidden entryway, then followed with the still-unconscious Moira.

Afterwards I went outside and searched the bodies of the two guards. No identification, which did not surprise me. I did find two cell phones, which also appeared to function as walkie-talkies. I smashed one and pocketed the other. One of the men wore an expensive-looking black metal watch with an emblem that looked military, its hands and numerals glowing. I put it on my own wrist. Then I carried the two corpses into the living room and hid them behind the sofa for the time being.

After a quick clean-up to hide the worst of the night's violence, I moved the wrecked pickup into the cavernous garage, then closed the door. My head buzzed from all the blood I had drank in the space of just a few hours, and even with a demolished front-end the vehicle gave me little trouble. Afterwards I found a tall tree next to the incoming road with limbs relatively close to the ground. A moment later I was perched in it, a good twenty-five feet overhead.

Now nothing left to do but wait.

Around seven a.m. the phone vibrated. I looked at the screen, ID blocked. I ignored it, as well as the one that followed.

Then a third vibration, text message. *Problem?*

The phone was so much like Moira's that responding was simple enough: *Phone trouble. Hurry up and get here, we're freezing our nuts off.*

I half-expected to hear them coming through the woods, suspicions aroused, but no, they drove right up. The tricky part was subduing them without killing them. Fortunately, it was enough to leave them alive. Whole would have been a bonus, but was more or less incidental.

Once they had been rendered unconscious, I removed — none too gently — their clothing. Relatively little blood had been shed after subduing them, so an additional donation was necessary. I made sure the cuts were superficial, as it would not do at all for them to bleed out. At least, not yet.

Now to set the stage. I carried the unconscious guards, tightly bound and gagged, into the basement and locked them in with the others. Then I went back upstairs and pondered the upcoming tableau before retrieving the deceased guards from their hiding place.

Tearing a dead body apart, limb from limb, is harder than it sounds. In the end I did a lot of twisting. A knife would have meant less work, and the kitchen contained a wide and varied assortment of gourmet cutlery, but it was important for this to look like something no human being could have done. And since my plan required the appearance of not just two, but four murdered guards, it had to seem as if there were multiple missing parts. So in the end it was necessary to strew the remains both inside and outside of the house, in various locations, using the extra set of uniforms to create the illusion of the missing two in the basement.

Then I ransacked the closets, ripping a selection of male and female clothing as I had the guards' uniforms, then using the civilian garments to mop up what little blood remained before scattering them about the grounds.

I closed the front door, locked and dead-bolted it, then broke it down with my shoulder using more strength than was necessary, splintering the wood into literal shards.

The plan, such as it was, depended on a great many suppositions, chief among them that there had been no more than six guards, at least within eight hours travel time. The arrival of a literal squadron would ruin everything. My plan depended on there being only two living guards left, and that the three Breed would not willingly part with their remaining security until sunset at the earliest, since the relieved mercenaries would not be returning.

I checked my new watch, but there was no real need. By now I could sense the coming dawn.

A quick search of the garage revealed a thick coil of old hemp rope. I hoped it would be strong enough.

Broad red fingers of light brushed against the tops of the enormous cedars as I searched the wooded area to the rear of the house. There were no rocks, but I found several chunks of broken concrete, left over from some renovation project. I piled them behind the largest Sitka I could find within sight of the front porch. Then I sprinted what felt a reasonable distance before snapping off a thick limb at chest height from the only tree I could find with low branches, splintering it lengthwise before flinging it as far away as I could.

Spotting the muskeg took little time. It looked as Horace had described it, broad and flat, punctuated by a few short scraggly pines. I had considered hiding in the basement, but could not take the risk that my little scenario, designed to sow both confusion and fear, might work too well and inspire something drastic, like setting the house on fire.

I dug into the mud underneath the frigid water with my hands, searching while simultaneously cursing the coming sun. Finally I found what I was looking for, a thick root. I sank my arms in up to the elbows, while wishing my previous life had allowed for a stint in the Boy Scouts. As it was, I fumbled with a make-do knot around the root, then tied the other end of the rope around my waist before crawling into the muskeg. It sucked at my legs, and I almost panicked before reminding myself that I could no longer drown. Despite that knowledge I still experienced a moment of terror as the waters closed over my head, then another electric shock of fear at how quickly I sank. I promised myself that if I somehow got out of this, the first thing I was going to do was learn how to swim.

Now the only thing left to do was wait.

Seven hours later I braved the surface of the water, now rimmed with ice. While not quite dark yet, the sun had dipped beneath the tree line, reminding me how Penelope's appearances had always taken place during the most overcast of days Though given my experiences up to that point it still amazed me how well she had coped with being outside during the daylight hours, despite her precautions. Fortunately (for once) there had been no clouds in the sky to encourage an early arrival by the Malakhars. And as I kept my head at surface level, I heard the sound of at least one, possibly two, vehicles.

But it was not until I heard voices that I dared to move. Using the calling of names to mask the sucking sound, I used the rope to pull free, then crept low to the ground as I circled the house.

Two men in the same black military garb as the others wandered about, weapons shouldered, heads turning as they tried to see in every direction at once. Two large black SUVs idled in place. Beside the second stood three men.

I knew them for what they were, though I cannot tell you how I knew. Perhaps it was their bearing, curious but not fearful, as if pondering the answer to a riddle. Unlike the mercenaries, they wore plain clothing with no distinguishing characteristics, speaking to one another in low, puzzled voices.

Which went silent when the head of the first guard exploded.

I quickly hefted the second chunk of concrete, flinging it so fast that the first must still have been traveling through the air when I launched the second. That one caught its target full in the face when the remaining mercenary turned instinctively in my direction.

I scooped up the remaining third piece and threw it at the rear of the house before taking off in the direction opposite of Wicker.

Already fifty feet away by the time I heard the glass shatter, I made as much noise as I could while running. If fortune finally chose this moment to smile in my direction, instead of taking its usual piss on me, two of them would investigate the broken window, leaving the third in hot pursuit.

But, typically, no such luck. Two sets of feet pounded the ground behind me.

I reached my spot and leaped high, before they could get too close. They slowed to a halt, looking — as I had hoped — around at ground level.

Had I given them time to think, they might have spotted me. So before that could happen (and before I had time to question the sanity of my actions), I dropped from the tree and charged the nearest one.

Despite my preparations, he must still have believed he was dealing with humans only, judging from the widening of his eyes as I reached him in seconds, hitting him below the waist and driving him against the tree with the branch stub I had broken earlier, impaling him.

While this should have finished him off (it had in every vampire movie I had ever seen), I could not risk otherwise, so I continued on past him, his fading screams chasing me as I fled.

One set of feet behind me now. But before I could take any comfort in that, I heard my remaining pursuer calling out from behind. "He's one of us, Justin! Hurry!"

Any temptation to turn and face Justin's friend had been dispelled by the strength I had felt of the one I had pinned to the tree. Had I not taken him by surprise, I questioned whether I could have overcome him in a fair fight, and I had to assume his friend was equally formidable.

A fact soon reinforced when something slammed against me with such force that I crumpled against the base of the tree I had been driven into.

Vision blurred, head throbbing, I looked up at two sets of eyes staring down at me, their twin faces like smooth stone which could be moved only by the most extreme of emotions. Like the ones they appeared to be experiencing now.

"Where did it come from?" the one I assumed to be Justin said.

"Jayde missed one, perhaps?" the other replied.

"We'll know soon enough," Justin said as he grabbed my right arm, twisting it with the sureness and grace of an expert. I tried to fight back, but still could not stand without assistance, much less resist. "Take the other arm, Fredrick, and pull it off as well. Then Anton can question him at leisure, once we've returned."

Fredrick grabbed my other arm, not nearly so gently as his friend, and braced himself.

"Wait!" I cried, as I struggled unsuccessfully to free myself.

Justin smiled. I had in my younger days seen a neighborhood child smile that way once, after removing the legs from a Japanese beetle with a pair of tweezers before tossing it on the ground to watch its wings beat furiously at the uncooperative air. "For what?" he said.

I looked up, then lowered my head and braced my legs. "For this."

They fell from above, lips parted in matching snarls with fresh blood on their lips. Blood from the remaining two mercenaries.

George took Justin, the largest of the two. The thick arms of the ex-sergeant wrapped around his opponent's, pinning them to his side. The two of them fell to the ground.

Melanie clung to Fredrick's back like a wildcat, tearing at him with tooth and claw, ripping at his eyes. As both disappeared in gouts of blood and other fluids, I turned back to assist George, who was starting to lose his grip. I grabbed Justin's head and twisted, not stopping until it and his body had parted ways.

I flung the head, its mouth still struggling to speak, then turned back to Melanie and Fredrick. But before I could move forward, George grabbed me by the arm.

"Moira," he said with a motion of his head back towards the house.

I looked at him, then at Melanie as she leapt lightly down from Fredrick's back to dance away as he howled in rage and pain, slashing at the empty air.

"Hurry!" George said with fierce urgency before joining Melanie. I did not pause for questions. Instead I spun and ran.

It took little time to make it back to the house. I leaped over the front railing, then through the shattered doorway—

And promptly ran straight onto the blade of the fourth Breed.

He stepped forward, forcing me to retreat. I felt one of the tree trunk pillars holding up the porch's roof against my back. He pinned me there, with the tip of his saber pressed hard against my chest, its point just piercing my flesh. Had he not struck my breastbone, the blade would surely have gone all the way through. With his other hand he held a still-unconscious (at least, I hoped only unconscious) Moira, dragging her along by her hair.

"So where did you come from?" he said, as his eyes flickered behind me.

Despite the razor's edge of his weapon (and the obvious fact that it was pure silver), I could not turn my gaze from his other hand as it held Moira's scalp with a grip so tight I knew it would take but a flick of his wrist to snap her neck.

As if he could read my thoughts, and for the sake of added emphasis, he shook her, the way a dog shakes a rat in its jaws.

"Yours, I take it?" He pushed the sword forward, and I felt more of my flesh part. "And almost dry, at that. Still, since the cupboards appear to be bare, what's left of her will have to do." He frowned. I could sense his growing awareness that his companions might not be rejoining him anytime soon. And I knew the moment he became aware of this Moira was dead, if she wasn't already.

I shifted my gaze to the sword, now pricking the vulnerable space between my fourth and fifth ribs. *Filthy metal, and that is its secret*, Argenta had said while caressing Andracéil's polearm. *But the unrepentant blade strikes pure, and you must welcome its kiss . . .*

Then I understood.

So before he could react to the dawning comprehension that he was now alone, I grabbed the blade, just above the hilt.

Then I impaled myself on it.

His eyes grew impossibly wide as I slid towards him down the near three feet of sterling silver. In his sudden shock, and subsequent error, he released Moira, instead using both hands to grasp the hilt.

Releasing the blade, hands weeping blood and eyes tearing from the pain, I took a chance and shoved him hard in the chest. Startled, he released the sword while stumbling back, half from the sudden impact, half from fear.

Before he could collect his wits, I yanked the sword from my chest and, with a scream, lopped his head from his shoulders, along with the forearms he had raised to protect himself.

Then I collapsed.

Sometime later, I could not say how long, I heard footsteps on the planks. I looked up from where I had fallen, covering Moira with my outstretched arms, and saw Melanie and George standing over me. Both were bloodied, and George appeared to have lost an ear, but was otherwise whole.

Jester had been right. Slain, after having consumed a quantity of my own blood in the drinks I had made for them (a la Penelope), they had risen the following night.

I did not allow myself to think of the likely outcome had they not done so.

Melanie noticed the sword in my hand and sniffed, then backed away. "Is that? . . ."

"Silver, yes," I said, as they stared down at me in frank wonder.

And I recalled Argenta's fingers as they had stroked the dark blades of Andracéil's poleax while she whispered, *Filthy metal*.

Silver, yes, I repeated inside my own head as I flung Anton's blade away. But not tarnished.

A fact I decided I would keep to myself.

It took a moment to realize I was no longer the focus of attention. Melanie and George both had shifted their gaze to the surrounding woods, as now did I.

They slipped quietly from the shadows of the forest, taking form as they circled us. At their head, Jerome. Behind him, Jester, and Nathan, and many others I did not recognize.

Jerome stood over me, staring down the length of his six and a half foot frame as he took the scene in. Melanie and George, after a moment's pause, interposed themselves between us. The giant looked at them as a wolf might have two small rabbits defending their den.

"We have come for you," he said. "Now you will return with us, to face the judgment of the White Lady." With a flick of his fingers, he indicated that my newly sired Breed should step aside.

"Death first," Melanie growled, and George nodded his agreement.

Jerome shrugged. "As you wish," he said, moving forward.

"No!" I said. All three looked down at me.

"You will step aside," I told my erstwhile protectors. "You will respect the representative of the White Lady, and you will do as you are told."

Melanie lowered her eyes. "My Lord . . ."

"No arguing," I commanded. "Now, help me stand. The Valyar of House Ember will not be dragged through the doors of Winterfax like an escaped felon. I will walk, unrestrained and unassisted, to the foot of Andracéil's throne and there face the Lady's judgment."

Each took an arm, and I rose. Then I turned to Jerome. "You will do as you will, but I ask for permission to walk the path of judgment on my own feet, and of my own free will. Will you allow me that dignity?"

He stared at me, a sullen rage warring in his gaze with what almost appeared a suspicious respect. "The responsibility shall be mine," he said. Then he looked down at Moira.

I nodded. "She requires medical attention."

"Her father can provide it. We intercepted him and his group before they reached town." He gestured to what I assumed was a group of topovar. "See to her."

I turned to Melanie and George. "These two . . ."

"All shall stand before the White Lady," Jester said from behind Jerome as he surveyed the carnage, along with the blood and wounds covering the three of us. "And who might this fellow be?" he said, pointing down at Anton.

"House Malakhar," I said.

Jerome frowned. "Then it is war after all."

"Not necessarily," Jester snapped with uncustomary ill humor. "We know nothing, and these three less than nothing, other than what they have apparently been told. Which I trust not at all, either from their own lips or from his," he finished, pointing down at Anton's unmoving corpse. "Are there others?"

"Not anymore," Melanie almost purred.

Jester regarded the woman as if seeing her for the first time. "Clearly there is much to discuss," he said. "We shall do so, but in transit. Jerome, see to the Valyar. I will deal with these two. Now, let us leave this place."

*   *   *

They had parked half a mile down the road. It occurred to me that this could not have been coincidence, they must have followed the two odd-looking vehicles brought by the Malakhars (Jester referred to them with a snigger as 'Hummers'). Coordinating the large group, swollen by the addition of the Ember topovar, went surprisingly quickly.

I kept my promise not to resist, but when Jerome once more revealed a coffin layered with garlic, it took some time before I could summon the courage to lower myself into that stinking prison. I almost lost control again when I heard the locks being engaged, though they were unnecessary. By then the pungent herbs had begun to take effect, and I could barely move.

Time blurred into a meaningless, endless now. I knew nothing, and recalled less, until the moment my body was unceremoniously dumped onto a familiar stone floor. Once again, I was a prisoner of House Winterfax.

A steaming copper tub sat in the center of the room. Jester, along with Candide and several other members of his hashna, stood nearby.

"Bath," Jester said to me. "And scrub well. Let not a hint of the scent remain, use the brush if necessary. For if Jerome is not satisfied with your efforts, he will take over and use a wire one in its place."

While I bathed, other members of Jester's hashna entered and left repeatedly, removing my clothing and replacing it with simple garments in what I now knew to be my House colors. No one spoke to me, nor did I attempt to engage anyone in conversation. I knew what must come now. All that was left was to discharge my remaining responsibilities.

When I had scrubbed and scraped the last of the hated garlic from my skin, I toweled myself dry, then dressed. No one offered to assist me, but even if they had done so, I would have refused.

Then we waited, though not for long. Soon Jerome, accompanied by a dark-skinned female Breed I had not seem before (but whom Jester introduced as Winda), came for me.

"Now we bring you to Andracéil's throne," Jerome said as he waved me forward.

"Will I be allowed to defend myself?" I asked as the female Breed circled me like a panther.

"There is no need," Winda said as Jester took a position next to the doorway. "Judgment has been entered. Now comes sentencing."

"Efficient," I murmured.

There was no reaction to my sarcasm, as though I had dropped a stone into a bottomless well. "Should you have any final requests prior to judgment being issued," Winda said, "You will be given the opportunity to make them. I recommend you couch your petitions with the courtesy commensurate with your desire for their fulfillment."

After that there seemed little left to say, so I allowed myself to be escorted out, Jerome preceding me, Jester following, and Winda accompanying me on my immediate right.

As vast as the reception hall was, it seemed smaller once we reached it. Perhaps it was the figures in the outer shadows, filling the dark spaces. At that moment I was overwhelmed by the sensation of hidden depths, that Winterfax was much larger and of far greater breadth than I had previously assumed.

On her gilded throne, as pale as winter's shadow, sat the White Lady. And at her feet knelt Argenta, staring at me through the veil of her coal-black hair.

I looked about. What remained of Ember's topovar, and Melanie and George as well, stood in a cluster to my far right. I kept my gaze turned away from them, and hoped none allowed themselves to be suddenly inspired into a moment of mindless stupidity.

"Judgment has been entered," spoke the White Lady in that husky whisper so characteristic of her. "However, it pleases us that the accused understands both what he has been found guilty of, and why." She gestured with her fingers.

I heard footsteps, and when he stepped into view — accompanied by two more of the Breed I did not know — I experienced a moment of genuine surprise. "Charles?"

He had already looked old. Now he looked ancient. What little fat he had once possessed had melted away, leaving behind pouches of skin hanging from a brittle skeleton. The only part of him burning with life were his eyes.

As soon as he saw me, he retreated backwards towards the two who had led him out. "You promised not to let him hurt me!" he wailed.

"You may speak without fear," Andracéil assured him. "Do so now. Repeat before us in public what you said to me earlier in private."

Charles moved still further away from me, though he had little reason for fear. Alone, Jerome could have brought me down before I had taken more than a handful of steps. And with Jester and Winda nearby, Charles was perfectly safe.

But even if I could have reached him, he still had little to fear, as I was as curious as anyone else present to hear what he had to say.

After some more nervous shuffling, he began to speak.

"For reasons the Lady Ember did not understand, our House had been targeted for annihilation," he said, the formality of his speech at odds with his typical drawl. "But our enemies clung to the shadows, and no one knew who they were, or why they did what they did."

"So she chose *him*," he continued, pointing at me. "She prepared him, keeping him beneath the house for nigh onto thirty years. Then she disappeared."

"At first, I suspected nothing. True, I did examine him not long after it became obvious some harm had befallen my Lady. And though his body had been cleaned of dust and webs, I assumed my Lady had done this prior to her disappearance, for I had known her to clean his corpse on occasion."

"Then, one night, I heard the screaming. It woke me, and filled me with terror. I stumbled to the secret door which led to the basement, and there I found him, crouched over a small child, now dead. When he saw me, he commanded me to dispose of the body, which I did."

"Then he slept again. But periodically he would wake, and hunt. At first he was merely careless. Then he grew reckless, and I had to expend great effort and no small amount of funds to cover his excesses. He would kill, then sleep, then rise and kill again. Fortunately his depredations took place over prolonged intervals, weeks at a time would pass between his risings and his feelings. I tried to warn him, but he was more beast than Breed. And what choice did I have?"

"After rising from his last killing he seemed different, and appeared to have no memory of what he had done. But after he attacked his own sister, I knew I could keep silent no longer. So I played the proper servant, and bided my time."

During Charles's testimony, the White Lady had not taken her eyes off me. Nor did she now. "Did he cause the accident which led to your hospitalization?"

He shook his head. "Not so far as I know, though he could have arranged it easily enough."

I felt dizzy. The urge to scream *Liar!* was overwhelming. But was he? What did he have to gain?

But he had to be lying! I could not have done the things he was accusing me of!

Could I?

How do you know what you might have done, or not done, during your long sleep?

Then the White Lady shook her head.

"I know not who you are, nor what you are, or even if you have memory of that which you have been accused of," she said to me. "However, it does not matter. All that I know tells me that a great terror is about." She lowered her hand and stroked Argenta's cheek. The mad girl leaned against Andracéil's palm, a sly smile on her face, her eyes focused on me to the exclusion of all else.

"What you are or are not may be beyond me," the Lady of Winterfax continued, "But action is not. Tradition, however, remains. Before I pronounce sentence, ask what you will."

How about a pardon? I almost said before catching myself. While I was both frightened and furious, I could tell nothing I said was going to change anything. All that was left was damage control.

"If I might have your indulgence," I said to her, "I have two requests I would like to present for your consideration."

"Do so," she replied.

"First may I ask, does Moira Bingham yet live?"

The Lady looked to Jester.

"Her father continues to see to her," he said. "While grievous, her injuries no longer appear to be life-threatening."

I nodded. "Then, if it please you, I request that Moira Bingham be returned to Jerome." It did not occur to me to include 'If she so wishes', since that would have presumed she had a choice in the matter.

Andracéil tilted her head. "Jerome?"

He lowered his head. "I am, as always, in the service of my Lady."

She nodded. "Done, then. And the second request?"

I turned to look at what remained of House Ember. "I sired two new *dashlas* since last we met," I said, using the term Jester had taught me for newborn Breed. "I ask that they be fostered under the cloak of your House, that they might one day do honor both to your family and to Ember. I also ask that what remains of Ember's topovar be sheltered along with them within your walls. The status of Ember itself I leave to your discretion."

"This will be done as well," she said. "Is that all?" Her tone implied that it would be best if this were so.

"Yes," I said.

"Then let the sentencing be carried out," she said as she stood, grasping the enormous poleax from its place over her head. I observed the dark stains of blood and tarnish on its blades as she spun it the way a drum majorette would a baton.

"Will you kneel on your own?" she said while descending the steps from her throne to the floor. "Or will it be necessary to restrain you?"

I turned to look at Melanie and George, who stood in front of the remaining members of the Ember topovar as if to protect them. I could not change what was about to happen, but perhaps I could leave them a legacy to guard them against whatever horrors might yet wait for them.

It all seemed so goddamned unfair. But I could not think of anything to change Andracéil's mind, or challenge Charles's lies.

Assuming, of course, that they *were* lies.

"I honor my House," I said, first kneeling at the White Lady's feet, then lowering my chest to the floor, my head turned so that I might press my cheek to the stone, hoping the strength she displayed wielding that monstrous axe would ensure a quick death.

Then I remembered the eyes of the Malakhar whose own head I had twisted from off his shoulders, and knew my death would be neither without pain nor quick.

As the shadow of Andracéil's polearm spun against the floor, I stared at Charles as he watched the coming scene with fierce intensity. His face grew indistinct, as if I saw him through ancient glass. And as the shadow of the polearm stilled, and I waited for its descent, I saw his lips move to form a familiar phrase.

I win!

The blade crashed through my flesh and into the floor. The pain of the tainted silver bit like acid, and I howled in an agony unlike anything I had yet experienced.

For a moment there was silence. Then I heard the White Lady speak.

"No," she whispered. "You have not won. Not at all."

I twisted on the floor, head still attached, though in such pain it took a moment for me to realize it. My hand went to my face, where Andracéil's ax had split my left cheek. Blood poured through my fingers, and showed no signs of slowing its flow.

She tilted her head. "Take him," she said, indicating Charles. The two Breed who had escorted the old man grabbed him. Charles looked from one to the other in confusion.

"Bring him to me," the Lady said. "Jester, would you see to our guest's wound?"

I felt arms pinning my own to my sides. "This will hurt," Jester said as he opened a green bottle he had produced from a pocket inside his jacket. "But it is necessary to stop the bleeding." He drenched my face with the contents. I could not stop screaming, so he shoved something between my teeth I could bite down on. I almost snapped it in half.

A second hand caressed my brow, damp with blood and sweat. "You will always bear a scar," Andracéil said as she knelt near my head, her frozen eyes gleaming with something that almost resembled emotion. "But it was necessary."

Then she stood to face Charles. Tilting her head, her eyes wide with curiosity, she regarded him.

"Is there anything of the man left?" she asked. "Or has he been consumed entirely?"

"Ma'am?" Charles replied, his voice full of confusion.

"So that is to be the way of it." She sighed. "Very well. Jerome, take him below. Do with him as you will, but no mortal wounds. And when he is ready to speak, return him to me."

It was like watching some expensive special effect. While Charles's face did not actually change, something behind it flowed beneath the skin, assuming an expression I cannot adequately describe. He coughed, a phlegmy sound.

Then he spat in the White Lady's face.

A dead silence filled the hall. Then one of Andracéil's hashnaids, a regal woman who resembled a 1950's movie star, wailed in dismay before rushing to her Lady's side to wipe the spittle away with her hair.

A shadow passed over me. But before he could take a second step, Andracéil lifted her hand to Jerome's chest. "Stay," she said.

The giant halted, though his face was — if possible — even paler with anger than usual.

His Lady, however, did not so much as change expression. "Thank you," she said to Charles, as she tolerated her hashnaid's ministrations. "For some time I have wondered if your kind could abandon a host, once taken, of your own volition."

Jerome looked from Charles to his queen. "My Lady?"

"It has possessed him," she said, still keeping her gaze on the old man in front of her. "But it cannot take its leave of him. At least, not so long as its host's body yet lives."

Jester stepped forward. He stared at Charles with an expression alien to that typically mocking face, pure wonder. "What is it?" he breathed.

"A mystery," Andracéil said, reaching out to caress the arm of Argenta, who now stood by the White Lady's side while staring at Charles as though he was a scorpion she had found in her shoe. "One I have gleaned from the whispers of my Little One here over quite literal centuries, though until recently I had begun to question whether or not the creatures she has spoken of truly existed at all, or — as she insisted — had found a place among us. But how to trick them into revealing themselves?" She smiled. "That was the unanswerable question. Until now."

Jester leaned closer towards Charles. "What are they?"

The White Lady frowned. "That has yet to be determined. This one is clever, though. It almost succeeded in freeing itself, hoping to trick us into slaying its vessel for its effrontery."

Charles, or rather the thing that inhabited his body, laughed, a rusty sound. "Torment me for a time, what does it matter?" He shifted his gaze to Argenta and grinned a rictus grin as he leaned forward, his eyes locked on her own.

"*Shi'Naith is coming for you all,*" he said.

Argenta screamed, her face a mixture of terror and rage, before flinging both the Lady and Jerome aside as she launched herself at Charles, her fingers curled into talons, prepared to shred his face as he shut his eyes with a smile.

Which disappeared as she fell to the floor.

I had hit her behind the knees with my shoulder, tackling her to the ground, then wound my limbs around her. She continued to scream, flaying my arms in an attempt to reach him. I buried my face against her back, desperately hoping to keep my eyes from meeting the same fate as Fredrick's.

In a moment, Andracéil had crouched by us, to stroke Argenta's face. "Sweeting, my sweeting, pay him no mind," she cooed. And when Argenta had calmed sufficiently to cease her struggles, the White Lady turned her regard to Jerome.

"Take him below," she said. "And sew his lips together, that he might not cause so much mischief."

Then, as his captors grabbed Charles to lead him away, I saw whatever it was that had possessed him submerge once again, leaving only a broken old man screaming in my direction.

"IT SHOULD HAVE BEEN ME, GODDAMN YOU!" he cried, the poison and hate in his voice staining the air. "NO ONE LOVED HER AS I DID!" He struggled in a vain effort to free himself. "IT SHOULD HAVE BEEN ME!"

He continued to repeat himself, his voice fading into the distance, as they dragged him away.

"You have placed me in your debt," Andracéil said as she stood over us, her eyes attuned to some distant place. "This makes me . . . uncomfortable."

I nodded, still maintaining my hold on Argenta, until others came and took charge of her.

"Rest easy," Andracéil whispered into her ear. "And if you can maintain your calm, when Jerome is done I will make you a present of the creature, and you may play with it in the catacombs as you will."

Argenta's eyes grew dark and wide, and she smiled as her escorts led her away.

Then the White Lady shifted her attention to me.

"A storm is coming," she said. "With you as its harbinger. And while no one loves the stormcrow, we ignore it at our peril."

I shook my head, understanding little of what I had heard and seen, but storing it all for future consideration.

"We will arrange for transportation for you and your topovar, to return to your home," she said. "And as promised, we will foster your *dashlas*."

I heard a howl from the hallway down which Charles had been taken, Jerome following closely behind. "He is possessed?"

Andracéil shrugged. "It is as good a word as any."

I shook my head. "By what?"

"All I know is what I have managed to glean from Argenta's whispered ravings," the White Lady said. "There is here, then there is what comes after. And then there is that which occupies the space in between."

I could not look away from that dark passageway. "What do they want?"

"That too," the White Lady said, "Is a mystery."

And though she said no more, instead simply walking away, I could hear the unspoken words hanging in the vacuum of her absence.

They have subverted one of our own.

Now none of us are safe. . . .

*   *   *

I reclined, my eyes shut. Warm air circulated throughout the vehicle, another Mercedes. The serendipity of the memory made me smile.

"Sir?"

I lifted my head. Constance Wingate looked at me via the rear view mirror from her position in the front seat. My new driver looked at least ten years younger, the result of multiple feedings. I think the uniform made her feel uncomfortable, a lady normally attired in the finest haute couture. But she suffered the transition admirably.

"Yes?" I shifted my attention from her to the scene outside my window. Patches of melting snow exposed brown grass near the corroding single-wide trailer. A man stood just outside the front door, the glowing coal of a cigarette visible between his fingers.

"I wanted to add to what I reported earlier, that the initial contact went quite well. As you instructed, I kept the conversation brief. The corner store stocks a local brand of strawberry jam, canned by a farm just outside of town, which I made over in effusive detail, to explain my frequent visits."

"Well done," I said.

In the front yard, a small figure patted at a dirty snowman, the child's mittens dark and wet. Little of her face was exposed outside of the knit cap and thick scarf, which I highly approved of.

I shifted my attention to the book beside me. Penelope's journal. I opened it and retrieved the single sheet of paper hidden between its final pages, reading its contents once more.

Dearest Ace,

Current events have blended together into a rushing river, and as I look at you now before I take what may be my final leave of you, I can only wonder where its flow will take us. You do not know, cannot know, how much pleasure I would take in the simple sound of your voice. When will I hear it again?

The shadow of a horde, and whatever it is that they serve, has fallen over me. And not only myself, but everyone I know and love, everything I hold dear. It is a swelling darkness, motivated by an unending hunger. And (I have been told by the same one who has seen this) they fear you.

I closed my eyes, recalling as I did the alien voice of a father who sought to slake his possessor's lust for the death of his family. The thing behind the mirrors of a young girl's eyes as she surrendered herself to torment and death. The entity which had consumed Charles, who had loved his Lady beyond reason, whose jealousy of me had been subverted by the creature for its own ends.

And I could see them.

I returned to the letter.

I have to take my leave of you now, Ace. My fondest hope is that, despite all that has and will happen, that there might be a future for us where we might sit together, and in which you can be made to understand all of the reasons why I have done as I have. So please, if you can find it within yourself, keep that door unlocked till such a day comes and I can stand outside of it, waiting for you to invite me in.

Until then,
Penelope

And as I had multiple times, over multiple readings, I reread the date above the greeting. Three days before. How she had slipped it into the outside mailbox, unseen, I had yet to puzzle out.

Once more I leaned my head back. So many mysteries remaining. These things, which Jester has named the In-Betweeners. Are they demons? Parasitic aliens? Or something outside of either? Something completely unknown, and unknowable? Are they collaborating with House Malakhar? Or has the family of the Great Hunt been duped as well? What of the other Houses?

And, most important, what is this danger Argenta saw in a distant past, and which now rushes towards us? A terror so overwhelming it has all but destroyed her mind?

Questions. So many questions.

But for this brief moment, I will concern myself solely with my own.

The current dangers did allow me to kill two birds with one stone. A request to the White Lady resulted in House Winterfax's vast resources being made available to provide a secret security for my sister and her family, giving me time to work on rebuilding House Ember while allowing Andracéil to quickly discharge her perceived debt to me. A very political solution, that, Jester had remarked with one of his trademark grins.

I return my attention to the child in the snow. Noel has grown since the last time I saw her, in the brightly lit Denny's just inside the Virginia state line. Her hair is darker, no longer the pale color of white ash.

But the eyes, the eyes remain the same.

Her foster father makes a noise from the shaky metal steps, and reluctantly she leaves her frozen creation. Soon the packages will come, waterproof boots to replace the wet sneakers, a woolen coat to take the place of the ratty sweater. And, with time, dresses with designer labels, shoes with names whispered in reverence by her peers, and the creamy vellum of an ivy league graduate degree. But no teasing absences, no playing of the heartstrings.

It will be different this time.

Truly.

I swear it. . . .

Cast of Characters

House Winterfax

Andracéil: The White Lady, Visconté of House Winterfax
Argenta: Favored of the White Lady
Jerome: Descendent of the topovar clan of Andracéil, the royal family of Livoire se Andolé, the Valdelords.
Jester: Chantéque to Andracéil
Nathan
Winda

House Ember

Penelope: Visconté of House Ember
Mordant: Formerly Eugene (Damien) Evans
Joshua: Missing and presumed deceased, brother of Priscilla
Priscilla: Missing and presumed deceased, sister of Joshua
Eli: Missing and presumed deceased
Juliet: Missing and presumed deceased
Anatolia: Missing and presumed deceased

Penelope Ember's Usoleté

Charles Jefferson
Arthur Bingham
Tracy Bingham
Melanie Scarsdale
George Tanner

Juliet's Usoleté

Horace Fowler
William Sinclair
Constance Wingate

Jester's Hashna

Candide
Robert

Glossary

Chantéque: The right hand of the Visconté.

Coffeyar: Literally, the Walls. A term used to denote the protective secrecy relieved only when solely within the presence of House members.

Coloque: The Separation, the splitting of the Breed into separate clans, which ultimately became the Twelve Houses.

Daylaire: Literally, Elevation. The selection and subsequent transformation of a topovar into one of the Breed.

Dalavar: The language of the Breed.

Dashlas: New Breed, less than a year old, who are not yet allowed to feed in private.

Hashna: A blood harem of a member of a particular House. Reserved for topovar promising enough that they might one day be considered for Daylaire.

Hashnaid: A female member of a hashna.

Horshno: A male member of a hashna.

Khompah: The informal term for the Lord of an Usoleté, as opposed to the more formal Tenegar. Khompah would only be used by a member of one's own Hashna, all others would refer to him or her as Tenegar.

Livoire se Andolé: A small country on the westernmost border of Russia. Also the name of its capital.

Rhejmar: Literally, the Hunger, though it is more commonly used to refer to the potential loss of control due to the Hunger.

Sinégar Ink: An ink effectively invisible to human eyes, but legible to the Breed.

Sireling: A newly created member of the Breed.

Som na Idilque: The Ecstasy. The altered state of mind of a human which occurs during a feeding, marked by heightened euphoria and a willingness to allow one's self to be literally drained of blood during the process.

Topovar: A collective noun used to refer to those who both serve the Breed and who act as sources of blood. But while all Hashnas are Topovar, not all Topovar are members of a Hashna. A Hashna lives under the same roof as its Tenegar.

Tenegar: The formal term for the Lord of an Usoleté.

Usoleté: A term used to refer collectively to the various members of a given Breed's followers. Not the equivalent of family, yet more intimate than 'servants'. While all members of a Hashna are included within the Usoleté, not all members of the Usoleté are considered members of a Hashna.

Valyar: One of the twin rulers of a particular House. As opposed to the Visconté, who is the final arbiter over internal House matters, the Valyar is charged with the responsibility of dealing with all external matters, particularly threats to the House. The position has fallen out of favor over time since the Great Reconciliation. Typically, though not always, a male role.

Visconté: One of the twin rulers of a particular House. The Visconté rules the Hearth, and is the final word on all matters dealing with House traditions and etiquette. While the Visconté may not always deal with House business matters, she will always appoint and oversee those who do. Typically, though not always, a female role.

Four Months Later . . .

The first coffee of the day sits like hot mercury in my stomach long after I leave my car parked at The Warming Hut, my head down, my shoulders hunched. It's cold. Or perhaps I should say colder than usual for San Francisco during this time of year.

A stiff wind blows my way from the nearby shoreline as I navigate the length of the Promenade. It whips my skirt against my bare thighs, a familiar sting. I keep walking.

In the distance I spy the length of the Golden Gate Bridge, rising from a sea of fog as it leaps across the bay. Its orange vermillion struts stand out in sharp contrast against the cloud it appears to rest on, as though the sky has fallen to earth. I neither stop nor pause.

Shortly thereafter I strike a path next to the parking lot on my way to the east sidewalk. As I do, I look up into the face of Joseph Strauss's statue, posed atop its white circular pedestal as though the somber gentleman has been waiting for me.

Then, suddenly, I hear them again. Footsteps. Still some distance behind me, but just a bit louder, just a little closer.

My name is Marie Abigail St. Claire, and I have fifteen minutes to live.

Afterword

Writing is like becoming a parent. You conceive and then nurture to full growth this rambunctious infant who matures into a belligerent adolescent who sneaks the keys out of your pocket to the good car so he can go cruising for femme fatales of easy virtue and a pronounced lack of discriminatory intuition . . .

Okay, you know what, scratch that. Yes, it was cute once, but before long everyone begins to expect a similar expository exhalation, and there's eleven fricking more of these books in the pipeline of my brain all clamoring to squeeze through the same damn door.

Let's talk about something else. Let's talk about pleasure.

And pain.

Because (and believe this if you believe nothing else I ever tell you), when it comes to writing, writers experience both.

For those of you not similarly blessed/cursed, writing is a compulsion. Or rather, the need to write is a compulsion. The actual talent/craft/skill required in order to tell a story which does not inspire one to fling a book face down as hard as one can in a dark parking lot (which I have done) is an entirely separate matter.

I have, at one time or another, struggled to acquire a modicum of skill in a multitude of areas in which I have at best questionable talent, such as music, mathematics, and chess, all of which (I just remembered) are fields of expertise known for producing child prodigies. Which I was not, in any of the three.

But I did consider myself to have a bit of a literary bent. And I knew from the age of twelve or thirteen that I wanted to write. I even remember my first attempt, a puppet play for Columbus Day done for a school project. What I most remember is how poorly it compared to another classmate's magnum opus, another manikin melodrama written to celebrate old Chris's discovery of the New World. As I recall, it was so much better written than my own that I can still remember the stifling heat suffusing my downy cheeks while watching their far-superior production shame my own by sheer proximity.

(I do occasionally comfort myself with the thought that no contemporary of mine of such tender years could have possibly produced something that good, that they must have found the script in a book out of the school library.)

It's okay to suck at something. Most of us do, while those who suck at virtually nothing at least have the good manners to typically occupy a more elevated plane than the rest of us, freeing us from being forced to endure their company on a daily basis.

The true nightmare, the kind that keeps waking one up at night, is the fear of sucking at something you love. And what's worse than that is the concurrent curse and capability of being able to recognize one's belletristic shortcomings, and not quite knowing how to fix them.

So one adopts the attitude of that great standby, the American Can-Do spirit, trudging forward with the sanguine expectation that if one simply works hard enough, the ninety-eight pound weakling can transform himself into Dwayne Johnson and the ditch digger — if he just shovels hard enough — can become the next Donald Trump. (Though he may have something there. . . .)

So one continues, driven by the aforementioned compulsion that allows for neither rest nor relief, and though there is the occasional bright shining moment when it all seems to come together, suddenly one blinks and then Poof! There it goes again.

And you begin to despair.

But that doesn't matter. Because, like any obsessed human being, you just can't stop. You're on a roller coaster ride on the outer circles of Hell, a self-absorbed Sisyphus unable to learn from history and thereby condemned to repeat it.

So you simply say, screw it. And you do it for yourself.

Not for any imagined audience. Not for the editor who will proclaim you are surely the next Stephen King (because, and let's be serious here, there will only be one Mark Twain). Not for fame and recognition, and sure as hell not for the money.

You do it for yourself. For you. And no one else.

And then, something happens.

Oh no, you don't suddenly get magically better. This isn't one of those movies.

You just simply don't give a damn. Because (for the first time in you cannot remember how long) the words are flowing like cheap wine at your cousin's biker wedding, and you're just having so much goddamned fun you'll need a crowbar to rip the smile off your face (with apologies to Chevy Chase).

And you wonder, while this is going on, if you have found some secret doorway, one that only a very few ever find.

Then you hope not. Most sincerely so. Because, like great sex, you find yourself floating on a cotton candy cloud, wishing and hoping that it can be this good for everybody.

And then you hand it over to the readers, hoping they feel the same way about what you have given birth to as you do. (And here we come full circle.)

But if not? . . .

Well then, that's okay.

Because you had a ball.

Walter Spence, April 5, 2012

Acknowledgements

First, I would like to thank the various folks who together, and at one time or another, comprised the Unknown Writer's Group (later Schrodinger's Petshop after its members began getting published). It would be impossible to list everyone by name, and I shall not try, but please know that your friendship and your feedback was crucial to the development of what storytelling craft I have come to possess, and I thank you for both. Though I began this novel long after the inevitable diaspora that scattered us over the years, you remain in memory yet green.

I would also like to thank the following friends and family members (listed in no particular order) who gave so generously of their time as test readers: my niece Heather Spence, my cousin Jennifer Collins-Mancour, my stepmother Sherry Spence, and my friends, Eileen Landreth, Ted Nolan, and Isabel Perez, the Gnomie Queen. Your encouragement and your input meant a great deal to me.

Lastly, a very special thanks to my wife, Debbie, who never stopped believing.

And to answer the question most everyone has asked, book two is being written as we speak.

About Walter Spence

From an early age Walter Spence channeled his fascination with life, the universe and everything into an obsession with the literary and dramatic arts. After years of splitting his attention between writing and acting, he realized a choice had to be made. You are reading the results of that decision now.

After collaborating with fantasy author and Compton Crook Award winner Holly Lisle on *The Devil & Dan Cooley* (book two of the Devil's Point trilogy) he began working on various projects, including a novel called *The Caballa,* which he describes as *"The Lion, the Witch and the Wardrobe,* as written by Stephen King." During this time he was "sideswiped" by the idea for a multi-volume tale of humans and vampires joining in common cause against a mutual enemy, a series he titled The Breed Wars. *House of Shadows* begins this tale, which will be continued in book two, *The Secret Room.*

If you'd like to be kept up to date on future releases, you can subscribe to his newsletter at http://eepurl.com/8Q8uv.

His constantly evolving (writer-speak for 'selectively-improved') website can be found at walterspence.com.

www.ingramcontent.com/pod-product-compliance
Lightning Source LLC
Chambersburg PA
CBHW060929180626
46817CB00004B/1458

* 9 780985 483708 *